CASSIDY'S BLUES

STEVEN DANIELS   KELLA DANIELS

Cassidy's Blues.

To request permissions, contact the publisher at TenThousandThingsPublishing@gmail.com

Hardcover: 979-8-9864428-1-5
Paperback: 979-8-9864428-0-8
Ebook: 979-8-9864428-2-2

Library of Congress Control Number: 2022911099
Second edition January 2025
Edited by Keight Editing
Cover designed by MiblArt

From Steven:

Thank you to Kella for thinking up the idea of Cassidy. Without you, she doesn't exist.

Thank you to Brittany for smoothing out the rough spots that began on page one and ended on the last page. Cassidy's story would have lived only on a hard drive without you.

Thank you to Lesli for always being my first reader and giving me hope.

Eric, Mom, and Dad – I love and miss you.

From Kella:

Thank you to Dad for taking my idea and creating Cassidy's world with me.

Thank you to everyone who helped and believed in us along the way.

Chapter 1

Mondays should be outlawed. Well, most of them anyway. Aside from those occurring during spring, summer, and winter break, Mondays were the worst. But the unquestionable, absolute worst of them all was first day of school Mondays. Once a year was simultaneously enough and too many. And today was that day.

"I don't want to get up," Cassidy groaned to the world. The queasy stomach she'd gone to bed with the night before greeted her as she woke. "Why does it have to be Monday?"

For the last two months, the morning sun meant the beginning of a day of summer fun. Now the bumblebee-yellow rays streaming through her bedroom window blinds took on an ominous meaning. Cassidy yawned, pulling the covers over her head. Maybe she was wrong about the day, and it was Sunday. Even better, maybe she was way off, and school was a week away. She peeked her head out. The new school clothes she'd laid out last night were on top of the thick blue cushion of her window seat, but that didn't mean anything; she could have been wrong yesterday, too.

Searching under her covers and pillows, Cassidy found her tablet. *Please, please, please.* She pressed the power button, and the day and date appeared on the screen. She had never known her tablet to lie, and the truth it showed stung. "Darn. It is Monday."

Cassidy slowly crawled out of bed, bearing the added weight of reluctance, wanting to climb back in and pull the covers over her head once more. Resisting the urge to hide from the day, she halfheartedly dressed, brushed her hair straight, and headed for the kitchen.

Cassidy sat, pouting, on a tall stool at the island in her kitchen and stabbed a fork at the food on her plate. She contemplated the last bite of breakfast she could bring herself to eat — part scrambled egg, part syrupy pancake. The last bite of breakfast was a woeful reminder that it was nearly time to leave for school. She unenthusiastically chewed and swallowed.

A sad-looking, half-eaten pancake remained on the plate atop a layer of sticky brown syrup. Cassidy pushed her finger into the syrup, revealing the white plate underneath. She made two eyes and traced a curved line for a smile. She scrutinized her sugary art. *At least the plate is starting the day with a smile.* Wiping away the eyes, she rotated the plate and made two new eyes above the curved line, creating a frowny face. *There. Now we match.*

Her dad, the chef, was plopping dishes into hot and sudsy sink water. He wore his daily uniform of messy blond hair, pajama bottoms, and a t-shirt that today read, "The soft overcomes the hard. The weak overcomes the strong. Lao Tzu." Working from home as a freelance writer meant he didn't have anywhere to go or anyone to impress, so he mostly went with the lazy, homebody ensemble. He turned toward Cassidy after recognizing the sound he'd heard a hundred times or more — the *tink* of her fork placed on a half-empty plate. She pushed the plate across the white countertop and sucked the syrup from her fingertip.

Dad eyed the half-eaten pancake left on the plate. "All done?"

He asked that question every time, whether her plate was clean or not. She usually welcomed the offer of another pancake or two, but this morning her stomach was not in the mood. She managed a grin and nodded in response before wiping away a glob of syrup from the corner of her mouth with a cloth napkin. Dad dumped the pancake remnants into the trash and dropped the plate into the sink with a plop, sending tiny soap bubbles into the air for a couple of seconds before they returned to their cleaning duty in the sink.

The microwave clock read 8:05. Cassidy tensed. *Ugh. I have to leave in five minutes.* The walk to school took ten minutes. If her timing was perfect, she would arrive just before the ringing of the opening bell and head straight for her classroom, avoiding the hallways swarming with kids.

"Are you ready for fifth grade, Blue?" Dad asked.

He sometimes called her "Blue" because of the color of her eyes. At birth, they were blue — a bright blue, a noticeable blue, a what-the-heck-blue. And though her father looked at her with blue eyes of his own, her mother was Japanese and brown-eyed. Cassidy should have had brown eyes, too. That wasn't the complete story, though. Cassidy's great, great, great — well, many greats grandma had blue eyes, the same as hers. That's what her parents said. Not satisfied with their explanation, Cassidy researched on the internet and found out that a mutation could cause someone Japanese to have blue eyes. A *mutation.* Really? The idea of having a mutated eye color wasn't the biggest confidence booster. How was being a mutant cool if she couldn't control the weather, shapeshift, or be invincible? Every person she met gushed over her "beautiful" eyes. It was like her eyes were the star of the school play, and the rest of her was just in the background. It just so happened that was Cassidy's favorite position in plays — somewhere in the background, or even better, in set design.

Was she ready for school? She wrinkled her nose. "I guess," she responded, as unconvincingly as the meaning of those two words when combined. Every first day of school was a reminder of the worst day of her life. All week she'd been trying not to think about that day, and now it was practically dancing in a spotlight of her memories.

Dad tossed the dish towel aside and leaned elbows first onto the counter. "Are you thinking about that day?"

Cassidy winced, nodding. It had come to be known as "that day" as if giving it a vague title would hasten its departure from her long-term memory. She'd gotten lost in a crowd at an amusement park on "that day" and was struck by the fear she would never see her family again and would forever be lost. Of course, those were silly fears, but she was just a little kid at the time and didn't know better. Soon after, doctors diagnosed her with social anxiety. Cassidy used simpler terms like "scared of getting lost", "hating crowds", and "a fear of strangers". She wished to be like every other kid, but her school days came with loads of anxiety from trying to avoid as many people as possible.

"It's day one. A fresh start with brand new opportunities." Dad tapped his temple. "Remember, yesterday is —"

"Yes, I know." Cassidy rolled her eyes. "Yesterday is an illusion and has no power over me," she finished mockingly. "Today is the first and only day of my life."

Dad had used that line on her at least a bazillion times. He wasn't wrong, but it wasn't that simple. When bad stuff happened, it wasn't always like a horrible haircut she could grow out of in a few months. Bad stuff could be more like glittered slime — even after smushing it into a plastic container, there was glitter somewhere forever, even if she couldn't see it right away. But, if she debated him on the topic, he'd repeat the story about the two monks and the lady wearing a long dress trying to cross a muddy street. He called it a parable or something, and the lesson was to let the past be the past. The concept of forgetting about the past made sense, but again, not that easy, Dad.

"There's still time to switch to homeschooling," she offered.

"Yes, but we talked about that already. You wouldn't see your friends as much."

"Friend, Dad, not friends."

He smiled apologetically. "Right. Friend. Besides, you have some fresh new clothes and awesome shoes to show off."

Cassidy rolled her eyes and scoffed. "No one says 'awesome' anymore."

"Okay, then 'ill' or whatever."

"Sick, Dad. We say 'sick'."

He chuckled. "Thanks for keeping me cool."

She raised her eyebrows and gave him a look.

"What?" he said, feigning hurt. "I'm still cool, aren't I?"

Cassidy stood from the stool and pushed it under the counter. "Borderline. So, enjoy what little coolness you have left."

Dad straightened. "You'd better get going. Maisy will be prancing by soon to walk with you."

Cassidy grabbed her mint backpack from the floor, scooted around the long kitchen island, and hugged him.

"I'm going to the grocery store today, but I'll be here when you get home. Mom will be home around six." He kissed the top of her head and gave her a gentle, encouraging shove toward the front door. "Watch out for traffic. It'll be crazy out there. And Cass... remember to breathe."

After "that day", Dad had taught her to focus on her breath to battle her anxiety. A deep breath in for five seconds, a breath out for five seconds, and repeat. The technique never completely quelled her queasy stomach or dried her sweaty palms, but it saved her from any more full-blown panic attacks. She'd had just about enough of those. They exchanged I-love-yous, and Cassidy left for her sixth first day of school, her first day of fifth grade, and what would be the first day of her new life.

The summer heat in Farmington, Utah was like an oven. The air was dry enough to parch and crack the skin of an ornery desert rattlesnake. But it was nothing a layer of coconut-scented lotion couldn't cure. It was that scent that emanated from Cassidy as she walked down the cobblestone sidewalk leading from the front door of her house. Maisy was waiting for her — Maisy Bijou Davis, to be exact — her best and only friend.

Cassidy grinned as Maisy smiled big and bright, performing a perfect pirouette — level chin, square hips, plié, passé, and ending in fourth position.

Cassidy wasn't quite sure what all that fancy dance talk meant, but she had heard Maisy's mom say it over and over and over. Her mother, a lawyer or something, also owned the dance academy where Maisy practically lived when not at school or home.

"Do I look fabulous?" Maisy posed as she always did when showing off a new outfit, flamboyantly raising her hands. She wore a yellow, flower-patterned sundress, sandals, and her black hair was pulled back tight into two buns. Her brown skin shimmered in the morning sunlight. Maisy did look fabulous, there was no denying it. No, there was no need to deny it. She was just that way — the landscape was better and more fabulous just by her being in it.

"When do you *not* look fabulous?" Cassidy countered.

Maisy pursed her lips, cocked her head, and looked to the side. "Ummm... *never.*" She broke into a gorgeous smile that could flip the mood of a surly troll. "Mmm, coconut lotion, like I told you," Maisy said as they hugged. "Smooth skin with the bonus of smelling delicious." She stepped back and looked down. "Are those the shoes you've been keeping secret? What color is that? They match your backpack."

Cassidy held her long, dark brown hair behind her ears and looked proudly at her new pair of Vans. "Mint. It's my color theme, for at least the first half of the year. I'm thinking of going with yellow for the second half." Maisy loved yellow.

"What about a mint shirt and mint pants?"

"No way. If everything I wore was mint, I'd look like a tub of mint ice cream."

"Yeah, that would look kinda odd."

"Exactly," Cassidy said. "That is the kind of attention I do not need. I'll just wear my mint backpack, mint Vans, and if I can find one, a mint scrunchie. Do you like the color?"

"Uh, *yeah*."

Cassidy looked at the front door of her house and silently sighed. If only she could talk with Maisy all day. Honestly, she'd love to go back inside and hang out with Maisy in her room, as they'd done for hours a day during summer break. When Maisy wasn't at dance or working on a summer study program her mom created, they watched TV, YouTube videos, made slime, danced, sang, and planned their futures. They were inseparable, best friends who called themselves sisters, as neither had siblings.

As sisters, they imagined they'd graduate high school together, attend the same college where they'd room together, and even live together after college. They would get married — though the thought of boys repulsed them — and live next door to each other. Eternal sisterhood was their master plan, and the only way to continue pursuing that plan was to get to school.

"Are you ready?" Maisy asked.

Cassidy shook her head and blinked. "Oh… yeah." She headed down the sidewalk, keeping in step with Maisy.

The walk to school took them through their neighborhood, a line of homes set on yards of lush green grass and adorned with trees of green and maroon leaves and colorful flower beds. Kids from ages 7 to 13 darted from their homes through tall doorways, saying goodbyes, I-love-yous, and have-a-great-days to their parents. Most kids were required to pose on the front steps for first day pictures. Some boys hated the photo tradition, but humored their parents with fake smiles and good posture before slouching and scurrying away. Most girls were eager to pose, looking like models for a new school clothing line. Pictures were never Cassidy's dad's thing, thankfully, and her mom always left for work early. She hadn't been there for a first day of school in years.

"Kids..." Cassidy contemplated.

"Huh?" Maisy asked.

Cassidy stepped back onto the light grey sidewalk from having trailed off into the grass in thought. "Huh, what?"

"What did you say?"

"I was just thinking, there's a lot of kids in our neighborhood."

Maisy took in the dozens of kids parading along sidewalks ahead of and behind them on both sides of the street. Kids walked, ran, and zoomed along on their bikes and scooters. Helmets, apparently, were optional.

"Yeah, so?"

"I don't know." Cassidy firmly gripped the shoulder straps of her backpack. "It's just a lot compared to when we first moved in. It seems... crowded."

Their neighborhood had been growing like crazy. A couple dozen homes were built and moved into over the last couple of years. Every new family seemed to have two or three kids.

"Cassidy? Are you in there?" Maisy placed her hand on Cassidy's shoulder, appearing to examine her. "Don't fall apart on me already. We aren't even at school yet."

Cassidy shook her head and forced air from her mouth. "Yeah, sorry. Present."

"BEEP BEEP!"

The girls screamed and jumped to opposite sides of the sidewalk, narrowly avoiding a boy zooming by on a scooter.

"Move it, slowpokes," the boy yelled. He laughed ruthlessly as he zipped away. The culprit's identity was no mystery, even with his back to them. His voice and laugh, an annoyance to Cassidy and most everyone she knew, were dead giveaways.

"Watch it, Brody," Cassidy scolded.

"Yeah, ya jerk," Maisy added, one hand on her hip and the other pointing an angry finger at him. Maisy had one heck of a pointer finger. When someone upset her, they knew it. She wielded her pointer finger as a ship's captain would a map. She'd point to let you know where she was coming from, and she'd point to where she wanted you to go. Brody may have scootered away from this confrontation with Maisy and her pointer finger, but the day was young.

"I wish he'd grow up," Maisy said, smoothing out her yellow cotton dress.

"I wish he'd move."
They laughed.

Ten, thankfully uneventful, minutes later, the parking lot of Canyon River Elementary stretched out before them. Cassidy often pondered over the school's name as it was neither in a canyon nor near a river. Canyon River Elementary was in a valley, with the Wasatch Mountains to the east and the Great Salt Lake to the west. The girls stood stoically, staring at the school grounds, taking in the commotion and emotion. Kids in new clothes blanketed the shredded rubber playground of the two-story center for learning. Boys were playing tag. Girls were swinging on swings and climbing various contraptions. Clusters of sixth grade girls were stealing glances at groups of sixth grade boys and turning giggling faces back to equally giggly friends. The boys didn't pay much attention in return.

Cassidy slouched and stared at the ground, imagining worst-case scenarios — all of them ridiculous after second thought — that could result from wading through the crowd. *Yesterday is an illusion and has no power over me.* She took a deep breath in for a count of five, breathed out for a count of five, and repeated. "Thanks, Dad," she murmured.

Maisy grabbed Cassidy's hand, sweaty palm and all, and smiled confidently — an expression of promise for what the day, the school year, and their lives held for them. "Okay, straighten up and eyes forward. Let's do this, sis."

Cassidy unenthusiastically smiled back and nodded, but she knew better. She would certainly not look forward, but instead avert her eyes to avoid attention. Slouching only helped with that goal. Maisy stepped crisply toward the school doors, pulling Cassidy along as the five-minute warning bell rang.

Chapter 2

"Okay, Cassidy. You can open your eyes," Maisy said. "We made it through the crowd. We're inside the school."

"What do you mean?" Cassidy said defensively. "My eyes were open."

"Really?" Maisy said, sounding doubtful.

"Well, mostly."

Maisy took in a deep breath. "Ahhh. The smell of education."

Cassidy scanned the expanse of the familiar school interior. The main office was to the left, where the assistant principal stood behind her desk, hurriedly stacking papers into piles. The school auditorium loomed to her right, which when used for its purpose, was loud and crowded and not one of Cassidy's favorite places at school or on Earth. The lunchroom and stairs leading up to the second level were also to the right. Another set of stairs was ahead to the left. They led to the library — her safe and quiet space — and the hall to her classroom.

Cassidy breathed deep and exhaled, unimpressed. "It just smells clean. Like a school that hasn't been used in months."

"Exactly. And I am here to use it. To make it my best year yet." Maisy pointed to a brick wall to their right. "On that wall over there will be my posters asking students to vote for me as their class president." She stood with her shoulders back and chin high.

Cassidy studied the empty wall, envisioning the posters. She smiled. "You have my vote, that's for sure."

Maisy scoffed. "I better."

A murmuring of voices and commotion seeped through the glass doors behind them. Soon dozens of sweaty kids would be rushing through the doors like crazed maniacs in preparation for the opening bell. At least, that's what Cassidy imagined.

She cringed. "We should get to class."

Maisy nodded. "Agreed. Let's go."

Their backpacks hopped up and down as they trotted up the stairs. At the top, they turned right toward a long hallway with doors to classrooms on either side. A blue banner with white letters hung above that read, "Welcome to 5th Grade." Maisy's feet did a little pitter-patter, and she made a sound that may have been a squeal.

Cassidy chuckled and shook her head. "Enthusiastic much?"

Maisy beamed. *"Much."*

Cassidy tried to keep up as Maisy speed-walked down the hallway, eyeing the doors to the right.

She abruptly stopped in front of a room with "107" on a small plaque above its door. Maisy opened the door just as the first bell rang. Cassidy hurried her into the room, anxious to find their desks and get situated before their classmates poured in.

Rows of empty desks filled the center of the room. On top of each stood place cards folded into the shape of miniature roofs with students' names written in blue Sharpie block letters. A wall of cubby holes lined the bottom half of the far-right wall, each marked with a student name. Windows with a view of the mountains made up the back wall, and posters with positive affirmations and faces of famous scientists, mathematicians, and leaders covered the remaining walls.

Maisy circled the desks, repeatedly muttering, "They had better…" until she stopped at a group of four desks at the end of the third row. She nodded with an affirmative, "Mmmhmm."

Cassidy shuffled over to Maisy. On top of three of the four desks were place cards that read Maisy, Cassidy, and Alex. The fourth desk was apparently not assigned to anyone. Cassidy's desk being next to Maisy's was no coincidence, as previous teachers would have warned Mrs. Higgins, their fifth grade teacher, of the predictable pleading from the two of them to sit next to each other. The seating arrangement was nearly perfect, just Cassidy and Maisy, but Alex had unknowingly ruined it. He was a nice guy who smiled bunches at her, but if he could just sit somewhere else… anywhere else. *Maybe she could just move his card to another —*

The classroom door opened, and the invasion of classmates commenced.

Cassidy turned to Maisy urgently. "Hurry. Let's find our cubbies."

Cassidy and Maisy were stowing their supplies of pencils, paper, tissues, and lunches, when Josie Pemberton squeezed between them, sniffing a box of number two pencils.

"I love the smell of new school supplies," Josie said with a smile grand enough to close her eyes. Josie was perpetually happy; a smile was her resting face. Her every word was said on the edge of joyous laughter. The saying of "someone has a bounce in their step", well, that someone was always Josie.

They exchanged hellos and talked about their summers. Cassidy said her summer was fun, then let Maisy do the rest of the talking. Painful small talk complete, Josie bubbled away. Cassidy exchanged a wide-eyed look with Maisy, and they giggled quietly. She liked Josie heaps and thought she was brilliant, but the girl was challenging to keep up with. Josie was the person who could be handed a five-hundred-page book on a Friday, and she'd return it Monday, read cover to cover, prepared to offer a synopsis. If asked, she'd grade the book based on its level of emotional resonance. Cassidy would need an internet search to find out what that meant.

Maisy considered Josie the number one threat to her goal of becoming class president. She had talked about it all summer, about how she would win the election and how nothing —not even Josie

Pemberton — would stop her. When Maisy wanted something, she would do whatever it took to win it, accomplish it, or get it.

Cassidy got comfortable in her seat and took a deep breath, now ready for the day after conquering the morning schoolyard. Yes, Maisy had dragged her through the crowd, head down and eyes closed to slits, but she conquered it, nonetheless.

"Hey. *Psst.*"

That voice. Please, no.

"Hey. Hey. Turn around."

Cassidy groaned, and for a reason she couldn't explain, knowingly swiveled in her seat to respond to Brody. Brody had short brown hair, a broad head, and always appeared to be on the verge of laughter, usually at someone else's expense. "What, Brody?"

"How cool, Cassieroll; I get to sit behind you *all* year."

She rolled her eyes. "Cassieroll? Really, Brody? We're doing that again this year?"

"I had considered 'Blue-eyed freak' but—"

"Brody," Maisy said harshly, inserting herself into the conversation. "You do realize your name rhymes with grody? You know, like Grody Brody?"

Brody stared at Maisy with his mouth open as he absentmindedly scratched his cheek.

"You do know what grody means, right?" Maisy asked, not hiding the condescension.

Brody scoffed. "Duh. Yeah." His cheeks reddened and he turned to Adam — his less annoying best friend. Adam, pencil-thin and narrow-faced, was like Brody-lite. He pointed at something to Cassidy's left. She followed his gaze and finger until her eyes fixed on a girl she didn't know, sitting alone near the teacher's desk. She had dirty blonde hair with straight bangs, and her freckled cheeks were a blotchy red. A pool of tears welled in the girl's brown eyes.

I don't remember seeing her come in. Was she there the whole time? Cassidy couldn't take her eyes off the girl. A heaviness grew in Cassidy's chest, starting behind her ribs and spreading to the ends of her limbs. The world around her faded into the background, except for the new girl who came into a singular focus. The classroom sounds were muffled and wavy, like two conch shells had been placed over Cassidy's ears. *What is happening?*

The girl erupted from her seat and bolted from the room without as much as an "excuse me" or "I'll be back," running past Mrs. Higgins, their teacher, who had just entered. She didn't even grab the hall pass hanging from a hook next to the door.

"Help her," came a faint and oddly familiar voice.

Cassidy snapped out of the trance she'd been in, scanning the classroom for anyone else who may have seen and heard the same thing. *What the Frappuccino?* She cupped her ears with her hands, removed them, and shook her head. The usual sounds of the classroom had returned. The heaviness receded from her arms and legs like an outgoing tide, settling again behind her ribs. A kind of pull replaced the heaviness, like the strange girl had her own gravity, drawing Cassidy to her. *"Help her,"* the voice came again. It sounded like… Cassidy's own voice.

Maisy was talking to Alex, who had just made it to his seat. Cassidy lifted her hand in an I'll-be-back-in-a-minute manner and muttered, "I gotta go. Be back in a minute." She eased out of her desk and walked over to Mrs. Higgins, just outside the classroom door. "Mrs. Higgins."

Her teacher glanced down at her, then peered down the hallway. "Hello, Cassidy. Get in your seat. I can't have anyone else run off."

"I have to go to the bathroom, too. I'll make sure…" Cassidy paused, not knowing the girl's name, "… she makes it back to class."

Mrs. Higgins looked at her disapprovingly. "You should have taken care of that before class."

"I know. First day nerves, I guess."

"Fine." Mrs. Higgins pulled the hall pass from the hook and held it out. "Be quick. Class has already started."

Cassidy grabbed the pass, which was nothing more than a ruler with a strand of red yarn pulled through a hole at one end and tied into a knot. "Quick. I promise."

She took a step, then stopped. *What am I doing?* She looked over her shoulder. Mrs. Higgins nodded toward the bathroom at the end of the hall and mouthed, "Hurry." Cassidy nodded and swallowed hard. She took another step with a death grip on the ruler, muttering over and over with each subsequent step, "What am I doing? What am I doing?" She hadn't seen the girl run into the bathroom, but she sensed it in a way she couldn't explain. Cassidy reached the bathroom door a few wary steps later, took two shaky breaths, and pushed open the door.

The smell of the bathroom was a sanitized clean, and the white tile floor, white sinks, and mirrors were spotless. On the right side were six swinging green stall doors — one door was closed. Cassidy couldn't see the crying girl, but knew she was in the stall, hitched breathing and sniffles echoed off the walls. So, Cassidy waited. She didn't really have to use the bathroom, so she just stood there. She opened her mouth to speak more than once, to say something to the girl, but couldn't figure out what to say or ask.

How did most conversations start? *Duh.* "Hello," she called out, just as the stall door eased open with a squeak.

The girl walked over to the sink, looking at Cassidy from the corner of her eye. The pull came on strong, like the girl was the Earth's gravity and Cassidy was a failing satellite, crashing down. Her feet moved toward the girl, unable to stop. The girl splashed water on her face, not noticing Cassidy only an arm's length behind her.

Cassidy finally regained the strength to speak. "Are you okay?"

The girl straightened. "I'm fine." Pulling a white paper towel from the wall dispenser, she wiped away water clinging to her face.

Cassidy uncontrollably reached for the girl's shoulder. A brilliant light overwhelmed her vision, followed by darkness. Followed by nothing.

Chapter 3

THE OTHER WORLD

Iwa pulled a dark gray kettle from a hook above a low burning flame and poured steaming tea into a white ceramic cup. The green-tinted liquid swirled clockwise inside the cup, reaching just below the rim when she stopped pouring. She returned the kettle to its hook and took the cup with her to a shin-high table in the middle of a sparsely decorated room. The floors were slats of yellow-brown wood, and pillars, equally spaced throughout the room, supported the roof. Around the table, tatami mats covered most of the floor.

She wore a maroon linen kimono with a white robe underneath, and a dark gray sash around her waist. Her grey hair was neatly fastened into a bun on the top of her head, held in place by two hair sticks. She gingerly bent at the knees and sat the cup on the low table. Rising with a wince and modest amount of effort, she walked the few feet to a pair of wooden sliding doors. Leaning into it, she pushed the doors apart, revealing the landscape beyond the four walls of her small home. A crisp breeze blew the sweet smell of evergreen into the room, bringing a smile to her face.

With a relaxed gaze, she took in the panoramic view of the world outside her home. A narrow wooden porch stood just outside the doors, with five stairs leading to the ground. Beyond the porch was a narrow strip of land covered in clutches of long grass from which sprouted various-sized grey stones. Several feet farther stood a sparse row of tall pine trees, and beyond that, miles in the distance, was a line of mountains.

Iwa returned and sat at the table on a square yellow pillow. The full cup warmed her chilled, weathered hands. She sipped the tea and closed her eyes, smiling at the perfection of the temperature. Quiet mornings like this were part of why she moved away from the village. The sound of wind through trees, songs from birds, the chittering of bugs in the day and night were all welcome interruptions to the silence. Nature didn't intrude on her mind; it didn't need anything from her, it didn't chatter as incessantly as people did. In fact, everything was per—

A jolt of pain struck the center of her forehead, as if she'd been pierced by an arrow. The room blurred around her. The cup fell from her hands, crashing to the table and splashing tea in all directions. Iwa pressed her fingers to her head and screamed. The pain was familiar but had never been this piercing, this intense. Then… it was gone, leaving a pulsating throb through her skull as if her brain had its own pounding heart.

Gasping for breath, Iwa looked about the room with stars dancing before her eyes and pushed herself to a wobbly stand. Her fastened hair came loose of its bindings, cascading over her slumped shoulders. The hair sticks clacked against the floor. Iwa leaned against a pillar, the room and her mind beginning to settle. It grew quiet except for the pounding of her heart and the rush of air in and out of her lungs.

As time passed, her breath and heart slowed, the pain in her skull easing, only to be replaced by a weakness she had never felt before. It was as if her life-energy had been drained from her body. "What is this?"

Slowly, realization crept across her consciousness as her trembling fingers found her lips. There was no mystery here. It was expected, foretold, but her heart skipped a beat anyway.

"The day has come. It's Cassidy's turn."

Miles away from Iwa, in a tiny village nestled in a valley surrounded by mountains that reached beyond the clouds, sat Kazuyasu's home. He lived alone, which was generally not a notable achievement, except he was only twelve years old.

In his cedar wood home, he sat on a tatami mat at the base of a dark wood cabinet shrine built to honor the memory of his parents. He held up a narrow strip of wood, tip aflame, to light the wicks of the candles on each side of the cabinet. When he was satisfied they were adequately lit, he doused the burning stick in a small iron pot of water at his side, emitting a sizzle and a puff of steam. He pulled a green incense stick from a stout and narrow wooden container, broke it in half, and held the individual pieces against the candle flames until the ends produced flames of their own. *That should do it.* A few waves of his hand extinguished the flames, filling the air around him with the fragrance of sandalwood. He jabbed the incense sticks into a small bronze pot filled with ash.

Using a cushioned striker, Kazuyasu rang a bell no larger than his hand, sending a pleasant *ding* reverberating through the room. He steepled his hands, saying a silent prayer to honor his parents. As the ding of the bell faded, his prayer ended, and he gave a final solemn gaze at his parents' names engraved on the small stone tablets standing in the cabinet. He doused the candles with a metal snuffer, finishing the ritual.

He couldn't say he missed his parents because he never knew them, nor did he have any memory of them. His parents had been the providers of fish for the village and were on the water when a torrential storm passed through, breaking their boat into tiny, jagged pieces. They were never found. For a time, he'd felt cheated seeing other children in the village with their parents. They had someone to play with, learn from, take care of them, and love. But Kazuyasu had a parent of sorts, Iwa, who took care of and educated him until the day she moved away from the village. He was only eight years old when she left and quickly learned what it meant to be an adult.

He gave a final nod toward the shrine and stood, stretching the cramps from his legs. He wore a white linen kimono decorated with images of light blue carp, a white robe underneath, and a narrow light blue sash wrapped around his waist. His long black hair was tied into a knot on the back of his head. With the monthly ritual to honor his parents complete, he turned his attention to the daily routine that Iwa called "a life and death responsibility." He walked barefoot down the tall, narrow hallway of his home, passing white paper latticed doors to other rooms. The walls and floors were dark wood planks, but the ceiling was open, revealing support beams for the roof.

A noise from the end of the hallway brought him to a stop. Kazuyasu squinted, craning his neck forward as if it would help him better hear and identify the sound. Iwa sent a sea eagle every couple of weeks bearing messages and English assignments. *Maybe she was a few days early.* His eyes widened. *What if the sound wasn't a sea eagle? What if it was... the box?*

Sprinting to the end of the hallway, he slid open the door on his right to reveal a large but sparsely decorated room. In the center of the room lay a sunken fire pit surrounded by four tatami mats. Gray stone slabs surrounded charred but unlit wood in the center of the pit. Above the charred wood, a large metal pot hung from a hook tied to the end of a long rope fastened to a ceiling beam several feet above. Kazuyasu used the room to cook his meals, keep warm during the cold months, or sit around with his best friend, Maku — a friendly spirit that visited him nearly every day.

He focused on a rectangular lacquered box sitting atop one of the tatami mats. He plopped down next to it and placed it on his lap, staring as he had done for more days than he could remember, waiting for a sign. If the box did anything out of the ordinary, emitted a bright light or a sound, it would be time to act. Time to take on the responsibility Iwa had bestowed upon him. Instead, the box was just as it had been for years — dark and silent. He sighed. *I guess it wasn't the box.*

He removed the woven bamboo lid from a small round container on his right and grabbed a rice cake. When he was not adventuring with Maku or training as a samurai, villagers who cared about his well-being would stop by to ensure he had food, clothing, and firewood. He politely thanked them for their concern while internally wishing they would allow him to take care of himself. Though, he never passed on their gifts, especially Baba-san's sweet rice cakes. She always brought enough rice cakes for two, claiming he was too skinny. The trick was to finish the rice cakes or hide any leftovers before Maku came over and gobbled them down.

Kazuyasu took a frustrated bite of the rice cake and set the lacquered box to the side. Watching the box every second of the day was impossible, and he often wondered if it had ever moved when he was not around. He had slept next to the fire pit the previous night with the box by his side. Every hour or so, he questioned if the noises that awoke him were the box moving, something else, or just his imagination. However, today's agenda did not include sitting around and watching the box. Today he would secure it in a secret place while away, and start the watch again, begrudgingly, when he returned. It was a sunny day in the valley with clear skies, and his samurai training awaited.

The pitter-patter of feet came from outside, and a smiling young girl with black hair materialized in the room out of thin air. *That's who made the noise.* Kazuyasu swallowed a bite of rice cake, grinned at the spirit, and deftly slid the container of rice cakes behind him.

"Hey, Maku. Perfect timing."

Chapter 4

Cassidy's hazy vision focused first on what was before them — textured, white squares. But they weren't squares. Well, they were square-shaped, and after a clearer-eyed inspection, she identified the squares by their actual name: ceiling tiles. An odd feeling met her as she woke — or was it come to? The feeling was barely there, an itch on her brain, a single flea on a grizzly bear. It was like knowing she had something important to do but could not remember what. Then came the voice again, the one she heard in the classroom, the one that sounded like her own but softer. *"Help her."* However, both the feeling and voice were forgettable for now.

Two adult-sized figures were standing next to her, and one of them spoke. "Cassidy, are you okay?" Cassidy recognized the voice — older, female. A voice she hadn't heard in a few months. It was —

"Cassidy. This is Principal Ramsbottom."

Mystery solved.

Principal Ramsbottom's hair was short, permed, and black with bits of gray; she was wearing one of her many slacks and blouse combos. Her name was just as it sounded and spelled how it sounded. The students at Cassidy's elementary school had a lot of fun with it. At least they did until parents were called in to discuss "behavior befitting the school."

Cassidy scanned the room. *Where am I?* The ceiling tiles offered zero help, being in every room of the school. She was lying on a cushy cot that felt like a bed, and a zoo animal mural covered the wall to her right. Cabinets lined the walls over and around a stainless-steel sink on her left. She knew those cabinets; they held all kinds of medical type stuff. *Nurse's office. Oof! How did I get here?*

"Cassidy, can you hear me?" Principal Ramsbottom asked.

Cassidy couldn't speak. *Okay. Let me make a mental list of what is working: I can see, check. I can hear, check. I can feel, ugh, check.* She could not only feel, but also hear her head pounding. The second adult-sized figure in the room moved, their face hovering over Cassidy's.

"Hi, Ms. Jennie," Cassidy croaked as her pupils focused. *I can speak, mostly. Check.*

Ms. Jennie had kind eyes and a cute bob hairstyle. She wore brown slacks, a white button-up shirt, and a fitted red blazer that hung past her waist. This was her second year as the elementary school's guidance counselor. Thankfully, she must have liked it enough to return. Technically

Ms. Jennie was an adult, but Cassidy imagined her as an older friend. Heck, if Ms. Jennie was fifteen years younger, she figured they'd be best friends. Cassidy spent a lot of time in the guidance office last year. Full disclosure, she was a frequent visitor of school guidance counselors since the first grade. Her anxiety was an annoying acquaintance that often came for uninvited visits.

"Hi Cassidy," Ms. Jennie said. "How do you feel?"

There had to be a metaphor — or was it simile? She could never remember — to describe her current condition, but Cassidy used neither. Though not known for having a potty mouth, "crappy" was her reply.

Without knocking, Nurse Becky strode into the room with quick steps and an "Excuse me, ladies," prompting Principal Ramsbottom and Ms. Jennie to let her by. She wore a blue uniform — for some reason, they were called scrubs on the medical shows — and bright white shoes. Her hair was pulled back into a tight bun, her face bronzed from the summer sun. She stood next to Cassidy, still lying on the fake bed. "I'm going to ask you a few questions and check your blood pressure, okay?"

Questions? Great. A test on the first day of school, Cassidy thought. "Sure. Okay."

"Can you tell me your full name?"

"Yes."

Silence.

"No. I mean, tell me your full name."

"Oh. Sorry." *Duh.* "Cassidy Kenner. Or did you want my middle names too?"

"No, that's okay."

The smell of lavender wafted from Nurse Becky.

"I love the smell of your lotion."

A smile cracked the nurse's straight lips. "Thanks, I like it too."

"You're welcome."

"Can you count backward from ten?"

"Sure I can." Cassidy giggled, realizing Nurse Becky actually wanted her to count. "Oh, never mind." She counted backward without missing a number.

Nurse Becky nodded. "Very good. Now, let me see your right arm."

The rip of Velcro preceded the application of the blood pressure band. Nurse Becky pulled the strap tight around Cassidy's arm, put on her stethoscope, and squeezed the black, squishy ball as she held Cassidy's wrist. Cassidy grimaced at the uncomfortable pressure before the air escaped with a woosh. Nurse Becky removed the band and jotted the numbers on Cassidy's student medical history sheet. There were numerous entries on that piece of paper. As it turned out, the nurse's office was an excellent place for Cassidy to hang out while waiting for the pressure in her chest to ease, the knot in her stomach to release, her breath to calm, and in general, to give her time to become friends with the world again.

"All good?" Cassidy asked.

Nurse Becky smiled. "All good."

Some adults had a way of looking at kids who were sick. The look was soft and caring, and they wore gentle smiles. Cassidy imagined, suspiciously, that some adults who smiled during these trying times for children were only a few sadistic brain cells away from laughing. And maybe, just maybe when they left the room, they did laugh. Nurses and doctors deserved the most suspicion, wanting to be around sick people all the time.

It wasn't a daily or monthly thing, but Cassidy had fainted before, and this time it felt different. She swallowed. "So, I'm really okay, and I'm not going to die? I just fainted or something?"

Nurse Becky grinned and handed her a lollipop. "No, you're not going to die. I'll talk to your dad when he gets here. You just go home and get some rest." She said something to Principal Ramsbottom and Ms. Jennie about going to the other room and left. Cassidy listened for laughter after the door closed behind her, but there was none. Or maybe the door kept her from hearing it. Until she could be sure, her suspicion of Nurse Becky remained.

"Cassidy," Ms. Jennie said. "Can you tell us what happened? What's the last thing you remember?"

That is a good question: what happened? The memory-wheel in Cassidy's head kicked into gear as effectively as an out-of-shape gerbil, languidly plopping onto a stationary wheel and immediately falling into a rodential sleep. It took a few focused moments before she locked on to the memory of breakfast with her dad. She told Principal Ramsbottom and Ms. Jennie that breakfast was delicious because pancakes were her favorite, but that she couldn't enjoy them due to her anxiety over the first day of school. She told them how Maisy walked with her to school and how there were so many kids in her neighborhood. "They just keep building new homes," she explained, though it sounded like a complaint, and it was. And no way could she forget to tell them about how Brody nearly ran over her on his scooter and laughed about it. Principal Ramsbottom appeared to make a mental note of that particular event. Cassidy described the crowd of students outside of school and how she would have never made it in the door without Maisy. "Maisy said my eyes were closed, but they were open, even if just barely."

"Cassidy?"

Cassidy focused on Ms. Jennie looking down at her. "Yeah?"

"Can you skip to the *last* thing you remember?"

Wait. Was I rambling? Absentmindedly, Cassidy nodded while studying the ceiling tiles — still there, still square-shaped, still white and textured. The strange feeling had returned, and so had the faint voice, her conscience maybe. *What does it want from me? What is it trying to tell me?* She pushed the voice to a corner of her brain and looked at Ms. Jennie. "I'm not sure what the last thing is until I get to it."

"Okay, but —" Ms. Jennie started.

"You *need* to let me in there," came a voice from the other side of the door.

Principal Ramsbottom opened the door just enough to fit her permed head through and spoke firmly but friendly. "Maisy, I understand you want to see Cassidy, but we need you to wait. You're welcome to have a seat or I'll have to send you back to class."

"Let her know I'm out here."

"I will, Maisy. I will. Now take a seat."

"I'm out here, Cassie. I'm here for you!"

Principal Ramsbottom closed the door.

Cassidy could always count on Maisy. The day's events were coming back to her foggy memory, but one thing she already knew for certain was at the end of this retelling of her day, Maisy would be on the other side of that door. That was what sisters did for each other.

"Cassidy, your dad is on the way. He was at the grocery store, so he'll be here in about fifteen minutes," Ms. Jennie said. "Want to finish telling us what happened?"

Cassidy searched her mind, found the spot in the memory stream where she had left off, and dove back in. This part of the day was more difficult to recall, like trying to get on the internet with bad Wi-Fi. "I was in class. Mrs. Higgins' room. Maisy… Maisy and I were putting our stuff in our cubbies." She sat up on the cot. "That was when I saw her. After I sat at my desk."

"Who did you see?" Ms. Jennie prompted.

Cassidy scrunched her face in thought. "I… I don't know her name. The new girl." She looked questioningly at Ms. Jennie and Principal Ramsbottom, who exchanged glances. *Surely they knew her name.*

"The new student's name is Anessa," Ms. Jennie said.

Cassidy silently mouthed the name. *Anessa.*

"Did Anessa hurt you?" Principal Ramsbottom asked. "Did she… push you down?"

Cassidy thought back, slowly shook her head, stopped, and shook it more confidently. "No. Nothing like that. She… Anessa was sitting alone. I didn't notice her at first. She was sad." Cassidy looked at Ms. Jennie. "She looked like she was about to cry."

"Do you know why she was sad?" Ms. Jennie said.

Cassidy pushed her hair behind her ears, twirling a long lock of it around her finger. "I don't know, or I guess I didn't know at the time. But she left the room fast, like *super*-fast. Just got up and left without asking. Mrs. Higgins called for her, but she kept going. I think Mrs. Higgins was going to go after her until I said I had to go to the girl's room. I said I'd make sure she made it back to class. I had a strange feeling that I should help her."

Cassidy paused to gauge the adults' response to that last odd detail. It even sounded odd to herself when she said it. She wasn't ready to tell them, or anyone for that matter, about the voice. If she couldn't make sense of it herself, it was probably best to not talk about. When they didn't look at her like she was crazy, she continued. "When I pushed open the bathroom door, I heard her. She was making that sound, you know, when someone's just finished crying or they're trying to stop."

"What did you do?" Ms. Jennie asked.

"Anessa was in one of the stalls, the second one.

She must have heard me come in because she got quiet. I didn't have to go or anything, so… I just waited."

"And she eventually came out?" Ms. Jennie asked.

"Yeah, a few seconds later. I said hello, and she came out and stared at me, but from the side, like she didn't want me to see her face." Cassidy rested her chin on clasped hands and continued thoughtfully. "I walked over while she was splashing water on her face and asked if she was okay." Her eyes narrowed as the memory flooded her mind. "She said something like 'fine' or 'I'm fine', and that's when…"

Ms. Jennie placed a hand on Cassidy's shoulder. "That's when what?"

Cassidy spoke slowly as she focused on the exact moment, her memory now crystal clear. "That's when I touched her shoulder." She pulled her knees to her chest and hugged them tightly. How could she explain what happened next when it was unlike anything she'd experienced before? How could she describe what she didn't understand?

"Cassidy," Ms. Jennie said, leaning her head down to meet her gaze. "What happened?"

"There were lights… images. There was," Cassidy's expression soured, "sadness, and hurt, and embarrassment."

"Lights?" Principal Ramsbottom asked. "You mean the lights flickered off and on?"

Cassidy shook her head. "No, not the lights in the room. They were in my head, like pictures in my head." She had said more than she would have liked, but she was just coming to the realization of what happened, and it was spilling from her mouth without a second thought. Judging by the curious looks on Principal Ramsbottom and Ms. Jennie's faces, it seemed best to backtrack some from the talk of visions. She tittered. "I guess I hit my head pretty good."

"Anything else you want to tell us?" Principal Ramsbottom asked hesitantly, as if what she had already heard was more than she expected and more than enough.

Cassidy's eyes widened at realizing she had made it to the end of her memory. "And *that's* the last thing I remember."

Chapter 5

THE OTHER WORLD

Niji slunk and snuck in the manner of despicable things. Though despicability was not her true nature, the behavioral trait was a defense mechanism brought about by circumstance and the dangers of the world in which she was forced to live. Self-preservation was presently her top priority, having traveled on a mission for her empress, far from the protective walls of the palace and its guards.

Niji slid and scurried far below the cedar tree forest's canopy, in and under brush and branches — a canopy more her height. She moved carefully and quietly so as not to draw the attention of keen-eyed creatures, land-bound or winged, who would do her harm or worse, have her for a meal. Her paws pushed her along in a slide atop the topsoil and damp leaves, her fur changing colors to match her surroundings. Her furry tail followed along, as straight and rigid as bamboo. From it hung an iridescent gem attached by twine. Niji stopped mid-slide, her black nose twitching at a familiar smell. It was the scent of something deliciously awful — the reason she had traveled this far from home — the scent of poison fire coral.

For Niji, the trip was an opportunity to munch on her most favorite food, however the impetus of the trip was the empress' need for a fresh batch of poison, for uses that were never disclosed to Niji. Poison fire coral, a fungus, meant certain death to humans and most creatures who dared or mistakenly ate them. For Niji, the more poisonous, the better. She had a genetic immunity to poison, so to her, the fungus was a delicacy. Two months had passed since her last trip to the fungus garden. Not long enough to feel like the first time, but long enough to have been dearly missed.

Her long, narrow pink tongue slid past her pointy white teeth. It rested outside of her mouth, giving her the appearance of being on the edge of insanity. It dangled, tasting the air, then licked the dead leaf colored fur around her long muzzle. Niji lay still as death at the edge of the clearing where the delicacies she came for grew. The poison fire coral sprouted from the ground, resembling burned, gnarled fingers of the dead, digging their way out of the earth. Ears the length of her body pulled from Niji's sides and poked their way through the sharp underbrush, breaching the surface like two leaf-green, furry periscopes. Using her unmatched sense of hearing, she listened intently for the padding of sneaking paws, the rustle of feathered wings, or the breath of anything with teeth or a beak.

Straying far from home was neither easy nor safe — the farther from the empress, the farther away from her protection. The empress and her sibling, the emperor, ruled the known land, or "Everything under the shine of the sun and moon," as the empress would say. But ruling and influence were two separate powers. Someone announcing themselves as ruler, king, or empress in this case was one thing, but influence only carried so far. If something — or someone — happened to Niji out here, who would know? Who would come to her rescue? Cries for help in the forest were answered by the brave or the foolish. Both brave and foolish did inhabit this land, but they were the self-serving kind, not the righteous. The answer was no one; no one would come to her rescue.

Niji peered past the fungus garden and beyond a row of shrubs and a cluster of trees at the grand snowcapped Gadian Mountains standing behind what prevented the empress's power from reaching any farther — a barrier of pure, nearly invisible magic. Viewing anything on the other side of the barrier was like staring at objects in a freshwater creek — everything was crystal clear but slightly distorted. The barrier was not so much a spell or incantation as much as it was a powerful energy emanating from within the valley. A troublemaker who could read minds, amongst other utterly annoying abilities, had created it.

Niji snarled at the magical barrier protecting the mountains, the valley, and the arrogant people who lived there. The empress and emperor wanted nothing more than to gain access to the valley and punish its uninvited residents for banishing them from it, but no one could bypass the barrier. No clawed creature could dig deep enough to go under, nor could any winged beast fly high enough to go over. The mountains and the valley were, alas, inaccessible. As bad as Niji wanted access to the mountains and valley, as sickeningly amazing as they were, all beautiful and serene, the land there didn't grow poison fire coral. The fungus only sprouted from this bleak ground.

Only hearing the creeping, crawling, and skittering of bugs, she pulled her ears back to her sides. Niji slowly poked her head from the underbrush, surveyed the area, and cautiously crept into the clearing. Encircling the clearing were towering cedar trees. In the center stood a single enormous cedar, taller and broader than the others, with a twisted rice-straw rope wrapped around it. The emperor had hung the rope, signifying that a kodama — a tree spirit, harmless and rarely seen — dwelled in the ancient tree. Aside from a few fallen limbs, only spongy green moss and dozens of her beloved fungus covered the ground. Niji's creep became a scamper toward the closest clump. Her damp black nose pressed up against one of the red fingers and she breathed deep, pulling in and holding the aroma with an intoxicated grin. The fur of her face burned a dull red, reaching past her eyes to the tip of her ears. Neck down she remained a bright green to match the mossy ground. "*Oh*, how I've missed you."

The crack of a tree crashing to the ground came from the distance. Niji's head jerked in the direction of the sound, then to the center tree, spying to see if the kodama would show itself to mourn the loss of the tree's life. Seconds passed, but the kodama did not appear. "That was no falling tree," Niji muttered, scowling. Someone was playing a trick. "Keep your distance tengu, I don't need your distraction and bother."

Knowing the tengu, if it indeed was him, he was more than a mile and many minutes away. Niji refocused on her purpose. She reached out a greedy paw, but paused as her claws met her palm around the fungus. The red faded from her face like the end of a sunrise as her eyes closed to slits and her ears rose and rotated to the left. *What now?*

Something was odd; something was different. Not the poison fire coral, it appeared as delicious as usual. Something else was off, something faint. Something that should be there but wasn't. Something less... whole.

Niji lovingly patted the fungus like a child patting a puppy and whispered, "You wait here. I'll be right back."

Facing the direction of what was missing, she stepped slowly and deliberately as her ears rotated and twitched, taking in every sound and the silence in between. The garden of poison fire coral only slightly distracted her hunt. Reaching the far side of the clearing, she shuffled under the brush. She scurried a few feet forward until her muzzle gently scrunched up against the barrier. Niji placed her paw on the translucent barrier, a solid impediment against her. Curiously, the barrier did not impede nature entirely. Tree branches could grow through it, clouds and rain could pass through. This close to the barrier, a breeze from the other side cooled Niji's face. She moved low along the barrier, sliding her paw against the smooth surface. If her instincts and ears were correct — she stopped, wide-eyed, and yanked back her paw. The smooth surface was gone. Niji reached toward the barrier, stopped, shook her paw, and felt into the space of the other side.

A thin layer of whatever energy made up the wall remained in the open space. The gentle breeze was a blustery wind on the other. Niji's furry eyebrows rose, and her jaw dropped. She pulled back her paw with a gasp fitting a creature her size. The fur of her arm resembled thin droplets of water, having changed to match the translucency of the barrier. Shaking was not required to change her fur back to its natural color, but she shook her paw anyway, like the change had to be forcefully removed. What did this mean? Why was there a hole? Why now? That witch on the other side, was she losing her power? In a flash of brilliance, the importance of the hole became evident.

"A way in," Niji muttered. "A. Way. In." A devilish, toothy grin crawled across her face.

Tentatively, she felt for the hole's edges to determine its size. She feared it might close in an instant, leaving her on one side and her foreleg, of which she was quite fond, on the other. Estimating the size of the hole to be that of a small pumpkin, she placed her arm back to the ground at her side, paw still attached, with a relieved sigh.

"The empress. I must inform the empress." Niji's imagination bloomed. The empress would be delighted at the news. Niji would gain great favor, and her status would elevate above that of a spy, messenger, and courier. She would be a trusted advisor to the empress and emperor, a most valuable asset. Land would be allocated to her; she'd have her own guards. She'd have more responsibility, more power. Beyond all of that, she would finally see and experience the valley.

Under the influence of euphoria, Niji shot from the underbrush without regard to stealth. She scampered across the clearing, passing her precious fungus without a second thought. Yes, some things were more important than a satisfied belly and pleased tastebuds.

Her scamper came to an immediate and painful stop only a few feet away from the other side of the clearing. First came the sensation of flipping through the air, followed by the pain of being forcefully slammed to the ground with a thud. The sooty gray legs of a bird with long, piercing talons gripped around her skinny torso came into view through her disoriented vision. Her eyes followed the length of the black-feathered bird up to its long black beak and single functional eye staring down at her. Where its left eye should have been was a raised, straight scar.

Niji fought for the breath to force out a distasteful greeting. "Ugh. Hello, crow."

The crow, who was not a crow but a raven — a freakishly large one — laughed a deep croaky laugh, raising its head and spreading its wings in a victorious flourish that spanned several feet across. The raven leaned down until the tip of its beak touched Niji's wet nose. "Hello, weasel."

Niji scoffed. "You shall address me by either my name or my title — the Empress' Ears. And I am a kitsune, not a weasel. Meddlesome little creatures they are. You should know, you saved me from them once."

The raven nodded. "Ah, yes, the kamaitachi. One creature more annoying than you, but they don't pretend to be something they are not. Have you not examined your reflection on pond water? You are not a kitsune. I've known kitsune. Your empress and emperor are kitsune. Never have I seen a kitsune as tiny as you and with color-changing fur. You can't even shapeshift. And those ears," he laughed. "Those long ridiculous ears. Tell me, *kitsune*, where is your second tail? Have you not reached your hundredth year? That hoshi no tama hanging from your only tail likely holds hot air instead of your soul." He paused, scrutinizing her. "Oh, Niji. Did I hit a nerve?"

Maybe she wasn't full kitsune, but her mother was. And her father? She wasn't sure. She had reached her hundredth year a month ago and hoped she'd grow a second tail. Perhaps she was a late bloomer, or maybe she had her birthdate wrong —

a hundred years is a long time. And, no matter what anyone said, her soul was most certainly in her hoshi no tama. It had to be. She'd never been parted from her gem, but if she had and her soul was indeed inside, she'd be dead. "You arrogant, cycloptic feather-head, you did not hit a —"

The raven pressed her into the ground with added force. "How about now? Now have I hit a nerve?"

Niji's ears reached for anything to grasp to pull her to safety but jabbed uselessly into the mossy ground. Words squeezed from her mouth, along with the last of the air in her lungs. "What do… you want… Sureto?"

Sureto thoughtfully tapped the foremost feather of his wing against his beak. "What do I want? You're right to ask, weasel." He examined her. "I'm sorry. Is there something more you wish to say?" He shifted his weight, relieving some of the pressure from her chest.

She gasped, taking in rapid breaths. "Stop calling me weasel. If the empress knew what you —"

"If she knew," Sureto said in a slow, dreadful squawk. "It's not if, but *how* could she know? How could she possibly know I caught the *Empress' Ear* so far from the palace?"

"It's Ears, not Ear —" Niji paused, comprehending Sureto's threat. "You would not! You would never —"

"Bite off one of your ridiculously long ears? Oh, I would." Sureto leaned back with his wings spread and croaked a loud laugh. "I most certainly would."

Terror bubbled up inside Niji and exploded as she fought against Sureto's taloned grip. Her paws pushed as her ears wrapped around his legs, tugging and pulling. She nearly broke free before the raven stepped on and gripped her neck hard enough to secure her, but not quite to the point of choking.

"Let me go!" It pained her to say those words. Niji never begged for anything.

"Oh relax, weasel. I won't bite off your ear."

Niji ceased struggling, awash in relief at the break in the clouds of impending doom. "You won't? Well, of course you won't. Clearly, you've come to your bird-brained senses. You —"

Sureto leaned in close, the rot of whatever rodent he had for breakfast on his breath. "Why stop at your ear when I can have all of you?"

Niji gasped. *This is the end of me.* Her mind raced, scrambling for a plan, a plea, a way to gain her freedom. *The hole.* She could tell him about the hole in the barrier. Surely it and the land beyond would interest him more than she, a nearly meatless meal. *No.* She couldn't tell Sureto before telling the empress. She could never do that. *Could I?*

Pain erupted where her left ear met her head. Sureto pulled back mid-nibble, just far enough to look into her wide, darting eyes. "Last words, weasel?"

"I am not a weasel," Niji huffed. Determination to keep the secret fought against her desire to live. What use was not telling Sureto if she never got a chance to tell the empress? The words flowed

from her mouth like molasses. "If you let me go…
I'll… tell you something. A secret."

Sureto croaked dismissively. "I have no need for
secrets."

"Yes, I too believe in your lack of desire to gain
knowledge. But this secret is something amazing,
something spectacular. A secret meant for the
empress, spoken by me, the Empress' Ears, the only
one who knows of this secret. It's — it's the most
important secret I've ever had to share. But if you
kill me, it dies with me."

Sureto straightened and tapped a single talon
against Niji's head, regarding her curiously. "What
do you know, Niji?"

She wiggled her head, attempting to evade the
tapping talon. "First… stop… tapping… my
head… with your stupid claw."

He stopped. Sensing an opportunity at accord
with the raven, she nodded at Sureto's feet, firmly
gripping her waist and neck. "Now, let me go."

Sureto shook his beaked head. "That I will not
do. But I will release one of my grips. Something
we can build upon." He pulled his taloned foot from
around her waist, placing it firmly on the mossy
ground. "There. You were saying?"

Imperfect as the situation was, it was as much as
she could hope for. Sureto would have to be stupid
to also release her neck. If he had, she'd be in the
brush in a second, running for freedom. "Fine. Here's
the deal. I tell you the secret, and you let me go.
You let me go so I can tell the empress. And none
of this ever happened. No harm will come to you."

Sureto scratched his head with his fore-feather. "I don't like the sound of this deal."

"What?" Niji said, dumbfounded. "How exactly would you like it to sound, bird?"

Sureto placed his wings together in a teepee shape. "It should sound like this: *I* will let you go after you tell me the secret."

Niji's furry jaw dropped, brushing against his leg. "What? That's the same thing! It's exactly the same thing!"

Sureto applied a slight amount of pressure to her neck and leaned down. "No. It's about power. It's about my power over you. I do the letting go, in my utmost kindness, after you tell the secret."

In whatever order Sureto arranged the words of the agreement, it was indeed the same. He simply always needed to be first, even when it came to sentence structure. Niji opened her mouth to say something unsavory about Sureto's ego but kept it to herself. "Very well. You incorrigible—" she sighed. "You know the barrier? The one around the mountains and valley?"

"Of course, who doesn't?" Sureto asked impatiently.

"Well… there's a gap. A small hole, wide enough for me to fit through." She paused at the raven's unimpressed expression. "Maybe even wide enough for *you* to fit through."

Sureto laughed, nearly losing his balance. "Lies. That barrier has been there for thousands of seasons. It was there soon after you were born."

"Y-yes," Niji stuttered, sensing her opportunity at freedom slipping from her grasp, "And now there is a beak — I mean a break — and I will tell you where as soon as you release your clammy claw. Then you can flippity-flap your way over to it, enter the valley, and eat whatever your cold heart desires." *Or maybe a sea eagle will have you for lunch.*

Sureto loosened his grip, appearing to carefully consider her offer. She could almost see the blue sky and green valley in the raven's eye, a memory of the time before the battle and their banishment. He broke from his reverie and brought his functioning eye close to one of Niji's, speaking urgently. "Where? Tell me where. I must know."

"Promise. Promise me, Sureto. You will let me go. You will let me live."

Sureto looked up to the sky with an expression of frustration. "Weasel," he croaked. "If you are lying…"

"If I'm lying, I'll be gone before you get back. So, there's no use in threatening me."

"Are you trying to talk me out of letting you go?"

Niji huffed. "I felt the full breeze on the other side. The hole is there. Honesty, Sureto. It's about honesty."

Sureto squawked. "Honesty? From you? Hilarious."

"Decide, raven," Niji said curtly. A tense moment passed before Sureto reluctantly released his grip. Niji sat up and winced, rubbing at her neck. "Thank you," she said with a sneer and not a single ounce of sincerity.

Sureto splayed a talon toward her, ready to resume his grip around her neck. "Tell me, tell me now. Where is this opening?"

Niji placed her four paws firmly on the ground and glanced at the brush behind her. She could run away, run from the clearing and away from the psychotic bird. However, if the time came in the future when their paths crossed again, she'd prefer to be in his good graces instead of his beak and belly.

"Niji, you promised. Where? Tell me where."

She nodded toward the shrub shrouding the hole. "There. Behind the far shrub. The hole is low near the ground. You can't miss it."

Sureto eyed her a final time, hesitating, then took off with a mighty flap of his wings. He reached the shrub, swooped down, and was gone.

Gone too was Niji. She left with urgency, fearing that if for some reason the hole had closed, the raven would be back to finish his meal. She ran for the palace to inform the empress of the way into the world they'd been locked out of for a century, a world that would once again be theirs.

Chapter 6

It wasn't yet lunchtime on the first day of school, and Cassidy was already on her way home in the backseat of the family SUV, sitting next to grocery-filled cloth bags. Dad bought groceries a few times a week, as he often cooked whatever came to his mind that day. Most of his dinners were great, but on occasion, Cassidy would push his food invention around the plate with her fork until she got the okay to dump it in the garbage.

Before unsteadily leaving the nurse's office, Cassidy had told Ms. Jennie and Principal Ramsbottom, with no uncertainty, that she had only fainted — Anessa did not hurt her. She asked them to promise that Anessa would not be in trouble. They promised. Though, it could have been one of those times adults promised something just to get a kid to do what they asked. Especially since a pinky swear was not performed. But Cassidy trusted Ms. Jennie — she could always believe in her.

Maisy had asked, no, more like *strongly recommended* that she go home with Cassidy. She wouldn't accept no for an answer until Cassidy's dad insisted she stay at school for the remainder of the day. He did, however, promise — that word again — that she could come over right after her dance practice. On this promise, a pinky swear *was* performed. It reminded Cassidy that Dad needed pinky swear practice. He treated it more like thumb wrestling.

Dad backed out of the parking spot and asked his Bluetooth to call Mom. She answered a few rings later.

"What's going on?" she prompted. "I have a client coming in soon."

Mom worked as a financial planner. "I help people plan for and reach their dreams," she told anyone who asked what she did for a living. The financial planner title always came after to clarify her actual job. On more than one occasion, she preached, "What we do in life is not our job or our title; it's what we do for people, it's what we do to make the world a better place." A sanitation worker is someone who helps keep our homes and streets clean, a fisher is someone who feeds the world, a police officer is someone who upholds the laws and keeps us safe, and so on. Someone once asked her about politicians, and apparently their job was, "Oh gosh. Don't make me go there."

Dad pressed the monitor to take the call off the car speakers and put the phone to his ear. "I'm leaving Cassie's school to take her home.

She's okay… she's okay," he said reassuringly. "She fainted and bumped her head. It's not too bad."

It was nearly impossible for Cassidy to make out Mom's words, but the worried tone in her voice was crystal clear.

"No," Dad said. "The nurse said she doesn't have a concussion, but I'll ask Bob to come over and check on her."

Mom spoke as Dad both nodded and, what he usually only did when not in Mom's presence, shook his head.

"Ann… Ann," he said in a calm tone, trying to get a word in. "You worry about your clients. I have this under control. But I think it may have started."

Silence.

"Sorry. I probably shouldn't have said that," Dad concluded. "We'll talk tonight."

Mom's final words were barely audible in the relative silence.

Dad pressed his phone screen and released a loud breath as he placed it in his lap. His troubled eyes met Cassidy's in the rearview mirror. He smiled. "Mom will be home later."

Cassidy smiled as she settled into her favorite cushy part of the couch and covered her legs with a fleece blanket. Nothing was quite as amazing as the combination of a comfy couch, soft blanket,

Capri Sun, and a good book bought over the weekend with her allowance.

Last year she scored low on reading comprehension, so she promised her teacher — and herself — that she would read one book every two weeks this school year. At the rate she had been buying books, she was ready for the challenge. Her to-be-read pile was nearly knee-high. She loved books that told stories of girls bravely overcoming overwhelming odds, girls who were secret agents and had to outsmart devious adults, girls struggling through school because they were different, and girls fighting against frightening monsters. The cover of her new book, *Sue and the Eight-Headed Dragon*, had the image of an armor-wearing girl holding a long, intimidating sword. Sue stood with her shoulders up and back, and her black braid flowed behind her as if blown by a strong wind, though it could have been by a dragon's breath. Certainly the pages of the book would explain. Cassidy wouldn't have to move from her spot on the couch in like, forever, or until she got hungry. But she only had to ask politely and Dad would bring her snacks.

Dad repeatedly asked if she was okay. Seriously, he asked every couple of minutes. He paced around the house, cleaning and straightening the already clean and straight, scratching at apparently rampant itches on his head and neck, and staring at the clock on his phone as if urging time to hurry.

Cassidy stopped mid-sip of her drink pouch, the straw resting on her bottom lip. *I should ask*

Dad what he meant when he said, "I think it may have started." But by looks of him — a crazy person — she opted to wait for Mom to get home. Dad wore a manic expression that she rarely, no, *never* saw on him. Dad was the calmest, most level-headed person she knew. He was all "mantras and meditation" in a hectic world. He was mister "everything will be all right", "you are what you think", "manifest your dreams", and all that stuff she had heard him preach over and over, but clearly, positive thinking wasn't working for whatever was wrong now.

What *was* wrong? What had started? She'd just been nervous about the first day of school and worried about Anessa. Why would any of this be a surprise? Who wouldn't be concerned about someone being upset? Well… Brody wouldn't. But what normal person wouldn't? But, there was something more. More than seeing Anessa sad, more than feeling sorry for her and wanting to help. The lights and images she saw when touching Anessa's shoulder were like movie snippets. They were brief and not all that clear, but each appeared to show Anessa in some state of sadness or embarrassment. Seeing them wasn't the worst of it either — feeling Anessa's emotions, that was the worst part. Cassidy winced, bringing her hands tight to her chest.

"Cassidy."

The images, the sadness, it was too much, and she'd fainted. It was all too much.

"Cassidy."

What did it all mean? How could she see *and* feel Anessa's sadness? And that voice, her own voice that said, *"Help her."*

"Blue!" Dad yelled.

Cassidy jumped in her seat and gasped. "What!"

"Did you hear me? Are you okay?"

Her heart pounded a heavy metal song. "Yeah. Geez. I'm good. What?"

"Doctor Shaw will be here soon to check on you."

Doctor Bob Shaw was a neighbor a few doors down. She had once heard Mom say Doctor Shaw was "mostly retired". Mom had helped with his retirement plan. Being mostly retired meant he was home a lot, and could come over for an unscheduled house call.

Cassidy nodded and tried to sound reassuring because the attention she had received today was already too much. "Okay, but I feel fine, really." But really, she didn't. She felt far from fine. It wasn't that she felt sick, like that one night a couple years ago when she barely made it to the toilet to throw up her lunch and dinner. She vowed to never eat lamb again. This was different. She felt off; she felt strange. Like she had something to do, and until she did it, her world wouldn't be right — it would be broken, out of order. She felt anxious, without an idea of how to relieve the anxiety. An invisible force gnawed at her, trying to push her into action, though what that action was, she didn't know. If her suspicions were true, it had something to do with Anessa.

The doorbell rang, sending Dad to his feet with a jump. "That must be Bob — Doctor Shaw. Wait here."

Cassidy nodded again, having no plans to leave her comfy spot on the couch.

The front door opened with an exchange of hellos.

"Where is that young lady of yours?" Doctor Shaw said, his booming voice traveling from the foyer to the living room. Seconds later, a short, stumpy, white-haired man wearing a stethoscope walked into the living room. He wore a plaid button-up shirt, brown shorts with a browner belt, and black socks with images of thermometers, medicine bottles, stethoscopes, and other doctor stuff across them. Without a pause in his step, he walked over to the couch and sat next to Cassidy. He peered down at her over eyeglasses clinging to the tip of his nose like an ocular daredevil risking a fall. His cologne was woodsy, like he had recently rolled around in a pile of pine needles or gotten into a fight with a Christmas tree and lost. "Cassidy. How are you feeling, young lady?"

She sat up and pushed her hair behind her ears, but her finger went to work, twirling away at a lock of it. "Okay, I guess."

"You guess?"

"Well, yeah. A little different, I guess."

Doctor Shaw took her by the wrist. "Breathe normally while I take your pulse."

Cassidy nodded, and though told to breathe normally, all she could do was think about her breathing and wonder whether it was normal or not.

"What do you mean, different?" he asked, checking his watch. He let go of her wrist and nodded approvingly.

"I don't know… different." Nervously, Cassidy went from playing with her hair to the scrunchie around her wrist. She wasn't about to tell him about seeing the images and hearing the voice. She might end up in a home for crazy people. "It's hard to explain."

"Where did you hit your head?"

She touched the back of her head and grimaced as her fingers found the sore spot.

"Lean your head down and let me look. Do you feel sick, like you need to throw up?"

A disgusting thought of lamb came and went. "Um, no."

"Now, look up. Do I or anything in the room appear blurry? Do you see two of anything?"

The objects of the room were all crisp, clear, and singular. "No. Nothing like that."

"Do you feel dizzy or off-balance?"

"She did faint," Dad said.

Doctor Shaw gave Dad a quick head shake and turned back to her. "How about after you fainted?"

"Yeah… I guess," Cassidy said. "I was in the nurse's office. I woke up and was, you know, dizzy at first."

"And now?"

Dad was biting at a fingernail, practically attacking it.

"I'm fine. Nurse Becky took my blood pressure with that thingy and said I was okay."

"Very good." Doctor Shaw smiled warmly and patted her blanketed knee. "You bumped your noggin, but there's no sign of a concussion." He stood and walked over to Dad. "I recommend scheduling an appointment with her pediatrician." He added something about her becoming a "young lady", bringing an expression of horror to Dad's face.

"You get some rest, Cassidy," Doctor Shaw said, pushing his glasses up the bridge of his nose. Comically his eyes looked enlarged behind the lenses, appearing more mad scientist than doctor. He patted the pocket of his button-up shirt and looked regretful. "Oh no. I'm sorry, I forgot to bring a lollipop."

"That's okay — no, wait." Cassidy reached into her backpack on the floor next to her, rummaged around, and pulled out the lollipop Nurse Becky had given her. "Here." She crossed the room and slipped the lollipop into Doctor Shaw's empty shirt pocket, smiling conspiratorially. "Now, did you bring a lollipop for me?"

He laughed and smiled pleasantly. "I most certainly did." He handed the lollipop to Cassidy with an exaggerated wink.

"Thank you." She plopped back onto the couch and wrapped up in the blanket.

Doctor Shaw left, giving Cassidy the time alone she desired. She sucked on the lollipop — lemon, not her favorite — and pondered over the most important question of her life: what the heck was wrong with her?

Chapter 7

Cassidy had moved from the couch to her bed, fighting against counting the hours, minutes, and seconds before her mom came home. Mom was good at fixing things. She would know what was going on and what to do. Cassidy passed the time with shifts of reading, watching YouTube videos, and thinking about Anessa and what she saw when touching her shoulder.

She laid back and stared at the textured, light brown ceiling, examining the lines and grooves that never quite formed discernible shapes. She focused on settling her anxious mind and closed her eyes, hoping blacking out the world around her would help pull the images from her memory. Minutes passed as she lay with her brow furrowed and eyes shut tight. The images were there, creeping at the edge of recollection as if waiting to be coaxed into showing themselves. Like when someone she didn't know came over for a visit, and her parents would insist she emerge from hiding to make an appearance and introduce herself. She was never hiding, she was just in her bedroom… avoiding. The introduction was always, "Hi. My name is Cassidy. Nice to meet you." Her parents were trying to get her comfortable with social situations, but still, she didn't like meeting new people and the horribly painful small talk that came with it. Adults always asked the same question, "What do you like to do, Cassidy?" She wanted to tell them that she liked to be alone or with Maisy, but to be polite and ordinary, she would say reading or playing video games. Adults assumed that all kids enjoyed playing video games, so it was an easy enough response though she had never picked up a controller in her life.

A long-held breath shot from her nostrils like air from an untied balloon. Her clenched fists relaxed as she focused on clearing her mind. Ambient sounds entered her room — cars passing on the street, birds chirping, a lawnmower somewhere in the distance, the cold air blowing from the floor vent. The sounds were a relaxing harmony allying with the softness of her bed, pulling her toward sleep. Like the beam of a flashlight illuminating an object in the dark, she found the images in the space between consciousness and unconsciousness — the visions of Anessa, as clear and bright as the screen of her tablet. They played like a personal video channel: free of hearts or thumbs up, and a viewer count of one — Cassidy.

She struggled to follow the images. The center was in focus with a vignette edge, but the movement was like a camera on a wobbling swivel, creating blurred segments: shots of a floor, of shoes tied by hesitant hands, then by adult hands. Cassidy heard voices. A young girl's voice, Anessa, saying she didn't want to go to school and a woman's voice — her mom, maybe — saying she had to, and no one would even notice her shoes.

The woman wore a uniform, the kind you would see at a restaurant, like the breakfast place that served pancakes with a banana and whipped cream smiley face on top. Anessa was wringing her hands in her lap when the vision blurred like water on a camera lens. No, not water... tears. Anessa was crying. "Mom, everyone will notice," she said, resigned.

Her mom returned with keys jingling in her hand. "Let's go, or we'll be late."

The vision changed to that of a school through a dirty window in the backseat of a car. It was *the* school, Cassidy's school — Canyon River Elementary. Words were exchanged — Anessa pleading and her mother saying something about "going" or "not going" and "getting out of the car" or "not getting out". Her mother offered a plea of her own, "Go today, and I'll see what I can figure out."

Anessa mournfully relented. "Okay. Promise?"

Her mother promised, but it sounded doubtful, desperate.

Then came hurried steps on the ground and quick glances forward and back. A cacophony of high and low voices came from all directions. Barely audible chuckles and snickers were near, directed at her. Stairs were climbed by tattered shoes. Anessa glanced at doors with numbers on them — 101… 103… 105…

She stopped outside room 107: her room, Cassidy's room, Mrs. Higgins' room. She yanked open the door, found her desk and sat, plunking her backpack on the floor to her right. She took a shuddered breath and sniffled, wringing her hands. She was alone, not even Mrs. Higgins was in the room. She glanced at the clock as the five-minute warning bell rang and ran a hand ran across her t-shirt and shorts like it would erase the wrinkles and stains. Maybe she was wishing her hands were magic, and by passing them over her old clothes, new and brilliant clothes would appear. But her hands were not magic. Stains resembling dirt remained. She swung her feet under her chair, hiding her tattered shoes.

The classroom door opened. Maisy entered the room and then… Cassidy watched herself walk in and over to Maisy, who was appreciatively nodding at the desks. *Do I actually walk like that? And what is my hair doing?* Moments later, more students piled into the classroom. Faces familiar to Cassidy: Josie, Adam — *ugh* — Brody — *double ugh* — Alex, and others. Anessa kept her head low, stealing an occasional glance at them, avoiding eye contact.

A voice grabbed her attention, Maisy saying, "Grody Brody." In Anessa's peripheral, a finger pointed at her. It was Adam, pointing at her shoes and clothes, laughing. He said something to Brody who had just turned around, red-faced.

I remember this part. Anessa bolted from the room past Mrs. Higgins, who had just said, "Good morning, class."

The vision cut to the bathroom. Anessa was in a stall with a wad of wet paper towels, scrubbing at the dirt on the sides of her canvas shoes. She sniffled and breathed a quavered breath. The bathroom door opened, and a voice called out — a familiar voice, Cassidy's voice. Anessa left the stall, glanced left, and Cassidy saw herself standing at the bathroom's entrance. Anessa looked at her reflection of red-rimmed eyes and splotchy cheeks, and then a hand touched her shoulder. Cassidy watched herself fall to the ground through Anessa's shocked eyes, and the image went dark.

Cassidy shot up to a sit on her bed with a gasp. She breathed raggedly as her eyes adjusted to the daylight streaming into her room. Through tear-soaked and squinting eyes, the clock read 3:50. She'd been asleep, if that's what it was, for only thirty-five minutes. She dropped down onto her pillow and wiped the tears from her eyes. *The visions were of Anessa. But how?* How could she see what Anessa saw? Did any of it really happen, or was it all in her imagination? Was it a dream, or a story her mind created to explain why Anessa was sad? It was all so real and accurate, the clothes everyone wore and the words everyone said — including her own. *How was there so much to see? I only touched her for a second. Heck, I don't even know if touching her shoulder had anything to do with it.*

Anessa's sadness somehow called to Cassidy,

urging her to *feel* it, understand it. But why would sadness call to her? Cassidy had read stories about mermaids, and not the pretty ones who could sing like pop stars and talk to sea creatures. She read about scary mermaids that would sing to unexpecting sailors, leading them and their ships to the doom of craggy rocks hidden beneath the murky water's surface. Was the sadness the mermaid's song and Anessa the rocks?

"What's wrong with me?" Cassidy said aloud, worried. "Why do I feel so sad?" She pressed her palms to her temples. She hadn't hit her head this time, but it pounded just the same.

Knock-knock.

She jerked up from her hands and breathed in sharply, turning toward her bedroom door. "What?" she asked, startled.

"Sorry," Dad apologized. "Mom's home early."

Chapter 8

assidy's mom stopped within view and earshot outside of Cassidy's bedroom. "How is she?" she asked Cassidy's dad, then whispered something Cassidy assumed she didn't want overheard. However, if Cassidy's ears did not fail her, Mom said, "It could be something else."

That word again — it. Whatever "it" was, Cassidy apparently had it, was infected with it, or was it. "It" must be a big deal — it brought Mom home from work two hours early, and that was no easy feat. Mom glanced at Cassidy, placed a hand on Dad's chest, and said, "I'll talk to her." She entered the room, wearing her black work pantsuit and black socks; her shoulder-length black hair in a tight bun, still perfectly in place at the end of her shortened workday.

Cassidy sat on the edge of her bed, the tips of her toes grazing the carpet. "Hi, Mom."

Mom kicked aside an empty shoebox, a few worn socks, and an empty cookie pack. She knelt in front of Cassidy, her expression soft and empathetic. "Hi, sweetie." She moved a strand of hair in front of Cassidy's left eye behind her ear. "How are you feeling?"

"I'm good," Cassidy said through a yawn. "I just got up from a nap." At least the nap part was true.

"I heard you fainted at school. Want to tell me about it?"

Cassidy sighed, having already told the story to Ms. Jennie, Principal Ramsbottom, Dad, and some of it to Doctor Shaw. She'd have to tell Maisy, and probably her classmates and Mrs. Higgins. Eventually, she imagined she'd share the horrid details with a famous daytime talk show host. Not that she could ever be a celebrity, standing in front of the class to read a report was terrifying enough. But she had considered being a secretive musical artist by wearing a mask, like Marshmello. She scrunched her nose. "Short version?"

Mom patted her knee. "Sure."

Cassidy tried to explain the weird experience of when she first saw Anessa, and how she followed Anessa into the bathroom to check on her because she seemed sad. She recounted how she touched Anessa's shoulder and saw flashes of light and images before she fainted.

Mom looked to Dad, who shrugged.

"These flashes... images, what were they?" Mom asked.

Cassidy crossed her legs on the bed and looked away for a moment. "Promise you won't think I'm crazy?"

Mom rose from the floor to sit next to her on the bed. "Oh no, Cass. I would never think you're crazy. No one will think you're crazy."

Oh yeah? Wait until you hear this. Cassidy hesitated, staring at her hands in her lap. "I didn't know at first, when it happened. I didn't know what the images were." She picked at a hangnail on her pinky. How could she tell them about the visions she saw during her nap and sound believable? It *was* the truth; she wasn't making it up. Cassidy mustered up her bravery. "When I fell asleep, I saw them again. But this time they were clear. Like watching TV, but through someone else's eyes. More like VR… ya know, virtual reality?"

Mom nodded. "What did you see?"

"I saw Anessa's morning before school, and what happened to her when she got to school. I saw what made her sad."

Mom shifted her weight and wrung her hands. She performed a single audible hard swallow. "Why —" She paused as if she was afraid to ask or afraid of the answer. "Why was Anessa sad?"

Cassidy frowned, finding a spot on her thumbnail to chew. Seeing and experiencing the visions, the underlying theme was clear. "Anessa was embarrassed to go to school, but her mom made her."

"Why was she embarrassed?" Dad asked.

"Because her clothes were old and dirty." Cassidy's chest ached at reliving Anessa's day. A tear slipped from the corner of her eye. "She didn't have new school clothes. I think, maybe, her mom couldn't afford any." The single tear was followed by another.

Mom pulled Cassidy into a side hug, often used to make things better, and said it would be okay.

"But that wasn't the worst part," Cassidy continued. "When Anessa got to school, she tried to hide, ya know, she tried to get to class first and sit in a corner to be alone. But it didn't help. Kids saw her —" She paused, surprised and ashamed of the anger welling inside her. "They saw her before she could get in the classroom, and they pointed at her and laughed before class started."

Mom stroked Cassidy's hair and softly shushed her. "It's okay, Cassie. It's okay."

Cassidy pulled away, tears blurring her vision. "Is something wrong with me, Mom? Is my mind broken or something?"

Mom pulled her close again. Dad knelt in front of her, patting her knee.

"Oh no, Cassie," Mom said reassuringly. "You're not broken, silly."

"Then," Cassidy's voice hitched, "what's happening to me?"

Mom and Dad exchanged a look.

"Cassie, I need you to trust me. Can you do that?" Mom asked.

Cassidy sniffled, took a double breath, and nodded.

"Grandma will be here tomorrow when you get home from school."

Cassidy pulled away, openmouthed. "Grandma? How? She's in Oregon."

"I called her. She's flying in tomorrow."

"But why?"

"This is where you trust me and know that you are *not* broken. I want her to talk to you. She knows more about what is going on."

Cassidy wanted to say something or ask everything to get Mom to tell her what was going on. Something *was* wrong, and definitely different. But at least, maybe, she wasn't broken. Mom wouldn't lie to her and Grandma was coming to see her tomorrow. Usually, the announcement of Grandma visiting would bring her joy, but a sense of uncertainty tightened Cassidy's throat, like waiting for the results of a math test she didn't study enough for. *Breathe, just breathe.*

"You okay, Blue?" Dad asked.

"Yes," she said, exhaling. "I'm good." *Kind of.* She took another deep breath.

"Good. Relax and breathe. You're gonna be fine."

The doorbell rang.

Mom checked her smartwatch. "Four-twenty. I bet that's Maisy here to see you."

"Can she come in?" Cassidy asked.

Dad scoffed as he stood. "Do you think we could keep her from you?" He grinned. "I'll go let her in and bring you some tissues."

"And I'll get you and Maisy some snacks," Mom said. "How does that sound?"

Cassidy's grin narrowly overpowered her frown. "Great. Thanks, Mom."

"Oh, and Cassie," Mom added. "Maybe not share too much about this with Maisy… for now."

Cassidy opened her mouth to protest.
"At least until after we speak with Grandma."
Cassidy hesitantly nodded. "Okay."
The doorbell rang again.

Chapter 9

Maisy stayed a full hour later than usual for a school night. After dinner, the girls hung out in Cassidy's bedroom, talked about the day, and laughed over YouTube videos. Maisy peppered her with questions while they watched: How do you feel? Why did you faint? What's wrong? What was up with the new girl?

Cassidy could somewhat answer each of the questions, but being honest, she didn't have a concrete answer for any of them. She only knew for sure what happened in class and the bathroom. Yes, she saw visions of Anessa's day, but could she say they were real? And what about the creepy voice, her own voice, saying "Help her"? Did she really hear it, or just imagine it? She, too, wanted answers, and she wanted to give them to Maisy — her best and only true friend. When panic threatened to take hold all those first days of school, it was Dad's breathing technique *and* Maisy who got her through. But before she could confide in Maisy with what she thought was the truth, she needed to talk to Grandma, who was apparently the only one with answers.

"Anessa was sad," Cassidy said, answering Maisy's last question.

Maisy set down the tablet, the screen paused on a funny chihuahua video. "Sad? Why?"

"She —" Cassidy gathered the visions from her memory. "She was upset because her clothes were old and dirty." She scrunched her nose. "Did you notice?"

Maisy shook her head. "I was too busy dealing with Grody Brody."

Cassidy smiled uncomfortably. Though preferring to be alone or with Maisy, she had always felt a need to make everyone around her feel comfortable and welcome; she felt protective of their feelings. Even though she hated when Brody called her names, or anyone for that matter, she worried about how it made him feel to be called "Grody Brody". Still, she appreciated Maisy being there for her. "Yeah, thanks for getting him to leave me alone."

Maisy smiled. "Anytime, sis."

Cassidy's smile faded as she peered into her closet through the crack of the open door, past the line of the bedroom light splaying along the floor into darkness. Kicking aside a pair of jeans, Cassidy walked to the closet and flicked on the light switch. Hanging clothes lined her closet, the size of a half-bathroom, from left to right. The top shelves held boxes containing once-cherished toys and stuffed animals she wasn't yet ready to part with. Clothes that may or may not have been clean and shoes covered the floor. But saying shoes covered the floor was an understatement. She had a gang of shoes, a load of shoes, a canvas army of shoes. She knelt and checked the tongues for sizes.

"What are you doing?" Maisy asked from the bed.

Cassidy shook her head and frowned. "I have so many shoes… a lot I don't wear anymore. I can't even fit into some of these."

"And?"

Cassidy pondered over the gaggle of shoes. "What size do you think —"

"Anessa wears?" Maisy finished.

Usually, they acknowledged finishing each other's sentences with a smile and their latest version of a handshake, but Cassidy's mind was elsewhere. "She's smaller than me," she mused. "I bet my smaller shoes would fit her." A wave of a smile curled across Cassidy's face, and she jumped to her feet. "I have an idea." She trotted to the bed and hopped on next to Maisy.

Maisy matched her smile, teeth for teeth. "What?"

"Well," Cassidy said, her hands moving excitedly, "if I'm right, and Anessa needs shoes and maybe clothes… what if we invite her over for a try-on, and she can have whatever she wants?"

Maisy's mouth opened in excitement but immediately closed to a straight line, her brow furrowing. "But what if she can't come over? Or… or what if she's too embarrassed."

Cassidy covered her mouth with her hand, considered Maisy's concerns, and perked up at an idea. "Exactly."

"Uh. Exactly what?"

Cassidy straightened and took Maisy by the shoulders. "You'll just have to convince her."

Maisy's eyes widened as she leaned away. "What? Me?"

Cassidy leaned in, nodding. "Everyone listens to you, and you get people to do stuff. It's like one of your superpowers."

Maisy tilted her head and pursed her lips. "It is, isn't it," she said with a smile.

Cassidy returned the smile and nodded. "Mmhmm."

Maisy left soon after hatching the plan they codenamed Operation Dress Anessa. With a shower taken and teeth brushed, Cassidy said goodnight to Mom and Dad, who were extra attentive with everything that had happened. She told them she was okay like a bazillion times. She laid in bed, thinking over Operation Dress Anessa.

She'll come over, won't she? What if Maisy can't convince her? What if Anessa's mom won't let her? I don't even know where she lives… what if she lives too far away?

"Wait. Dad can take her home." One potential problem solved.

Sleep pulled at Cassidy as she felt more confident with her plan.

YAWN.

I hope my old shoes fit her.

YAAWN.

I hope she likes them.

YAAAWN.

I can do it. I can make Anessa happy. I have to. I have….

Cassidy dreamed that night. And though she dreamed many nights, these dreams were unfamiliar, peculiar even. She dreamed of lush green mountains with tops of snow-capped craggy stone that stretched toward the clouds. She dreamed of well-traveled, tree-lined paths that meandered up, down, and across the mountains. Birds and unseen animals rustled in secret hiding places. The serenity and reverence of nature pulled her in like a warm blanket. Formless, she floated through the scenery like a ghost.

Next she lay in a field of long, flowing green grass. Above her, a blue sky filled with billowy white clouds drifted effortlessly by with a push from a gentle breeze. The clouds formed shapes as they passed. Not shapes she had to imagine, not "that resembles a dragon", no, a cloud became a dragon with a long spiky tail, four stubby legs, and a head emitting a flame-shaped cloud. Clouds formed fish and swam across the sky, swirling together in an aquatic dance around a turtle, or a man, or a turtle-man. A building appeared, a castle maybe, like one she had seen in a picture book about Japan with Grandma.

A cloud floated by in the shape of a boy holding a sword. He swung the weapon in a way that resembled a dance or a form similar to a martial arts performance she saw at the school talent show last year. The boy's eyes released two brief bursts of static electricity. *Wait. Was he staring at me?* But as quickly as the boy and his electric eyes appeared, the cloud was lost to the wind.

Chapter 10

THE OTHER WORLD

Niji neared the end of the day-long trek back to the Palace of the Divine, which would have taken less time had she not needed to take the long way and intermittently hide to avoid predators and shady characters. As she often did, she internally laughed when thinking of the name — the Palace of the Divine. The palace was a beautiful and impressive structure, but divine? Though, she couldn't blame the brother and sister rulers for naming it as such. Everything about them had to appear, feel, and sound like royalty. Their rule was tenuous. Not because they lacked powerful attributes or didn't have the mindset for ruling, they had both. Their rule was tenuous because the inhabitants of the land were… difficult, to say the least.

The palace came into view as the dirt road turned to gravel. As the thick underbrush gave way to unobstructed ground, she ran at top speed to the right of the road under the cover of rows of tall copper cypress trees. The area around the base of the trees was free of clutter, branches, and brush. The emperor wanted the guard to have a clear view of anyone approaching, so he ordered a team of servants to clear the surrounding land of fallen limbs every morning. Shrubs and other plants didn't grow around the palace; he would not allow it. Being a forest kitsune, allowing flora to grow or not to grow was one of his abilities.

Charred land lay on the other side of the path. Days earlier, a fire had ravaged the area. The trees that remained resembled burned pencils sticking from the ground. Niji shook her head yet again, seeing the destruction that had deeply disturbed the emperor. He had first believed his sister started the fire after an argument they had. Niji wouldn't put it past the empress to do something as vengeful, but witnesses claimed to have seen a lightning strike during a passing storm. Helpless, the emperor could only weep as he watched the tragedy unfold. He was the Son of the Forest, not the son of preventing lightning strikes and fire. Instead of blaming the gods for the destruction, the emperor thanked them for the opportunity at rebirth. Then, with great love and devotion, he nurtured the trees that lived and planted seeds to grow new ones. He told Niji, "In a single seed lies dormant generations of life." He was *that* kind of serious about trees.

Niji's paws struck a pebble path, and a few strides later she bounded up the stone steps that led to the palace's grounds. She passed through a thick open wood gate that stood a dozen feet high. The enormous five-tier palace was crafted of cedar with sturdy thick beams and stone as its base. From each of the five gabled tiers jutted a red slate roof. The top tier, being the smallest, looked as if it were a hat of sorts placed atop the palace.

The palace had taken years to build because the emperor only allowed the use of trees he selected. He said that trees were living things, and thus worthy of honor and respect. In some trees dwelled the kodama, and anyone caught felling a tree without the emperor's permission answered directly to him. And though the Son of the Forest was mild-mannered and docile by nature, he could be quite disagreeable when it came to the killing of trees.

Niji raced through the courtyard along the wooden walkways that wove over and around elaborate gardens – gardens of large stones surrounded by gravel raked into patterns resembling rippling water and gardens that were miniature representations of nature with small trees, colorful plants, and pools of water bustling with koi splashing around the surface, searching for their next meal.

Niji no longer ran out of fear of the world's dangers, but from the desire to tell the empress the fantastic news. Her regret at telling Sureto about the hole had not abated, however, she reminded herself, again and again, she didn't have a choice. This was mostly true, but if Sureto did something stupid and got caught, residents of the valley would know the barrier had been breached. The element of surprise would be gone. Who was she kidding? Sureto would undoubtedly do something stupid. But she couldn't worry about him now. She had one job — reporting back as the Empress' Ears.

"Open the doors!" Niji yelled to the guards at the entrance of the main hall leading to the throne room. The two giant figures wearing terrifying, devilish masks and dull iron and leather armor grunted as they banged the end of their long polearms against the ground. They unlatched and pulled open two massive red doors, nearly twice their height, and bowed to Niji. She hastily nodded at them as she ran past. Being their superior, she wasn't obligated to bow or nod, but being on the good side of as many people and creatures of the land was part of her live-a-long-life strategy.

Inside, she hurried down a long hallway with wooden tables on either side laden with potted bonsai — tiny, intricate trees the emperor meticulously manicured. Paintings of various landscapes lined the red walls. A grand entrance at the end of the hallway led to the throne room where the siblings would be waiting, and whether they knew it or not, they were waiting for her. What she had to tell them meant everything. She hoped that they were free from visitors. The empress and emperor occupied the main room during the day, making themselves available for messengers and residents of the realm. The latter typically came to air grievances or ask for favors. The siblings were lucky to have her. Most inhabitants of the land were useless loners with an inability to understand the meaning of loyalty and family. Truthfully, many of the inhabitants were either drooling lunatics, monsters, or tricksters who cared for the feelings of no one.

Niji slid to a stop a few scampers from the throne room. Blocking her path, bumbling and bounding in awkward ground-shaking hops, was Doa Heddo. He filled the entirety of the entrance with his enormous head, which was in fact, what he was — a gigantic head. Doa Heddo didn't have a body, he didn't have arms or legs or a neck to bring it all together. He was simply a head with all the typical components: two eyes, a nose, a mouth, and two ears. He was hairless other than a scraggly mustache and beard, which tended to become foul after a few days of eating and being unable to clean his own face. She felt sorry for the house workers whose job it was to give him a weekly scrub down. She never cared to ask how it all worked, you know, just being a head. Some things were better left unknown.

"Hi, Doa," Niji said, pretending to be perfectly pleased that he was blocking her way.

"Hi dere Nidi," Doa said in a deep voice. Enunciation was not Doa's strength due to limited jaw movement, with it being pressed to the ground under the weight of his skull. However, he did have the power of brute force, was worthy of the title of the royal jester, and could eat like a giant. Again, don't ask.

"I need to talk to the empress and emperor; it's most important." In a friendly manner, she motioned for him to move. "If you could bouncy-bounce out of the way."

He smiled. "Joke firsht."

Niji clenched her eyes shut and took a deep breath. Listening to one of Doa's jokes was the toll to be paid to pass. He would not move until the joke was complete. She opened her eyes, forced a smile, and relaxed. Many of Doa's jokes were horrible, some were okay, a minuscule amount were funny, but most didn't make a pebble of sense. The key to pass, however, was to laugh all the same.

"Okay." She feigned interest. "Ready."

Doa let out a deep guffaw before he started. "What did duh rat say to duh giant during an argument?"

Niji closed an eye and scratched her head. "Hmm. You got me. What did the rat say to the giant during an argument?"

Doa laughed again. "I can't undustand you. Stop using big words."

Niji filed the joke under "okay" and laughed. Honestly, it wasn't his worst. "That was a good one, Doa. You're getting better." She didn't only humor him to get him to move; she liked Doa. For as weird as he was and not all that pleasant to look at, Doa was a kind, gentle giant... of a head.

"Dank you," he said, thunderously hopping out of the way.

"You're welcome." Niji scrambled from the hallway and onto the tatami mat floor of the throne room. The siblings sat upon cushioned thrones on an elevated section at the far side of the room. This way, commoners and subordinates were literally below them. Sliding paper doors to other rooms and hallways lined the sides of the throne room, and the walls were painted gold. The ceiling was sectioned into hundreds of squares that currently displayed the sun, magically illuminating the room. At night, the squares became a midnight blue sky filled with the moon and stars.

Niji stopped at the steps to the thrones, laid her ears flat, tucked her tail, bowed deeply, and worked at suppressing her excitement. The empress's name was Subete no Musume, which meant the Daughter of Everything, and her brother was Mori no Musuko, the Son of the Forest. Niji called them sister and brother to herself, and empress and emperor in their presence or the presence of others out of respect. The siblings were kitsune through and through, every piece of fur, every ounce of blood, every bit of magic, and every fluffy tail.

Lingering jealousy reminded Niji of her lack of tails compared to the sibling's grand and flourishing tails. The jealously ramped up a notch, as it always did, when considering their incredible magic and ability to shapeshift between human and fox form. She would never tell them of her feelings, but when alone, she vocally expressed her displeasure to the Universe quite often. If only her life had been different. As it was, she was half kitsune — amazing — and half of something else; evidently something with ridiculously long ears. While she had hated her ears at first, she had come to appreciate them, as did the siblings. Her unsurpassed hearing was a fantastic ability that no one else had.

The emperor met Niji's eyeline as he stood, revealing his two tails. Barefoot, he walked toward her, moving fluidly and slowly, his arms forward and extended. Niji often thought it was just like a tree would walk if they could. His shoulder-length hair was naturally forest green, his eyes a lighter green, and his skin a deep brown. He wore a simple, brown kimono with a leaf green sash. His hoshi no tama hung from a thin chain around his neck. He spoke in a soft voice. "Niji, who or what do we thank for your early return?"

The empress scoffed as she stood. It was debatable if the empress was indeed the daughter of everything. Still, she was the owner of five tails — one for each of the hundred years of her life — and each one granted her an ability. Though not quite possessing the power of the gods, she was nearly all-powerful in these lands and not to be trifled with. She stared at Niji with close-set eyes set into a narrow face the color of an eggshell. She wore a long, deep-purple silk kimono that bunched up at her feet. A conspiracy of crows in flight covered the top half of the kimono, and colorful flowers decorated the fabric from the knee down. A thick black sash wrapped her waist. Where she wore her hoshi no tama was a secret, which fell in line with her trust issues. "I imagined you'd be sleeping off a belly full of fungus for at least a day," she said condescendingly. Her perfectly sculpted eyebrows rose. "You did return with it as I requested?"

Ooops. Niji, in fact, did not even have a single bite of poison fire coral, much less bring any back with her. She paused to calm herself and speak clearly instead of blurting the news. "If I may, I have something to tell you that is far more important than my favorite fungus… that I indeed forgot to bring back with me." *Do not say anything about Sureto.*

The Son of the Forest looked to his sister, sharing an emotionless stare as if they could communicate with their eyes. Maybe they could. He returned his gaze to Niji. "The empress and I feel you have information of great importance to tell us." He raised his hands, palms upward. "You are forgiven for returning with empty hands and may continue with what you have to share."

Niji took a deep breath and released it with a smile large enough to rival Doa's; her tail waved excitedly behind her, wildly flinging her soul gem. She scanned the room to confirm their privacy. Satisfied they were alone, she spoke. "When I was in the poison fire coral garden" — *do not mention Sureto* — "a strange sensation overcame me." Her ears perked up and moved as she relived the moment. "The sounds of the clearing were different than before. There was something more, which… proved to be something less."

The empress stepped closer, her five tails twitching behind her, with an expression of shocked understanding. She could not read minds but had a sixth sense, like she had access to the Universal stream of consciousness when needed. "Everything is connected," she had said a time or two. The Daughter of Everything raised a single black eyebrow.

The emperor interlaced his fingers and leaned down toward Niji, his green eyes gleaming. "What was this, 'more and less'?"

Chapter 11

Anessa's classroom chair was empty, just four thin metal legs and a plastic seat where she should be. Cassidy sat anxiously in her own seat. *She's late, that's all, just late.* The starting bell rang, forcing Cassidy's classmates to switch from being frenetic buzzing bees to the role of attentive students. Cassidy sat forward in her seat. *Hold on. Class can't start yet.* Mrs. Higgins began writing on the whiteboard. Class had definitely started, and still, Anessa's chair was empty.

"Where is she?" Cassidy asked Maisy quietly, mostly mouthing the words.

Maisy shrugged. Today she wore her hair pulled back tight and held in place by a stretchy white hairband with the back naturally escaping in a big puff. It gave her an air of having an even bigger personality than she already had.

She's just late, Cassidy repeated like a mantra. An hour later, Cassidy gave up on the mantra and the hope that Anessa would show up. She wasn't coming to school today, and maybe never again. *Good job, everyone, good job being mean to her.* But there was still tomorrow, Friday. Maybe Anessa needed a day off. Maybe her mom figured things out and took her shopping. That was it — she was out shopping. Tomorrow, Anessa would walk into class wearing new clothes head to toe, looking resplendent. Cassidy smiled as she sat back and slid down into her seat. Problem solved. She could get back to worrying about herself, though it felt a little selfish to think that way.

"Yes, Mrs. Higgins, I guess I'll do it," Cassidy said, garnering a curious stare from her teacher.

Mrs. Higgins stepped over to Cassidy and laid a thin stack of papers on her desk. "Did I ask you —" She shook her head. "Would you hand out the assignment for me?"

Most of the class gawked at Cassidy like she was a zoo animal that finally revealed itself. With so many eyes on her, she wanted to scurry back to the figurative hiding spot from which she had just emerged. Guarded chuckles slipped from a few brave mouths, testing the ire of the teacher. Embarrassment radiated from Cassidy's cheeks. *What just happened? All I did was agree to hand out the assignment.*

"Okay, class, faces forward. It's not polite to stare," Mrs. Higgins said, saving Cassidy from a class of ogling eyes. One set of eyes remained fixed on her — Maisy's. It wasn't the first time Maisy had given her that look like she was crazy, like she had said no to cash as a birthday present.

Cassidy quietly eased out of her seat as if she'd set off a hair-trigger bomb if she moved too quickly or, in this case, draw additional unwanted attention. She regretted agreeing to the task. One by one, desk by desk, she handed out the assignment — something to do with fractions. Most kids moved beyond the curious looks and giggles; some even said thank you and took the assignment. Alex smiled at her for what felt like an awkwardly long time. But Brody, of course, made a face, though she wasn't sure what the look was meant to convey. If anything, he looked meaner than usual. She handed him the assignment straight-faced, not offering him the pleasure of a reaction.

"Are you okay?" Maisy whispered, taking the assignment from Cassidy.

"I don't know what I did," Cassidy whispered back, sliding down into the safety of her seat.

"You —"

A purposeful cough from Mrs. Higgins interrupted the conversation.

"I'll tell you after class," Maisy quickly snuck in, drawing a disapproving scowl from the teacher.

"I did what?" Cassidy asked, mortified. If yesterday wasn't strange enough, today wanted its chance at being the Mayor of Crazy Town.

"You answered Mrs. Higgins before she asked you to hand out the assignment."

"What the Frappuccino?" Cassidy stopped in the middle of the sidewalk, sending kids behind her into the grass to get around. "But —" she started, then looked at Maisy.

Maisy, not one to fake seriousness, met her stare unwaveringly. When Maisy was serious, she'd stare at you with eyes like two brown daggers pinning a sheet of wide-ruled notebook paper to your forehead that read, "I'm not playing."

"That's crazy," Cassidy said, continuing down the sidewalk toward home, a death-grip on her backpack straps.

"Mmhmm, that's what the class was thinking too — crazy."

"Maybe I just expected her to ask me." Cassidy had heard Mrs. Higgins ask her to hand out the assignment, hadn't she?

"Half the class was looking at Mrs. Higgins, hoping to be asked. But sis, her mouth did not move."

Cassidy pushed her hair behind her ears and nibbled at a jagged thumbnail. She felt like a kid in general math given a calculus book — she wasn't sure what to do with this information. What does someone say when told they're a mind reader? Quit school, get a crystal ball and a small circular table, read palms, and tell people their future while wearing one of those ridiculous hats? Or do precisely what she was doing — hope her best friend, her sister, would say she was only joking.

"Are you sure you're feeling okay?" Maisy asked. "You did hit your head yesterday."

"Yeah," Cassidy said, nodding, "I'm good."

"Promise?"

"Promise."

She felt fine. Honestly, she did. Still, Cassidy focused on herself as they walked, searching for anything that felt out of place or wrong. She found nothing more than that underlying feeling she had something to do. Other than that, she felt right as rain.

The sight of her grandma passing by in the passenger seat of Dad's SUV pulled Cassidy from mulling over the mystery of her new mind-reading skill. Seeing people's memories apparently wasn't enough of a hassle.

"Grandma!" Cassidy screamed. "Come on, Maisy," she said with a jubilant smile, "let's go say hi to my grandma."

Maisy frowned at first, then smiled. "Okay, but we are talking about this tomorrow."

"Fine, I promise." Cassidy grabbed Maisy's hand and pulled her along in a trot. Questions would soon be answered.

Chapter 12

assidy's dad cooked as Grandma got settled in one of the extra bedrooms. When dinner was ready, they all sat on opposite sides of the rectangular dining room table. Above them hung a chandelier with dozens of crystals illuminating the room in a soft white light. Dinner tonight — rice, miso soup, and tempura shrimp — was made special for Grandma's visit. Dad made a good attempt at making a Japanese meal, though it is difficult to mess up shrimp. Grandma didn't rave over the food, but she gave her "compliments to the chef".

"Are we going to ignore the reason I'm here?" Grandma finally asked, sitting across from Cassidy at the table.

Cassidy wasn't ignoring anything. She had been ready to talk about her newfound abilities the moment Grandma got out of the car. She gently placed her fork on her plate and stole glances at Mom and Dad, who were acting quite sheepish as they lowered their forks to nearly clean plates.

Being out of food to stuff in their mouths, they could no longer stall the discussion. Dad strategically took a drink of his tea, leaving Mom to lead the occupants of the dinner table on the oral expedition of Cassidy's odd new affliction.

Mom narrowed her eyes at Dad, her mouth a straight line. She shifted in her seat. "So, Mom, we want to talk about Cassidy and what's been happening."

"Well, that's why I'm here," Grandma said. "Cassie, tell me about the last couple of days."

"Um," Cassidy eloquently started.

"Cassidy had a… strange event happen at school," Mom said.

Grandma kept her brown bespectacled eyes on Cassidy, asking for details without saying a word.

"Do I have to go through the whole story again?" Cassidy asked. She didn't want to revisit seeing and experiencing Anessa's sadness.

Grandma rested her wrinkled hands on the table. "You saw someone's sad memories," she said, a half-question, half-statement.

It wasn't entirely surprising that Grandma knew about seeing memories; her knowing about this stuff was the reason she was here. But what else did she know? Cassidy scrunched her face and nodded, then nodded again at hearing what Grandma was about to say next.

"You know what someone will say before they say it."

Cassidy froze, her eyes wide, glancing at everyone. *Did anyone notice?* Confident they hadn't seen her nod yes to the question before it was asked, she answered this time with words. "Yes, but that just started today, so I'm not exactly sure how it works. It seems to happen at random."

Grandma gave a knowing look to Mom and Dad, who held hands across the table. They may have been comforting each other, but it resembled the beginning of a séance. Like they would soon summon some otherworldly spirit to provide answers to what the frappe was going on.

Grandma sipped her tea and gently placed the cup on its saucer. "Is that all, Cassidy? Have there been any other experiences? Any stranger things happening?"

In the last two days, there had been more than enough strange things, but Cassidy went through a mental checklist anyway that indeed had strange boxes to check off. *Should I mention the other thing — the voice?* She still questioned if she really heard it, or if it was just her telling herself to help Anessa. Hearing voices was never a good thing in movies or TV shows. Either the character was going crazy, or something scary was coming after them. She decided to keep that part to herself for now. "No, that's all."

Grandma nodded. She leaned to the right, hefted a wooden box from the empty chair next to her, and placed it with a *thunk* in the middle of the table. The box was light brown and lacquered to a shine. Images of various colorful flowers decorated the sides. Across the top were golden dragons, their bodies bent in an "S" shape, mirroring each other.

A black and grey stone pathway passed between the dragons to an unknown destination.

"That is beautiful," Dad said. "What is it?" He collected everyone's plates and stacked them at the end of the table.

"This" — Grandma shimmied back into the center of her seat — "is a suzuri bako."

Questioning faces met Grandma as Dad returned to his seat.

"It's a writing box," she explained. "In Japan, it would be used for holding calligraphy tools."

"How cool," Cassidy said.

"I'm guessing there is more to this calligraphy box than what we see," Mom said.

Grandma smiled. "You'd be correct. This box," she said, giving it a tap, "should contain everything Cassidy needs to understand what she's experiencing."

Cassidy's shoulders relaxed. "Thank gosh."

"Your ancestor first owned it, a grandmother many times over. Her name was Takayama Iwa."

Cassidy opened her mouth to respond, then tilted her head like a dog hearing its favorite word. Why was that name so familiar? She had heard it before… but where? Her mind churned in the part that held lost or forgotten memories, a shadowy place that teased her by putting answers on the tip of her tongue until she spoke them or give up trying to remember.

"Cassidy. Are you in there?" Grandma asked.

Cassidy shook her head. "Oh, sorry. Iwa. That's a pretty name. Does it mean anything?"

"Roughly translated, her first name, Iwa, means rock." Grandma explained. "Her family name, Takayama, means high mountain."

Cassidy mentally arranged the names in the American way and gave a funny look to Grandma. "Her name was Rock High Mountain?"

Grandma, Mom, and Dad laughed.

"Yes, if you use the literal translation," Grandma said, pushing her glasses up the bridge of her nose. "Iwa is also the name of someone with outstanding character and good morals."

"Like Maisy," Cassidy said. She hovered her hand over the box, and if she didn't imagine it, she felt a tug in the space between, pulling her to touch it. Grandma smiled and nodded her approval. Cassidy let her fingertips skirt along the top of the box; it was as smooth as it looked. Gooseflesh rose on her skin.

Mom touched it too. "How old is this box?"

"I believe it is from seventeen-hundreds Japan," Grandma answered.

Mom pulled her hand back with an expression of astonishment. "You're telling me this box is over two hundred… maybe three hundred years old?"

"I am," Grandma said confidently.

Cassidy's fingers brushed against the rough corners where the lacquer had peeled away to exposed wood, and over the keyhole at the lid line. "It's locked?"

"It looks well-kept for being three hundred years old," Dad said.

"It's locked, Grandma?" Cassidy repeated. "Where is the key?"

Grandma flashed a smile as her fingers slid underneath a thin silver chain around her neck, pulling it until a key breached the top of her blouse. The key hung from the chain, swaying back and forth, hypnotizing Cassidy. It was metal, with a loop at one end wide enough for a pinky to fit and two ridges with a single notch, resembling the smile of an infant with only two gapped front teeth. "This key is just as old. And now both the key and the box belong to you, Cassidy."

All eyes fell on Cassidy. She sat back, wide-eyed. If the box and the key were hers, so was the feeling of being overwhelmed. How was she deserving of something this old, something this beautiful, something that had been in her family for over two hundred years? What was she supposed to say? Gee, thanks? More importantly, what was she supposed to do? "I… I don't know what to do."

Grandma unclasped the necklace, cupped the chain and key in her hand, and held it out for Cassidy. "First, take this key. Then I'll tell you about Iwa and how all of this started." She pointed at Cassidy. "I'll tell you how you got your pretty blue eyes."

Cassidy scrunched her face and tilted her head. "What do my eyes have to do with this? They're a stupid mutation."

Grandma slowly shook her head. "Oh, no. There is an amazing story behind your blues. It's time that you heard it."

Cassidy nodded in anticipation. Mom and Dad gave her half-smiles like they already knew. Finally she would learn how she got her blue eyes, her what-the-heck blue eyes, and, she hoped, so much more.

Dad took the dirty dishes and glasses to the sink, and they moved to the living room to get comfortable for Grandma's story. Cassidy sat on the couch with Mom and Grandma, and Dad sat in his recliner. Mom and Dad admitted that Grandma had told them the "blue eyes" story shortly after she was born. They had planned to tell her but were unsure when the time would be right. It was Iwa who had the blue eyes, so their story about a many greats grandma with blue eyes was partly the truth. Cassidy forgave them for keeping this nearly eleven-year secret. Grandma promised Cassidy wouldn't have believed them anyway.

Grandma settled in her seat, preparing to tell Iwa's story. According to her, she had shared the story many times, but it had never been more important than now. She explained that Iwa lived in Japan, near the mountains of the Gifu prefecture. A prefecture was like a state in the United States. Dad didn't even know this, and he read a lot. Grandma's face brightened as the words flowed from her mouth. "And this is where Iwa's story begins."

Chapter 13

Iwa headed for the mountains to trek her favorite trails after an argument with her father. She needed time and space to quell the frustration and anger swirling inside her. For years she had diligently studied her father's work. She knew how to make kimonos and how to negotiate with fabric traders. However, her father said her older brothers were first in line to take on the business' responsibilities. Even worse, on her sixteenth birthday a month prior, her father had reminded her she would soon be married, and had no say in the matter. Iwa had heard these explanations and demands from her father before, but this time she'd stormed off.

Fifteen minutes and nearly a mile away from home, she paused and considered her clothing. She wore split-toed socks, wooden sandals, and a large circular straw hat covering her head from the blazing sun. Her delicate blue flower silk kimono was not the best choice for hiking mountain trails, however, she was not about to return home to change. It was not a good time to be around her father or brothers, and her mother would only insist that *she* apologize. Iwa narrowed her eyes and huffed. She would not return home, nor would she apologize. She would get by in what she was wearing.

She trudged up and down the dirt and gravel paths, occasionally kicking innocent pebbles while calling her father unflattering names and crying over how he never listened to her. A torrential storm had passed through the previous day and muddied parts of the trail; every few steps, her feet sunk where there was more mud than stone. On either side of the path stood tall cypress trees and short yew trees with bright red berries hanging from their limbs. The bottom of the late day sun, a red-orange ball of flame, dipped behind the trees. The daytime bugs and birds quieted as they settled in for the night and were replaced by creatures of the dark. A breeze kicked up, carrying whispers of animals and unseen creatures through the trees.

Iwa stopped, balled her hands into fists, and stomped her feet. She spoke in harsh tones of what she wanted to say to her father, but respectfully could not, should not. After another minute of angry thoughts and words, her tantrum ended and she decided to head home, thinking better of continuing down the path into even more darkness.

Under the canopy of the trees, the darkness of night impending, Iwa paused at an unfamiliar trail, a way less worn and less traveled, leading deeper into the woods. Unventured paths were both alluring and frightening. Under the current circumstances, frightening was the better descriptor. A noise came from somewhere down the path, a sound like a gravelly voice. Iwa gasped, stumbling backward. The cluster of trees muted the sound, but if she wasn't mistaken, she'd heard a cry for help.

Her father would be even more furious with her if she didn't get home before dark. But someone had called out, and she might be the only one who could answer. She paused at the first step toward home, turned, and studied the trail. "I can't believe I'm about to do this."

She removed her straw hat and tossed it to the ground, not wanting it to get snagged on low branches. Tying her black hair back with a thin piece of cloth, Iwa slipped off her sandals, and slowly headed down the path toward the cry. The path, covered in fallen limbs and undergrowth, grew darker and eerier with each step. *Why am I doing this? I should go back to the village for help.*

Quiet blanketed her. The voice, if there ever was one, was gone, and the bugs had strangely stopped their nighttime singing. The only sounds were the snapping of twigs and crunching of leaves beneath her feet.

"Hello," she said tentatively, hoping no one would answer. She stopped to listen. At second thought, maybe her father's wrath was a better option than what might be waiting in the dark.

A voice cried like a beacon, breaking the silence. "Over here. In this hole."

Iwa's heart beat a rabbit-fast rhythm, the voice stealing her breath. She wiped her sweaty palms on her kimono, took a deep breath, and continued down the path in the direction of the voice, carefully stepping over and around the ground-covering. Several uncertain footfalls later, she stumbled and screamed. Something had grabbed her right leg, bringing her to the ground. Regret arrived in an instant. What a mistake she made taking this path! This moment would be the last of her life… or would it?

Scowling, she kicked her leg free from the fallen tree limb that had seemingly reached out and grabbed her with sinister, barkish claws. She fumed seeing a tear in her kimono. *Father will be furious.* She stood, straightened and adjusted her clothes, and begrudgingly continued down the path. Several yards ahead lay an enormous fallen cedar that was at least a hundred feet long. Its limbs, though mostly broken and bent, were full and green.

"There storm must have taken you down," Iwa said softly. Where the roots had been in the ground was a gaping hole, several yards across and deeper still. The root system, now exposed, gave the tree the appearance of being a wooden club for a giant, no, for a titan. Cautiously, she stepped toward the edge of the hole and peered inside. Half of the bottom of the muddy hole was visible in the remaining light; half was shrouded in darkness. She stepped closer to the edge, lost her footing, and stumbled backward as the ground gave way. A chunk of muddy earth landed with a splat at the bottom of the hole; she fell near the edge with a splat of her own.

"Careful," said a voice as rough and rugged as a tortoise shell from within the hole. "You don't want to be down here with me. Then we both would surely die." The owner of the voice, the same one that had cried for help, spoke slowly and deliberately.

From her seated position, Iwa asked, "Who said that? Who are you?"

"I'd better not tell you or you'd run away, and I'd be stuck down here and surely die."

Iwa stood and ineffectively brushed the mud from her kimono, leaving brown smears across the fabric. "Ugh, I'm filthy." A layer of mud coated the length of and underside of her socks. When she firmly planted her feet, mud squished between her toes. "Gross."

Directing her concern away from being covered in disgusting filth, Iwa leaned forward, attempting to project her voice down the hole. "Fine. Come into the light. Let me see you."

"I'd better not show you either, or you'd run away, and I'd be stuck down here and surely die."

Iwa huffed. "Then what do you want me to do? How can I help you if I can't see you?"

"Girl, young girl, what is your name?"

Iwa hesitated, wondering if this was some type of trick. Unable to imagine what it could be, she answered. "Iwa. Takayama Iwa. Why?"

"What a wonderful name, a trustworthy name. Can I trust you, Takayama Iwa?"

Anger rose from her toes to the crown of her head. "Listen to me, whoever you are. I wasn't in a good mood to begin with. Now my kimono is torn and dirty; I will have to throw it away without my father knowing. Speaking of my father, he is already upset with me, and I'm supposed to be home before dark. So," she placed her hands firmly on her hips, "if you don't tell me who you are right now, I won't help. I'll leave, and you'll —"

"Surely die down here."

"Yes. Surely you will die down there," she agreed mockingly.

"Iwa. The walls are too muddy for me to grip, and the remaining roots won't support my weight. Search the roots up there, and you'll see one firmly attached to the tree, one much longer than the others. Do you see it, Iwa?"

There it lay, a root longer than the others and still firmly attached to the tree.

"Iwa, simply direct the root into the hole and I'll climb out after you leave. Yes?"

Iwa approached the downed tree and grabbed the root at its end. It was muddy, wet, and somewhat pliant. She managed to move it with a firm tug and brought it to the hole's edge.

"Okay. I have the —" She froze. A streak of pale light shone on the face of the stranger. He was not a man; he was a beast with a face covered in fur — the face of an ape.

The ape-man receded to the shadows.

"You are not a m-man," she stuttered.

A low, growl-like sigh came from the hole. "I am not. I never said I was. Now, Iwa, drop the root and I shall climb free."

"I know what you are and I will not drop this root to you, you loathsome creature."

"What is it you think I am?"

"You're a satori. I know all about you. You'll eat me if I let you out."

Her father told her many stories as a child of yokai — supernatural spirits and creatures. One story was about the satori, ape-like creatures who had the power to hear the thoughts of others and read minds as if memories were books. Some of the satori were peaceful, but others ate those who happened across their paths, especially little girls. The stories frightened Iwa until she grew up and stopped believing in monsters and spirits, but ten feet below her was a real life satori. It must be.

"No, no, Iwa. I will not eat you. I am the peaceful kind your father spoke of."

"How did you know my father —" *Of course.* If the satori truly had the powers from the stories, it would know what her father had told her. She dropped the root at the hole's edge and waved her hand in front of her face. "No. I'm going to tell my father about you. He'll come back here with my brothers. They will decide what happens to you."

At this, the satori stepped from the shadows, fully revealing itself. It peered up at her with bright blue, pleading eyes. "Iwa, please don't. They will certainly not help me. They will most certainly hurt me... or worse."

Iwa's jaw dropped, suddenly at a loss for words. She studied the satori, which somewhat resembled a human; however, its face and fur-covered body were like nothing she had ever seen.

"Takayama Iwa, I know why you are sad."

"You don't —"

"I do know. I know your father doesn't respect you. Your brothers, they don't respect you."

"How — how are you —"

"I can see and feel your sadness. It surrounds you like a shadow. I can know your thoughts and what you intend to say before you say it."

Iwa didn't like the idea of the satori traipsing around in her mind, but it piqued her curiosity. She had to know for sure if the stories of the satori were true. "Prove it," she challenged, wearing a scowl.

"Of course. Of course. Now, dear Iwa, think of what you want more than anything and before you tell me, I will say it."

"Fine," Iwa said boldly. What did she want more than anything? A list formed in her mind, a long list. She considered the importance of each item, and it became clear what she wanted above anything else. She opened her mouth to speak, but her words were spoken by the satori.

"You want to be treated by your father as an equal to your brothers. You want to help the family business."

Iwa's eyes widened. A few seconds passed before she remembered to breathe. "I... I believe you," she said slowly. She shook the daze from her head, and an idea bloomed within her clever mind. There were stories of people receiving favors and being granted powers from yokai they helped or, in some cases, tricked. This could be her chance. "I'm still not letting you out, unless —"

"Unless I grant you my powers."

"Yes," she said plainly, uncertain if the satori could share its powers.

"I, I cannot. The powers of the satori are —"

"Fine. I guess I'll be leaving."

"No. No, wait!" The satori reached a pawish hand up to her.

She had turned to leave, but only as a ploy to get the creature to reason with her. "Do we have a deal?"

"Child, child, you do not want my powers. They are a burden."

"I will impress my father with them. He'll have to respect me. My brothers will admire me," Iwa said eagerly.

"Iwa, Iwa, my powers are no good for humans. Hearing the thoughts and seeing the sadness of a single human is tolerable, but you live in a village with many humans. Many humans would be a misery."

Iwa curled her hands into fists and glowered at the satori. Her voice rose. "Last chance, you hairy beast, or I'll leave."

The satori grumbled and lowered its head. It remained silent until it peered up at her with bright blue eyes, nodding in defeat.

Iwa's smile reached her eyes as she led the end of the long, sturdy root down the muddy hole. The satori grabbed the root with an expression of satisfaction and made a grunting noise, not quite human or beast, tugging the root to test its strength. It gripped halfway up the root with a jump and climbed hand over hand until it was chest high out of the hole.

Iwa slowly backed away. Deal or not, she didn't trust the satori and was prepared to run. Being honest with herself, she knew she wouldn't be able to outrun it. The satori's greedy hands grabbed at the bottom of the fallen tree, found a solid grip, and pulled itself up. It stood firmly on the muddy ground. Breath left Iwa, wide-eyed and frightened at the satori towering above her.

The satori brushed the mud from its fur-covered legs and furless stomach and chest with the same lack of success Iwa had with her kimono. It looked at her with what resembled a smile. "Thank you. Thank you, Iwa."

Iwa had been uncommonly rude, and now with the satori standing before her, she questioned if a bow was appropriate. To avoid risking additional offense, she slightly bowed. "How… how does —"

"How does it work? How do you get my powers?"

Iwa nodded rapidly. "Y-yes."

The satori walked closer to her and crouched. Iwa back peddled to maintain the distance between them, only to back into a cedar tree.

"Iwa, Iwa, I'm free, but please, please reconsider. My powers will be like a trap for you, a curse. You'll be in a figurative hole of your own for the rest of your life, begging to be freed."

Iwa vigorously shook her head. "No. No, I won't. You do what we agreed." She couldn't stop the creature if it decided to run away, but some yokai were known for being honest and honorable. Her bet, or at least hope, was that the satori in front of her was one of them.

The satori frowned; its broad shoulders sagged. "Very well. Very well." It studied her for a moment with impossibly blue eyes, then stepped closer with a fur-covered hand extended.

Iwa stood rigidly as the giant hand moved closer. She flinched as the satori's warm muddy palm covered the top of her head, pressing against her closed eyes and forehead.

"Iwa, listen," the satori said softly, with only a hint of gravel in its voice. "Listen to me before I grant you my powers. Listen carefully."

"I'm listening," Iwa said softly.

"When it gets to be too much — the voices, the images — go to the space between thoughts. Focus on your breath; clear your mind. Find the silence within yourself."

"What? What does that mean? The silence within me?"

"This, Iwa, is a journey you will have to travel on your own."

"Thanks," she said with a smirk, hidden underneath the satori's hand.

"I'll count to three. And Iwa, thank you for freeing me."

"As you said, I have a name you can trust."

"One."

Iwa inhaled deeply.

"Two."

She held her breath, squeezing tight every muscle she had.

"Three."

A brilliant light pierced her eyelids as immense pressure assaulted her forehead. Before everything went black, she saw the satori, its eyes sad. Its final words to her were, "This power will become part of you and shall pass to your descendants."

Chapter 14

Cassidy scrunched her face as she attempted to digest the story about Iwa and the satori.

Grandma paused. "Cassidy. Are you okay?"

"Sure. I'm fine." *Monsters and mind-reading are normal everyday stuff.* "Why wouldn't I be?"

Grandma nodded to Cassidy's hands that were gripping the seat of the leather couch like vices.

Mom pulled Cassidy's hands free and patted them. "Wow, Mom. That's the first time I've heard you tell the story that way."

"That's the first time you've paid attention," Grandma countered.

"Sounds about right," Dad joked, receiving a punch in the thigh from Mom as payment.

"Wait," Cassidy said. "That can't be the end of the story. What happened to Iwa?"

"Early the next morning," Grandma continued, "Iwa awoke next to the fallen tree. Her father and brothers were calling her name, and she yelled for help just like the satori did the night before. Her father found her, picked her up in his arms, and squeezed her tight. He was worried he had lost his only daughter."

"That was nice of him," Cassidy said pleasantly.

"Then he dropped her."

"What?" Cassidy exclaimed.

"He saw her eyes — blue as the clearest sky. Her brown eyes had become as blue as the satori's. Iwa told her family what happened, and they were astonished."

Cassidy crossed her arms. "Don't tell me. They didn't believe her?"

"Not at first, but with her eyes, there was no other explanation. She showed them the satori's footprints encased in the drying mud, too." Grandma sat forward. "And then she did something that made them believers."

Cassidy mimicked Grandma, leaning closer to her as if a secret would be told. "What did she do?"

"She finished their sentences, saying their next words before they could open their mouths. This was a known power of the satori, whether or not they were a myth."

"Then her life got better? Her dad and brothers respected her?"

"I'll never forget this part of the story," Mom said, sharing a pained look with Grandma.

"Are you kidding me?" Cassidy replied before Grandma could get the words out. "No? What do you mean, no?"

Grandma and Cassidy's parents exchanged stunned glances, witnessing Cassidy's ability for the first time.

"Cassidy. Did you just —" Mom started, then paused.

"Yeah." Cassidy laughed uncomfortably. "Crazy, huh?"

Dad smiled proudly while Mom appeared terrified.

Grandma gathered her focus. "I'm sorry, Cassie. What did you ask?"

Cassidy huffed. "Her dad and brothers still didn't respect her. Why?"

"Iwa's father forced her to hide away for fear the villagers wouldn't understand. He couldn't explain her blue eyes. He feared he would lose business. More importantly, he feared Iwa would be harmed, or even killed for what she became."

"Then what? What did he do with her?" Cassidy asked.

"He made beautiful eye patches for her to wear and told everyone she went blind. He ordered her to wear the patches whenever in public."

Cassidy frowned, her eyes narrowing. "That's horrible." She sat back, crossing her arms.

"However," Grandma added, "her father took her to business discussions and used her for an advantage in negotiation. Iwa heard the thoughts and whispers of the other merchants. She became invaluable to him."

Cassidy perked up. "So it's a happy ending?"

"Not yet. You may find out more about Iwa from what's in the box. But I'll share this final part."

Cassidy sat forward.

"After Iwa's seventeenth birthday, she became despondent."

Cassidy scrunched her face. "Despon — what?"

Grandma smiled. "She lost hope. When away from home, she had no control over hearing what people would say. And seeing their sadness was the worst of it all. So, she began to stay home… she stopped eating and laid around most days."

"Now, wait a minute. She was like my whole lotta greats grandma, and you're here. I'm here. She must have had a life. A real life. Something good happened for Iwa, right?"

"Yes and no. When her father realized that his daughter would never marry, he sent her away to work for another merchant who traded with the Dutch. In return, he received a reduction in cost for materials he needed."

"He did what?" Cassidy's gaping mouth could have caught a bucket of flies. She glared at her dad, silently asking him to answer for the indiscretions of all men. He just shrugged. "First, he tells her that she has to marry at sixteen, then he sends her to live with someone else. What did the merchant say about her eyes? Did she have to still pretend to be blind?" Cassidy asked.

"She kept her powers secret from the merchant and his family and told them she was born with blue eyes. Many of the Dutch merchants had blue eyes and they had no knowledge of the satori, so she fit right in. Though, she missed her family dearly."

"Okay, Grandma. Where is the good part? Because all of this still sucks."

Dad chuckled.

"I'm getting to it," Grandma said reassuringly. "The merchant she was sent to work for had a son her age who came to love her more than anything. They grew up together, married, had children, and lived together happily for the rest of their lives."

Cassidy smiled, relieved.

"And now there's you. Now it's your turn."

Cassidy let the weight of that statement sink in before pulling herself free of the thought before it sunk her. She had no fear of her father sending her away; he was her number one fan. Her parents loved her, their only child, more than anything.

"Why did it have to be me? There have been like a bazillion descendants before me."

Grandma shrugged. "That is a mystery I can't answer. I suppose only the satori knows."

Cassidy's brow furrowed. Finally, she got the answer to her blue eyes, only to have it replaced by the question of, why her? She met each of their stares and said with what she hoped was the beginning of her confidence, "I guess it's my turn."

"Now," Grandma said, "go get that box and take it to your room. You don't need us staring over your shoulder. This is your time to find out what's inside."

"Wait. You don't know?" Cassidy said, surprised. "You've never opened it?"

Grandma shook her head. "I heard from my parents, who heard from their parents, that it's believed Iwa's journal is inside, but that is all I know."

"That's crazy. Not even a peek?"

Grandma smiled. "Not even a peek."

Cassidy skipped to the dining room and pulled the box from the table. She breathed in sharply as an intense tingling coursed through her hands and up her arms. The box or its contents had an invisible energy that apparently only she could sense. Grandma didn't say anything when she held it, and Mom, though she only touched it with her fingertips, didn't act like she felt anything either. Of course, the box couldn't speak, but it seemed to be letting her know it belonged to her.

Mom's agitated voice came from the living room. "Are we sure about this?"

A swell of concern rose within Cassidy, similar to what she felt when she saw Anessa sad on the first day of school. The concern was accompanied by a kind of confidence, drawing her to her mother. Slowly, Cassidy walked into the living room with the box cradled in her arms.

Mom stood, shaking her hands. "What if Cassidy doesn't want this? What if *we* don't want this? We don't know anything about this… power, other than a story about a girl and a mythical creature."

Dad stood and held Mom's hand.

A steady heat radiated in Cassidy's abdomen, spread down her legs to her toes, up her shoulders and head, and down to her fingers gripping the box. An urgency came over her seeing Mom this way, hearing Mom's words before she said them. She could sense her mom's worry and sadness that her daughter was going through this… had to go through this.

The voice inside of Cassidy spoke. *"Help her."* Helping was precisely what she wanted to do, what she needed to do. Helping felt right, natural.

Grandma stood, too. "I don't think she has a choice. I know this won't be easy, and I have concerns, but it's not like she can be hurt."

Mom, wearing a worried expression, looked at Grandma. "Seeing people's sadness and hearing their thoughts? Maybe she can't be hurt physically, but what about mentally, emotionally. It can't be healthy. You said Iwa became depressed and stopped eating and… I just think… I think we —"

"Excuse me," Cassidy said gently. The adults looked at her as if they had forgotten she existed. "I'm right here. Does anyone want to know what I think?"

Dad put his arm around Mom; she put her fist to her mouth below teary eyes. "Sure, Cassie," Mom said. "Go ahead."

Grandma smiled supportively.

"Mom… it's going to be okay." Cassidy studied the box for a moment. "I can't tell you how I know, but I just feel it, you know? You don't need to be sad or worried about me. I mean, Iwa got through it, and we're all here. Right?" Confident words came from her, but at the same time, the timid and anxious Cassidy was there in her head, questioning every bit of it. However, the timid and anxious version was in the back seat for the moment.

The corners of Mom's mouth rose and fell, unable to hold the smile.

Cassidy tried again. "How about this, if I ever can't handle it, I will let you know, and I guess we'll figure it out from there."

Mom looked to Dad, then nodded. She didn't look all that happy about the situation, but the creases in her forehead had nearly smoothed, and forced or not, she smiled ever so slightly. The urgency Cassidy felt to help her subsided, like a squeezed fist slowly opening.

"I'm going to my room to open the box." Cassidy took a sidestep, waiting for approval.

Dad nodded this time.

"Okay. I'll let you know what's inside." Everyone stared at her like she was the quarterback calling a play in the huddle, waiting for her to say "break". "Later. I'll let you know later." With three heads nodding at her, Cassidy left for her room with an exciting sense of accomplishment at successfully handling the interaction with her mother.

She closed her bedroom door behind her, leaned against it, and released a long breath. "Wow. *That* was intense." That voice in her head, her conscience or whatever it was, went quiet, as if shutting up was its way of telling her she had accomplished the task. She had done what was needed. "Now, let's see what's in this box."

Chapter 15

With her bedroom door closed and locked, Cassidy sat cross-legged on her bed and gently placed the writing box in her lap, the box that held secrets and, she hoped, answers. Carefully, she positioned the key in front of the keyhole and placed her left hand on her right to settle it after several shaky attempts. The key roughly slid in.

It was the moment in waiting for hundreds of years. A simple turn of the key would reveal hidden secrets. Grandma never opened the box, so who knew the last person to open it? What would it hold besides a journal? Could there be something magical? A talisman or wand? As a little kid, she had believed in wizards and witches, dragons and unicorns. Part of her still didn't want to give up on unicorns. But she was not a little kid anymore. If someone had asked her a week ago if she believed in magic, she would have rolled her eyes and said, "Sure, anything's possible." Her dad had told her more times than she could remember that "imagination unlocks everything in the universe". What powers would this key unlock? Could it unlock magic?

"Here we go." Cassidy slowly turned the key. *Click-click-click.*

Nothing happened. She had imagined there would be a *whoosh* of released pressure, followed by a blast of light and a strong gust of wind blowing her hair everywhere, some kind of *whoa* moment. Or worse, a creepy spring-mounted smiling clown busting free, wavering left to right — the terror of young kids for generations. It should be no wonder why people are scared of clowns. Jack in the box? More like jerk in the box.

She wedged her short and uneven fingernails into the slit between the lid and the box and paused. A glance confirmed her bedroom door was still locked. A shaky breath escaped her lips. She couldn't do it, not with the door locked. What if something happened and her parents couldn't get in to save her? Again, Cassidy imagined ridiculous worst-case scenarios. What if the box contained a poisonous snake or a spider that had waited a hundred years for someone to bite? What if it was filled with poison gas or booby-trapped? She slid from the bed, trotted to the door, and unlocked it. She opened the door a crack and peeked into the hallway to see if anyone was secretly listening in. The hall was empty. She had her desired privacy, even with the door open a little. The tension in her muscles and stomach eased. *It's okay to be a little scared. I'm only ten.*

Setting aside the thoughts of worst-case scenarios and spring-loaded demon clowns, she returned to the bed and examined the box. She traced a finger along the golden dragons, then down the stone path between them. "You two are pretty," she said softly. "I wonder where the path leads." She shook her head, sending the daydream of flying dragons back to wherever daydreams come from, and again slid her fingernails into the gap between the box and its lid. She exhaled as she lifted. A sound of release accompanied the cracking of stiff wood. The lid's hinges creaked as it rose, a sound harbored for decades.

A smell wafted from inside the box. It was the smell of the used bookstores Dad would take her to as he scoured the shelves for first edition novels of authors he admired and loved, or like the smell of Grandma's basement on a summer day. Inside the box lay a book on top of a larger book. She picked up the smaller of the two, about the size of a composition notebook. The cover was reddish-brown leather with scratches and worn edges. *This explains the old book smell.* Loosely tied around the book was a frayed, yellowing silk strip that slid free and draped across her wrist. She gently opened the cover, revealing yellowed pages with fancy writing in black ink. "This is calligraphy."

The first page read, "Inside this box is the original journal of Takayama Iwa and a twin bronze mirror. The journal you hold is a translation of Iwa's journal. This box, now and forever, should only be opened by those bestowed with the power of the satori. Only those with the bluest eyes shall peer into the mirror and the world it awakens. Guard this box and its contents so it may pass on to a descendant of yours."

Cassidy reread the page, ensuring she got it right the first time, fearing she missed some critical piece of information. The journal was in the box, just like Grandma said, but what was the deal with the twin mirror? If it's a twin, where was the other one? And what did "the world it awakens" mean? She continued reading.

"May the following pages provide knowledge and comfort while adjusting to your new life." It was signed, "Kashiko, Sato Kiku". A brief online search using her tablet revealed "kashiko" was similar to "yours truly" when signing letters.

Cassidy gently flipped through journal pages with the tip of her finger, random words catching her eyes as the pages passed. "This is my guidebook. Like, instructions." As tempting as the journal was to read, there was more inside the box to examine. She placed the journal at her side and laid the silk strip across it. A red cloth lay draped half over the larger journal in the box. At first pull, it became evident it wasn't merely a piece of cloth, but a piece of cloth wrapped around something. *This must be the mirror.*

Her fingers slid under the cloth, grabbed the hidden object, and pulled it free. She lifted the mirror, a mirror heavier than any she owned. Unlike her plastic ones, this mirror was metal — bronze, as it said in the journal. Engraved flowers and a bird she couldn't name adorned one side of the mirror. The opposite side was not a mirror as she knew them. Instead, where there should have been glass, was a smooth unreflective surface, dull with a greenish tint. The same green shade covered the decorated side and handle. *Dad will know how to clean it.*

She placed the mirror to her right and peered at the larger journal, Iwa's journal, which fit perfectly in the box. The journal appeared as ancient as it was, two hundred years or even more. Older than Mom, Dad, and Grandma combined. It had a cream paper-like cover that may have been white but had aged over time. Neatly printed symbols were on the left side running top to bottom. Cassidy recognized the symbols as kanji, a Japanese writing style, but had no idea what they meant. She bit her lower lip as she lifted the journal from the box; its spine and cover creaked and cracked on the way out. Would she be the first to see the pages inside since Sato Kiku? Carefully, Cassidy opened the cover with a shaky hand, worrying it would fall apart with the tiniest of movements. The pages were thicker than her school paper, almost like a fabric.

Kanji — strokes of ink forming symbols that were actually words — covered the first page, but she recognized none of it. However, these pages of unrecognizable words, written over two hundred years ago, struck her more than any book she'd ever read. The ink on the paper was from another time, heck, practically another world. Words that were once no more than Iwa's thoughts were now being viewed in a time she could have never imagined. It was like written time travel.

"Oh, no." Cassidy gasped, turning a shade of red as one of the pages pulled free from the binding. She carefully slid the page back into place, closed the journal, and put it back in the box where it would be safe. She'd look at it only if necessary. The translated journal would tell her what she needed to know.

Knock-knock.

Cassidy's head snapped toward the door, eyes wide.

"May I come in?"

Cassidy relaxed and let out a slow breath. "Oh… hey. Sure."

The door opened fully, revealing Grandma. "Did you find what you expected in the box?"

Kiku's translation was on Cassidy's left, the mirror on her right, and Iwa's journal was in the box — the loose page would be her secret. She'd be lying if she said it was all she expected. Information on what was going on with her was expected and she assumed the journal had that covered. As for the mirror, she didn't know what purpose it served. Maybe the journal had an explanation. She shrugged. "I guess."

"Want to show me?" Grandma asked, wonderment in her voice.

Everything inside the box would be as much a surprise to Grandma as it had been to Cassidy. Grandma had never opened the box that she'd faithfully kept and protected for so many years, decades even. But for the last almost eleven years, from the day she first saw her blue-eyed granddaughter, Grandma would have known this day would come.

Cassidy smiled and raised a finger. "Wait a sec. Let me put everything back in the box to how it was."

Grandma walked over to the bed. "Great idea."

Cassidy returned the items to the box just as she found them, closed the lid, and locked it. "Okay. Your turn."

Chapter 16

THE OTHER WORLD

The greenest green meadow of tall grass, dotted with clusters of bright yellow sunflowers, stretched out for hundreds of yards in all directions. Far above the greenest green grass was the bluest blue sky, in which floated the fluffiest fluffy, whitest white clouds. In the distance in every direction, towering mountains reached higher than the limits of where the human eye could see.

Far below the sky, Kazuyasu sat silent and still on the grass. His brown eyes were barely open, his palms were positioned upward — right hand over left — on his lap. His black hair was in a tight ponytail secured by a thin piece of red cloth. He wore a gray linen kimono, a darker gray hakama, tight gray trousers that reached just below his knees, and white split-toe socks on his feet.

A sheathed katana — his sword — was fastened to a white sash wrapped around his waist.

A burst of gentle wind swayed the long grass, his ponytail, and played at the sleeves of his kimono. It was the perfect day for meditation, as were most days in the valley when it wasn't raining or snowing to replenish the earth. Eyes relaxed and staring at the ground in front of him, Kazuyasu had been meditating undisturbed for nearly an hour. His mind had settled like a leaf on a still pond.

Rustle-rustle.

His face twitched; his eyes slightly widened.

Rustle-rustle.

Kazuyasu's brow furrowed and the corners of his mouth turned downward. Slowly, his right hand slid across his waist and his fingers and thumb wrapped around the hilt of his katana.

The rustling grew louder, closer. His eyes cut to the right, closing to slits. *Something approaches; a treacherous enemy. My sword is ready.* He sprang to his feet and whirled around, prepared to pull his blade from its sheath and strike down his foe.

Excitedly bounding through the long grass came Maku, her black hair flowing as if moved by an underwater current. She wore a midnight blue silk kimono bearing the image of a waning gibbous moon in the middle of the chest. Her feet, just peeking from underneath the bottom of her kimono, were bare.

Kazuyasu's snarled lips relaxed and the tension in his body eased. He loosened his grip on the sword, and his hands dropped to his sides. "Maku," he said in a huff.

The excitement on Maku's face faded as she heard Kazuyasu's tone. Timidly she stopped before him. Pressing her palms together against her chest, she bowed, her long hair shrouding her ghostly face that appeared to be on the verge of translucency.

"Haven't I told you not to bother me during meditation?" Kazuyasu scolded.

Maku peeked at him with black eyes through the strands of her hair and straightened. Though she could hear, she was without a voice and used her hands to speak. "Yes, Kaz," she signed. "I'm sorry. It's just —"

"No, it's not *just*. If I'm to become a proper samurai, I need to train every day, and that training includes meditation. Diligence is required so that I may one day be accepted by the samurai."

Maku stepped forward and continued to sign urgently. "But —"

Kaz held up a silencing finger, pacing as he continued. "I'm on a path to greatness, and one day you will be a companion of a samurai whose name will be etched into the books of our history as one of our greatest warriors."

Maku failed to hide a grin behind her hands.

Kaz stopped pacing, stepped close to her, and leaned in. "Are you laughing at me?"

Maku fought against her smile and signed, "No." She looked away and frowned. "But by the time you are a great samurai, you'll be an adult, and you'll no longer believe in me. I'll disappear from your mind just like I do with all kids when they grow up. Besides, you can never be our greatest warrior."

Kaz took a step back, looking her up and down, stunned at her lack of confidence in him. "Why not?"

"Because there hasn't been a reason to fight in over a hundred years. We have no enemies, and with the barrier protecting us, we never will again."

"But Maku, imagine if the barrier was gone just like that," he snapped his fingers, "and there *were* monsters for me to strike down with my blade." He clenched his fists. "Wada-sama would marvel at my sword skills and would invite me to train with the samurai, to be one of them. I wouldn't just be the son of a fisherman."

"That's just it — the only monsters are in your imagination. Our most dangerous foes are bears and boars, and they mostly leave us alone."

"I may be imagining that there are monsters, real monsters, to fight, but you are pretending that the barrier will be there forever. You know it is not as certain as it used to be." Kaz unclenched his fists and softened. "Though, I hope you are correct and that the barrier remains. But Maku, there is one thing I am certain you are wrong about. You will never disappear from my mind. I will always believe in you. You're my best friend."

"Your only friend."

Kaz sighed and relaxed his shoulders. "Anyway. Why are you here?"

Her eyes widened above a grand smile. "The box. It moved."

Kaz squinted and tilted his head to the right. "The box?"

Maku nodded excitedly and signed with emphasis, "Yes, *the box*."

It hit him a few seconds later, like a confusing joke he finally understood. His eyes widened above his gaping mouth. "THE box?"

"THE box."

A rush of urgency coursed through his veins, igniting him into action. Kaz hurriedly slipped on his sandals and took off in a sprint without warning, yelling, "What are you waiting for? Come on, let's go!"

Maku chased behind him.

The trip to his home was an eight-minute run. Kaz scampered down a grassy path between terraced rice paddy fields that resembled large steps that stretched out dozens of yards in both directions, rambled across an arched, red wooden bridge stretching over a slow running stream, and sprinted down a dirt path past villagers in front of their thatched-roof wood homes. The villagers gawked at him, the "baby samurai" running through the village yet again.

"Where are you headed in such a hurry?" a white-haired man called as Kazuyasu darted by.

"No time to talk," Kaz said, barely glancing back. He leaped, skipping the first three wooden stairs, and landed on the fourth step leading to the door of his home. The dark brown door slid aside with a quick push to the right. He hastily loosened the rope securing his sandals, kicked them off haphazardly, and sprinted through the house, leaving sweaty footprints on the wood floor.

He ran down the main hallway of his home, past paper-covered doors to other rooms, slowed, then sprinted left down a hallway until he reached its end. He bent over at the waist, heaving breaths, and shook his head as Maku arrived, looking pitifully at him. A benefit of being a spirit was that she never tired, never had to fight for breath. She didn't even need to run as she could cover great distances by disappearing and appearing where she wanted, but she told Kaz she never wanted him to feel bad about being so slow.

A noise came from the other side of the wall.

Kaz stiffened and straightened. He took a final deep breath and wiped the sweat from his brow. He poked at the edge of the right side of the wall, and pushed at a small point that gave, creating a groove. With a pull to the left, the wall slid away, revealing a dimly lit secret room. He had been told the room was once used as a hiding place during dangerous times when monsters and bad people were in the valley. Now it was used for storage and a place for him to go when he wanted to be alone. He nodded for the eager-faced Maku to follow.

Various artifacts filled the secret room: a single set of black and gold laquered samurai armor loomed over as if worn by an invisible warrior, bamboo fishing poles hung horizontally, interspersed with paintings on wood and canvas, beautifully crafted pottery bowls sat on tables, pedestals, and the floor. Against a far wall was a small, squat table, on which sat a lacquered box no bigger than a tortoise shell.

He and Maku stood motionless, staring at the box, waiting for it to do something. Then it did. It moved — a quick jerk that would have been missed if they were not focused on it. They shared a look, said not a word, and watched in awe as a soft glow escaped the sliver of a gap in the lid.

Kaz swallowed away a lump in his throat and nervously reached for the box as it gently rattled. He slowly lifted the lid, freeing the golden glow to brighten the room and illuminate their astonished faces. He pushed away Maku's hand as she reached for the box's contents. She pouted and mouthed, *"Sorry."*

The box held a bronze mirror that lay nestled in a silk-covered slot of its same shape; the right side of the box had a twin silk-covered space, but its mirror was missing. Kaz pulled the bronze mirror from the box. Engraved images of sakura flowers and cranes decorated the mirror's backside; the bronze was polished to a mirrored shine on the other side. He examined his face, moving the mirror slightly to the left and right. His eyes narrowed, searching the reflection for something more, searching for the other world. Searching for the other universe where the mate to the mirror he held lived. A gentle gasp escaped his mouth. His eyes widened at seeing, though faint, a face in the mirror other than his own. It was the face of a young, blue-eyed girl.

After years of box watching, it finally happened — the connection between the mirrors was established, reopening the doorway between his world and hers.

"We should tell Iwa," Maku signed, staring into the mirror at the blue-eyed girl.

Kaz's expression soured. "Iwa told me that when this day came, she would feel it… feel her powers lessen. She said there wouldn't be much we could do at first. She said to wait."

"Wait for what?"

Kaz nodded toward the mirror. "For Cassidy to be ready to help us."

Maku seemed to consider this for a moment, then asked, "What do we do while we wait?"

"Be ready."

"Be ready for what?"

Kaz pulled his gaze from the mirror and looked at Maku, the space between his eyebrows creasing. "For things to get worse."

Chapter 17

After Cassidy finished examining the writing box and its contents with Grandma, she got ready for bed and said goodnight to everyone. She wanted to read more of the journal, but it was late. She would be a wreck at school without at least eight hours of sleep. The box was on the dresser where she left it an hour ago, but she checked to make sure it was still there to confirm, yet again, that the events of the day were not a dream. It was just as she had left it, between a framed photo of her and Maisy and a silver piggy bank stuffed with unspent allowance and loose change from Mom and Dad.

"What the?" She picked up a brown leather book from her pillow. *C A R K* was engraved in the bottom right of the cover. *My initials.* A folded piece of paper fell to the bed when she opened the cover. Cassidy picked up the note, unfolded it, and read, "Cassidy, this journal is to record your journey so that one day a little girl or boy like you can read about your adventures and learn from YOU. Love, Grandma."

Cassidy's gift-induced smile collapsed to a straight line as she considered the responsibility of sharing knowledge with her descendants. How could she? She was stumped on how to handle the situation herself. She hated feeling this way. Feeling too afraid and too intimidated to do anything. She wished she were more like Iwa — Iwa was brave. She had walked down a scary trail to save someone and didn't run away after that someone turned out to be a monster. Well, a satori. Maybe calling it a monster wasn't very fair.

Earlier in the day, when Cassidy reassured her mom that everything would be okay, she felt it — she felt brave. But where was that feeling now? Did being brave just come and go when she needed it? Maybe being brave was like what Dad told her about discipline. "Discipline is like a muscle, use it or lose it." Cassidy didn't care much about muscles, and discipline was easy when she stopped committing to things, but she wanted to be brave.

"If I'm going to be brave, I better start now." Her brow furrowed and she stood tall, looking around the room as she put her hair in a ponytail. "I can do this. I know I can." Her voice rose. "Do you believe me, Universe?" Her shoulders relaxed as she touched a finger to her lips, her eyes narrowing. "Do I believe me?"

She pulled a pen from her desk drawer and hopped onto the bed with her tablet and new journal. Pulling the covers up and over her head, she flipped to her stomach. She'd never given much thought to her initials that were now before her, engraved on the journal. "Cark," she said with a frown. "Car K" and "C Ark" did not sound any better. She Googled cark: to worry or be worried. *Well, I guess that fits me.*

Cassidy checked the time; it was getting late. "I have to call Maisy." A melodic dial tone sounded with a swipe across the tablet screen and a couple of rapid finger presses.

Maisy's cheerful and expectant face appeared on the screen.

"Hey, Maze."

"I was about to say, you'd better call me before bed. So… what happened?" Maisy asked.

Cassidy pressed her lips together. "Umm, it's kinda difficult to explain."

Maisy put her round face close to the tablet camera. "Thank greatness you have a bestie like me who is amazing at difficult."

Cassidy broke into a smile and laughed. "Yeah, that's the truth."

"So, spill it."

"It's… I found out I have this…" Cassidy's voice trailed off. She wanted to tell Maisy everything, but Mom said it was best to keep her powers a secret. But this was Maisy, and she already knew about it. Well, most of it. "Maisy, you have to promise not to tell anyone."

"No one? Can I at least tell —"

"No. One." Cassidy repeated emphatically.

Maisy pressed her lips, then nodded. "Okay, sis."

"Promise?"

Maisy stuck out her right pinky and waited for Cassidy to do the same. They faked a gripping of their fingers and made an "S" shaped movement. It was their version of a pinky swear, the "S" representing "sisters". It was their most sacred promise.

Cassidy told Maisy about the powers, and how she was the unlucky descendant of Iwa to inherit them. She skimmed over the part about the satori. Believing in a mythical creature wasn't easy; Maisy might think Cassidy's family was crazy with that particular detail.

Maisy was wide-eyed through most of the conversation. "We are going to have *so* much fun with this."

Cassidy offered a weak smile. "Yeah. Maybe."

"Tablet off!" Maisy's mom yelled from somewhere in Maisy's house.

Maisy clenched her jaw. "Uh oh. Gotta go. Night, sis."

"Night, Maze." Maisy's face disappeared, leaving the screen and the space under the covers dark. Cassidy released a held breath and stared at nothing. *How could this be fun?* She pushed the cover from her head, laid the tablet on the floor, and grabbed her new journal and pen. She shoved the pillow under her chest and propped herself up on her elbows.

Using the light from her lamp to see, she flipped open the journal and stared at the blank page with her pen uncapped and ready to write. The blank page stared back at her. She imagined if the page could speak, it would ask, "What do you have to write about that's so important?" And that was the question — what did she have to write about? The most interesting part of her life was "that day", and the most exciting part of her life was having Maisy as a friend.

Cassidy's face brightened. *Of course.* She positioned the journal and wrote the month, the day, and the year at the top of the page. "Well, that's a start." She pursed her lips. "Umm."

After a minute of thought, she put pen to page and wrote.

Journal Entry August 23

So. This is my journal. I'm Cassidy. My full name is Cassidy Anne Rumiko Kenner. I'm almost 11 years old.

My best friend is Maisy Bijou Davis. She's also 10. She's like my sister.

Anyway. I got some kind of powers from something called a satori, which is why I have these blue eyes. I shouldn't have blue eyes but now I know why I do. I'll know more tomorrow when I read Iwa's journal. Oh, Iwa is who started all of this.

Goodnight, I guess.
Cassidy
P.S. I almost forgot. <u>BE BRAVE!</u>

Chapter 18

Cassidy slept. She didn't dream of shape forming clouds, nor did she dream of Anessa and her sadness. Instead, she slept quietly and comfortably beneath her fluffy, purple-flowered comforter without a care in the world — not in hers or anyone else's. Everything was perfectly peaceful... for most of the night.

A soft light pierced her eyelids in the early morning hours while she slept. Somewhere in her subconscious, the light was identified as passing headlights — nothing new with her bedroom window facing the street — but without the accompanying sound of a car. A brief gust of wind accompanied the warmth of a summer night. Outdoorsy noises came next: wind blowing through trees and long grass, bugs playing their nighttime serenade. Cassidy turned from lying on her side to her back. She coughed away an itch in her throat and released a slow, tired breath.

Another noise broke the silence — clothes hangers moving, maybe. Her barely-there waking mind reconciled the noise as inconsequential and released its grip on the waking world for the continuation of sleep.

Movement. Gentle movement. Cassidy's head lifted slightly, then gently lowered. Her consciousness registered the movement worthy of the slightest slit-eyed peek. Two black orbs set upon white, shrouded by a curtain of black, hovered above her. *Something… someone is here, in my room.*

The whites of the eyes above her were hidden away by a toothy smile. The smile faded, and a finger was placed on pursed lips. No words came from this pale face with black eyes, only a sound. *"Shhhh."*

Cassidy's eyes closed, and all of her gave in to sleep. Quiet and peaceful sleep.

Chapter 19

Cassidy woke to Grandma's voice. She stretched her arms overhead and yawned. "Morning, Grandma. I'll be down in a little bit."

"Okay," Grandma said from the doorway. "Any special requests for breakfast?"

"Two pancakes with whipped cream and strawberries on top," Cassidy said through a yawn.

"I'll have it ready in a jiff."

"Oh," Cassidy said urgently, "and strawberry milk, please."

"Strawberry milk. Got it." Grandma smiled and left for the kitchen.

Ugh, morning. Cassidy closed her eyes to hide away from the morning light a little longer. Lying in silence, something seemed off; something was not quite right. The comfortable pillow, usually cradling her head, was gone. Her feet, however, were uncommonly comfortable. She lifted her comforter. Mystery solved — her pillow was under her feet.

"What the frappe?" She sat up, pulled the comforter from her feet, and stared at the pillow, waiting for it to explain itself — strange things *had* been happening lately. After a moment of contemplation, she placed the wandering pillow back to its proper place at the head of her bed. A cursory scan of her bedroom revealed nothing else was out of place. Still, an unexplainable odd aura she didn't like one bit stuck with her. She slid from the bed and checked the window — closed and locked. She studied the room. What exactly was she looking for? Giving up on finding the apparently unfindable reason behind the odd feeling, the box caught her eye. Today she'd read the journal to learn more about her powers, and hopefully, find out what she was supposed to do. But first things first — get cleaned up and eat some yummy, whipped cream pancakes.

After brushing her hair, Cassidy stood in front of the bathroom mirror. Her long, dark brown hair was straight as a board — boring, as usual — with mint-colored barrettes on each side to keep it out of her eyes. The night before picture day each year, Mom would intertwine Cassidy's hair with socks. When the socks were removed in the morning, her hair was voluminous, at least for that day. Her eyes were as blue as the clearest blue sky, eyes like her ancestor Iwa, and rather creepily, like the satori. *My eyes are the same color as the magical ape-like creature... fantastic. At least I didn't get its hair-covered body.* After digesting that bit of knowledge, she frowned at her reflection and went to get the journal.

She opened the dragon-covered lid of the writing box and gently removed Kiku's translation. It was not nearly as old as Iwa's journal, the original with the Japanese script, but it was old enough to be treated with more care than her math textbook. Math was not her favorite. Truthfully, if she could, she'd toss her math book in the road for morning traffic to run over. She considered creating a protective cover for the journal as she did for her textbooks. She loved decorating the covers with her own designs. She wasn't the best artist, close to the worst, actually. Still, she imagined and drew her own characters or recreated ones she loved — superheroes, faeries, unicorns, and mermaids — each one more whimsical than the pre-made covers bearing symmetrical shapes and Fibonacci patterns. Her fascination with the idea of dressing up the journal was surpassed by the tantalizing image of pancakes covered in whipped cream and strawberries. She left for the kitchen with a hungry smile and Kiku's journal in hand.

Cassidy's nostrils filled with the aroma of breakfast. She sat in her regular spot at the kitchen island and shined a wide smile at Grandma. She ran her hand across the countertop until satisfied it was dry, placed the journal next to her plate of food, and opened the cover.

"How's breakfast look?" Grandma asked.

Cassidy grinned with eager eyes at the plate of pancakes and glass of strawberry milk. "It looks delicious. Thanks, Grandma."

Grandma nodded at the journal. "Getting some reading in before school?"

Cassidy took in and released a deep breath. "Yep. I gotta figure out what the heck I am."

Grandma laughed. "What you are? You haven't changed. You're still Cassidy, you're still my granddaughter."

Cassidy scoffed and eyed Grandma incredulously. "I haven't changed? Grandma. Two days ago, I started seeing people's sadness and not just their frowns. I can literally see their sad life as it happened. I can hear what someone is going to say. I think that's a pretty big change."

"No matter what, you will always be my sweet Cassie," Grandma said encouragingly.

"And you know what?" Cassidy said.

Grandma placed a pan in the soapy water-filled sink. "What?"

"I heard you think that before you said it. I heard you think, 'No matter what, you will always be my sweet Cassie.'"

Grandma laughed.

"Now, that's creepy, not sweet."

Grandma nodded. "That is a bit creepy."

Cassidy smiled. "At least you aren't lying to me."

"Never." Grandma crossed her heart.

Cassidy filled her mouth with a fork full of syrup, whipped cream, strawberry, and pancake goodness.

She said, "This is good," but it sounded more like "Th eh goo." She focused on the second page of the journal. The shape of the letters written in calligraphy again caught her attention. A message from Kiku was near the middle of the page.

"On these pages is my translation of the journal of Takayama Iwa — the first of you — born 1618 and died 1678. You, reading this, are the next after her. May these pages help you on your journey, wherever it leads." Near the bottom of the page was "Sato, Kiku, Nineteen Thousand and One, January First." Unlike the first page that detailed the box's contents, this page was dated.

Cassidy swallowed a mouthful of chewed food she had forgotten.

Grandma leaned in with her elbows on the counter that she was only about a foot taller than. "Anything good?'

Cassidy took a sip of strawberry milk. "Sato Kiku translated the journal. Who was she?"

"Sato Kiku was your great, great, great... great grandma."

Cassidy smiled. "Only four greats. That's a bit easier to imagine."

Grandma grinned. "She was born in Japan and moved to Hawaii in the late eighteen hundreds."

"This page in the journal, it's dated January first, nineteen thousand and one."

Grandma's eyebrows rose over the top of her glasses.

Cassidy's brow furrowed. "New Year's Day."

"Mmhmm."

"Like she made a resolution… to translate the journal?" Cassidy asked.

"Perhaps. What else does it say?"

"May these pages help you on your journey."

"A journey? Oh my."

Cassidy leaned away, shaking her head. "I do *not* want to go on a journey." She related the word "journey" to hobbits and people who dreamed of traveling to the center of the earth. Those journeys never went well, despite the Hollywood happy ending. Journey to the mall — loads of fun and doable. Journey to school — painfully necessary. Journey to Narnia or Middle-Earth — not happening.

"Maybe she meant it metaphorically," Grandma said.

Cassidy tried to repeat the word that had way too many syllables.

Grandma smiled and clarified. "Maybe she meant the journey of life, not a journey to somewhere or someplace."

Cassidy mulled over the explanation and slowly nodded. "Yeah. I hope she meant it metaphorically." She managed to get the word out.

"Okay Blue, only ten minutes until you have to leave for school," Dad announced as he walked into the kitchen. Today his shirt read, "Don't just do something; stand there. Martin Gabel." "Good morning, Mom." He hugged Grandma. Technically, Grandma was his mother-in-law, but they were close. Dad's mom died years back, making Grandma the only person he could call mom.

"Good morning, Dad." Cassidy took another bite of pancake and turned the page of the journal. *Okay, Iwa. What do you have to tell me?*

Chapter 20

aisy wore an expectant expression while waiting outside of Cassidy's home. "So?"

"Hey, Maze," Cassidy replied casually, walking past her down the sidewalk. She gave an *are-you-coming* look over her shoulder.

Maisy slipped her arms into her backpack straps and performed a little hop to get it and the back of her dress in place. "Don't 'Hey, Maze' me. What's the story?" She took a step and paused. "No, wait. Let's give you a test." Her eyes intently focused on Cassidy. "What am I about to say?"

Cassidy stopped. She stepped close to Maisy, narrowed her eyes, and leaned in close, in case the ability to hear thoughts was a matter of distance. She pulled back after a few fruitless attempts, shaking her head. "I don't think it works like that." She frowned, confused and disappointed. She had heard what Grandma was about to say without even trying. "Or maybe it does, and I just don't know how."

Maisy raised an eyebrow. "Didn't you figure this out last night?"

"Not really." Cassidy trudged away. "Maybe it can't be on purpose, ya know? The conversation has to be natural. Like, I can't force it or make it happen."

Maisy skipped to catch up. "You'll figure it out when you read more of the journal."

"I hope so."

"Wait." Maisy frowned. "Will you be able to hear *everything* someone is thinking? Because that would be creepy. Not that I'm thinking anything bad, but, you know, thoughts are personal."

"No, it's only what you are about to say. At least for now."

"For now?"

"Right. I'm not one hundred percent sure how all of this works, but I'm figuring it out."

Maisy gave her an uncomfortable grin. "You'll let me know when you can read minds, and you know, hear everything? Then maybe turn it off around me?"

Cassidy grimaced. Hearing what someone was about to say was awkward enough, but hearing all thoughts? It sounded like an incredible power to have, but thoughts were personal, private, stuff for journals. She wouldn't want anyone to hear her thoughts, nor did she want to hear anyone else's. "I'll tell you when. I promise."

Maisy gazed longingly into the distance and sighed. "What I would do with that power." She immediately clarified, "For good, of course," and with a hint of a devious smile, "Only for good."

"Oh, I believe you," Cassidy replied with a sprinkling of sarcasm.

They shared a laugh and headed to school.

Cassidy stopped at the edge of the school grounds and grabbed Maisy's wrist, bringing her to an abrupt halt.

"What's wrong?" Maisy asked.

Cassidy stared at the horde of kids mulling about, running around playing tag, chatting about the day, working on unfinished homework, and doing general kid stuff. She examined their faces, hoping to see happy ones, excited ones, and even content ones. However, considering her power, sad faces like Anessa's on the first day of school were her concern. Those faces she desperately wanted to avoid.

Most of the kids had expressions of various forms of happiness. Josie was a picture book image of happy, ecstatic even. A few kids had vacant expressions — neither happy nor sad. She'd stay clear of them, just to be safe. Anessa's sadness was already more than she knew how to handle.

It was like the first day of school all over again: the anxiety, the nervousness, the imagined ridiculous scenarios. Would she have to go through this every day of school? Or worse, every day of her life? Would she have to watch for sad people in college or at the mall and avoid them? This power, or curse — the satori's words not hers — would be more of a pain than she thought. Iwa should have listened to the satori when it pleaded with her not to take the power.

"Cassie?" Maisy said with a hint of concern.

Cassidy shook her head. "What? Sorry."

"You okay?" Maisy asked.

Cassidy forced a smile. "Yeah. It's just… I'm not sure what to expect. Ya know?"

Maisy hugged her. "I'm here for you. We've got this, sis."

Cassidy let go of a held breath. Maisy was there for her again, and it was that knowledge that got her feet moving. "Let me know if you see Anessa."

"My guess is she's already in the classroom, hiding from everyone." Maisy glanced at kid's faces they passed, searching for Anessa. "It's probably a few minutes until the bell. Let's get there first and find out."

Cassidy nodded.

Still holding hands, Maisy dragged her through the crowd. Everyone was talking so much that conversations mushed together into loud nonsense. Like one hundred kids talking before the start of a school performance, or just when it gets too loud in the lunchroom and a teacher asks everyone to "take it down a notch". Cassidy didn't know if what she was hearing were what kids were about to say, or just them actually speaking. It was kind of a relief not knowing.

They stepped into the school.

The school's interior was quiet, still minutes away from the ringing of the warning bell. Most students were outside stretching their before-school-life for as long as possible. Many of them, like Cassidy, would love to live a no-school life permanently. Only a spattering of teachers and students with an aversion to being outside inhabited the hallways. The students inside were the friendless, the introverts, and the go-getters who wanted to get to class first just so they could give a victorious, smug expression to everyone entering the room *after* them. Some kids were like that, taking every little victory they could get. Cassidy was searching for the friendless Anessa. It was no fault of Anessa's; she was new to the school, so of course she didn't have friends… yet. Anessa just might be the most outgoing kid in school if she wasn't embarrassed about her clothes.

Cassidy, accompanied by Maisy and nervous expectation, headed down the hallway toward their classroom. *Anessa will be there. She has to be.*

Without a dramatic pause — no slow unveiling — Maisy grabbed the handle and pushed open the classroom door. She took two steps in and abruptly stopped: Cassidy stutter-stepped, bumping into her.

Cassidy peered over Maisy's shoulder and briefly locked eyes with a startled Anessa, who averted her eyes. Anessa wasn't first in the room to gloat. She was first in the room to avoid the disapproving stares from her peers. Stares typically accompanied by words or sounds of mockery. Anessa was hiding.

The feeling hit Cassidy, and that little voice urging her into action. *"Help her."*

Geez, give me a chance. I literally just got here. Cassidy hugged herself, opened her mouth to speak, but closed it without saying a single word. She gritted her teeth and closed her eyes for a breath. *I can do this.* She opened her eyes and blurted, "Hi, Anessa." Instinctively, she wanted to collapse in on herself and hide, but fought against it. Instead she stood a little straighter and taller, helped by a surge of confidence at being the conversation starter.

Maisy looked at her openmouthed, then whispered, "You just did that."

"I know. Crazy, huh?" Cassidy whispered back, then nodded toward Anessa, prompting Maisy.

"Hi, Anessa," Maisy said.

Anessa made brief eye contact and may have smiled. If it was a smile, it was likely forced through embarrassment and the desire to be left alone. At a distance, her clothes looked okay, not tragic. However, she wore the same shoes as the first day, and they looked just as worn.

"Ooookay… what now?" Maisy asked quietly from the corner of her mouth.

"Um," Cassidy replied. *Good question.*

The classroom desks were in pods of four — two desks facing two other desks to form a square. This way, you weren't facing the back of the head of the person in front of you. Instead you'd see the top of their head if they were diligently working on classwork, or their face if you were talking to them at appropriate or inappropriate times, or catching them staring at you like a creeper.

Anessa's desk was the odd one out with one next to her — yet to be claimed — and no desks in front.

Lightbulb.

"Maisy," Cassidy said quietly, but urgently. "Get your desk."

Maisy gave her a '*what do you mean, get my desk*' look. Maisy was forever good at looks.

"I'm changing desks. I'm going to sit next to Anessa. Push your desk in front of hers." Maisy stared at her, so Cassidy gave a look of her own. A look that asked her friend to be understanding and agreeable. The same look she once gave Maisy after asking her to ride the ski lift in Park City, knowing Maisy was terrified of heights. Or after she showed Maisy a video on piercing your own ears or the ears of a consenting friend. Luckily in hindsight, for both of them, Maisy had refused to be a consenting friend. Maisy was a doer, a go-getter, and had confidence for days. But heights and blood? No way.

With the task of moving her desk free of heights and blood loss, Maisy lifted one end of her desk and nodded for Cassidy to lift the other.

Anessa narrowed her eyes, either in confusion, bother, or both.

Cassidy smiled at her as they trundled over with the desk. "We're going to be pod mates."

Anessa's lips parted, but she didn't speak.

Cassidy cringed. She had heard and answered the question Anessa was about to ask —'What are you doing?' Luckily, Anessa didn't appear to give it a second thought. Cassidy's reply was an obvious enough answer to her confused expression.

"Why?" Anessa asked, a slight southern accent in her voice.

Cassidy and Maisy finished setting Maisy's desk flush with the front of Anessa's and what was now Cassidy's desk, precisely in the center of the two.

"I just thought —" Cassidy caught Maisy, grinning wide-eyed and nodding at her. "*We* just thought that you —" She froze. Anessa looked directly into Cassidy's eyes. Sadness assaulted Cassidy like an arrow to the head, the insecurity passing through the air like Wi-Fi. The room spun. Her knees gave. An arm was around her, and a hand firmly grabbed her wrist.

"Cassidy." The voice was distant, possibly from another classroom.

"Cassidy." The voice again, this time with urgency.

"Cassidy!" someone yelled as the five-minute warning bell rang.

Cassidy shook her head, trying to break the stream from Anessa to her. A few dizzy moments later, the spinning stopped and her eyes focused on Maisy's face — pretty as ever, but now caked with worry and a hint of embarrassment.

"Hi, Maze," Cassidy said hazily, dropping until her butt smacked her seat. Anessa wore a wary expression and scooted her chair back in quick, jerky movements.

Maisy, still standing, took over the conversation with Anessa. "We thought you could use some pod mates. Sitting here by yourself makes it look like you're in perma-trouble with the teacher."

The words forming in Anessa's mind reached Cassidy's mind before she said them, like echoes without the echoey sound.

"I'm okay. You don't have to," Anessa said, glancing up at Maisy before returning her focus to her textbook. Her fingers picked at a tear in the book's corner. The book was new, so obviously she had been nervously working at the tear.

"No, it's all great." Maisy sat and smiled her smile that won the hearts and minds of those lucky enough to witness it. "Oh, I forgot introductions. I'm Maisy. Maisy Bijou Davis."

Maisy always used her full name for introductions. Whenever asked why, she'd simply say, "Because it's my name." Years ago, she and her family had moved in a few houses down from Cassidy's. She introduced herself one day as "Maisy Bijou Davis", and the rest was history. Well, a brief history.

"I'm Anessa," she responded, raising her hand from the table and giving a lazy wave.

It was Cassidy's turn, and Anessa's eyes were already on her, giving a look of *'hey, aren't you that weird girl who followed me into the bathroom and fainted after touching my shoulder?'*

Yes, that's me. The weird girl. Nice to meet you… again.

Fake conversation in her head aside, Cassidy introduced herself, first name only. "Hi. I'm Cassidy."

Anessa gave a small smile and timidly said, "Hi."

Cassidy noticed something strange about Anessa she hadn't before. Maybe it had been there all this time, in the bathroom before Cassidy had fainted, but now it was unmissable. A dark haze surrounded Anessa, a black and gray smog hovering above and around her like a terrible blanket. It didn't have a discernible smell, nor did it make a sound. Cassidy wanted to reach out to touch it, but doing so would risk her looking like a total weirdo again.

"What?" Anessa asked uncomfortably, pulling her hands into her lap.

Oh, man. I was staring again. "Sorry. I guess I was daydreaming." Cassidy bit her lower lip and glanced toward the distracting sound of kids streaming into the classroom, the interruption saving her from further embarrassment.

"You have really blue —"

"Eyes," Cassidy finished. "I get that a lot."

Maisy's mouth stretched into an awkward smile as she nodded sideways toward Anessa.

Cassidy grimaced, understanding the non-verbal queue. Maisy wanted her to act on their plan — Operation Dress Anessa — but nearly fainting, again, had gotten in the way.

"Cassie, one minute until class starts," Maisy said.

Cassidy narrowed her eyes and nodded. "Anessa," she paused, awaiting acknowledgment.

Anessa looked at her in the same *'What, weirdo?'* way. Then her response came twice — once inside Cassidy's head and once from Anessa's mouth — "Yeah?"

"Maisy and I…" Cassidy started. She shifted in her seat and tugged at the end of her shirt. "We're hanging out after school at my place. Do you want to come over?"

"To hang out?" Anessa asked.

Cassidy nodded. "Yeah, at my place. It must be difficult being the new kid and not knowing anyone."

Anessa appeared to dissect the offer before answering. "Uh, I don't know."

"It's Friday," Cassidy said, followed by an uncomfortable laugh.

Anessa shook her head. "No. My mom's really busy. She won't be able to pick me up after."

Cassidy shifted in her seat toward Anessa, placing one hand on the desk and the other on the seatback. Anessa hadn't said no, so there was still an opportunity. "That's okay. My mom or dad can take you home. I mean, you go to this school, you can't live too far away."

"We'll have so much fun," Maisy added.

Cassidy flashed an appreciative smile at Maisy for helping.

"I don't know." Anessa said.

"What if… my dad talks to your mom, and she says it's okay? I'll give you my dad's phone number, and she can call him. We walk home every day, she doesn't even have to give us a ride."

Anessa averted her eyes before glancing at Maisy, then back to Cassidy. "Yeah, I guess."

A smile broke out across Cassidy's face, coupled with a smile from Maisy.

The barely perceptible black haze around Anessa compressed ever so slightly before snapping back to its original prominent shape and size. Movement in Cassidy's peripheral and giggles grabbed her attention.

Brody and Adam were laughing in their direction. Cassidy glowered at them and turned to see Anessa's reaction. She obviously thought they were laughing at her. If her sad expression wasn't enough to show how she felt, the growth of the sooty haze around her told the story. *The haze must be linked to her sadness.*

Maisy got Brody and Adam's attention and pointed a stern finger their way. Only the back of her head was visible to Cassidy and Anessa, but Cassidy knew the face Maisy was giving them. It was her *I mean business* face. It was a face from which Brody and Adam sheepishly turned away from. Maisy swiveled back around. Her expression, flipping like a light switch, was now all smiles. But to say Maisy's smile was glowing would be an understatement. In all the years of knowing Maisy, Cassidy literally saw her in a new light. A soft glow surrounded Maisy in the same way a haze surrounded Anessa. She appeared to have her own backlight. Maisy appeared as Cassidy imagined angels would.

"So, we have a plan? We're hanging out after school?" Maisy asked.

Anessa nodded.

Cassidy nodded absentmindedly, still in awe or maybe shock at seeing an illuminated Maisy.

"Cool," Maisy said. "We'll talk to your mom in the pickup line after school."

The bell rang.

Cassidy, in full creeper mode, stared at Maisy's angelic presence. Her friend, her best friend ever, had a glow like the kung-fu master from a movie she recently watched with her dad. It was part of his plan to introduce her to classic '80s movies over the summer. She scanned the room to see who else had the glow, or worse, the haze. At first look, no one else had a haze, thankfully; though, Josie glowed the same as Maisy. Cassidy rubbed her eyes. *What the heck is going on?*

She studied Anessa's haze from inches away, and ever so slightly pulled back her arm for fear of it touching it. After everyone drew quiet at Mrs. Higgins entering the room, a sound, barely perceptible, lingered. It was the type of sound you'd only notice when paying proper attention and all was quiet. It sounded like fingernails on a chalkboard during a windstorm. It sounded like miserable things, and it was coming from Anessa's haze.

Cassidy pulled her arms in close and hugged her waist. Immediately, part of her regretted asking Anessa over. But that something inside of her, a calling, maybe, and the voice, was intent on keeping her on the path. Like it or not, Anessa was Cassidy's burden.

Anessa looked over at her, and this time Cassidy shared her own forced smile.

Chapter 21

In the late day sunlight, Kazuyasu sat cross-legged on his home's mountainside veranda. A mosquito net hung over and around him, fastened at the corners to four wooden pillars holding up the roof. Near the veranda stood cherry blossom trees in full splendorous pink bloom. Far beyond the cherry blossom trees, cedar trees stood in tight clusters going up the mountainside.

Once every three months, Kazuyasu would clean and oil his katana, picking a day when the wind was calm. Today the slightest occasional breeze cooled the air, and birds chirped happy songs. He held the katana by its tang in front of him with one hand. The katana's hilt lay on the floor to his right. A small metal container of choji oil and wrinkled, soft pieces of rice paper were on the floor to his left — everything he needed to clean the blade and protect its integrity.

With his other hand, Kaz dabbed at the blade with a white cotton sack, covering katana's shiny surface in a fine white powder and filling the air around him. He said nothing as he worked, wearing a look of concentration, his lips pressed. Satisfied that the powder covered the side of the katana, he rotated it to its opposite, unpowdered, reflective side.

Kaz's eyes scanned the blade for imperfections. Engraved in the tang was the name of the katana's maker — Nakano Shojiro, known simply as Nakano. Nakano made each katana for a specific samurai. Kazuyasu's katana was made for someone else, a taller someone else, evident by its length compared to his height. Nakano offered it to Kazuyasu, saying its intended owner never came to retrieve it. When Kaz asked who the intended owner was, Nakano responded with a grunt, saying something about being respectful and having gratitude.

Kaz's inspection continued up the length of the katana's mirrored surface. Upon reaching the tip of the blade, he held it away from his face, regarding it thoughtfully. "The samurai sword, a blade that can cut through bamboo, a reflection — No. Too many syllables."

He had difficulty grasping one samurai passion: the haiku — a short poem of only three lines and seventeen syllables. What warrior needed poetry? Meditation, fine, he understood its benefit, but how would poetry help him win a battle? Why waste time on poetry when he could be practicing his sword kata? Kaz only practiced haiku when doing something that took a little less focus, like eating, falling asleep, and cleaning his katana. His best haikus came just after meditation when his mind was most still.

"A reflection… no." He pursed his lips. "Re… flecting back… reflection of a… of a… Oh, whatever. Stupid haikus." He sighed. "Samurai training would be so much easier if I was allowed to train with everyone else. I don't care what my parents were to the village. I don't want to be a fisherman like them." He brought the katana close to his face and froze; his face locked in an expression of terror. In the reflection, his eyes met eyes of sunken blackness with a gaping mouth meant for swallowing him whole. He screamed and shot up like a startled cat from his seated position, sending the katana flying into the mosquito net. He stumbled to his hands and knees and scrambled away from the creature behind him.

Kaz curled into a terrified ball against a wooden pillar. His screaming stopped upon finally recognizing his frightener. Maku winced, covering her gaping mouth as her monstrous face morphed into a more friendly appearance.

Kaz's fearful expression morphed as well, into a mixture of anger and embarrassment. "Maku!" he yelled, standing in a low part of the net. His angry hands grabbed and pulled until the net was off him. It slipped from the wooden pegs holding it up, and passed through the ethereal Maku. She was nearly formless, a ghost, with the image of the moon on her kimono less than half full.

His fight with the net over, Kaz stomped over to Maku. Heat radiated from his burning red face.

"Why, Maku? Why did you sneak up on me like that?"

Maku pressed her palms together in front of her chest and bowed, her hair cascading over her shoulders to cover her face. She always hid her face when embarrassed or caught being mischievous. The face that moments ago resembled a ghostly terror was now timid and remorseful. "I'm sorry," she signed.

"Sorry?" He raised his hands to his sides. "You're sorry?"

She nodded. "I didn't know I'd scare you that bad, like a little kid."

"You did not scare me." Kaz straightened, holding his chin high, trying to regain some dignity. "Just... surprised me a little."

Maku smirked.

"Just don't sneak up on me like that again. And that face... no more with that face. It's... it's just... no more with that face."

When Maku wasn't smiling, her natural expression was that of a ghost or a ghoul; everything and anything terrifying. But she usually kept her scary face hidden unless playing a joke on someone, like now.

"I thought samurai couldn't be snuck up on," she signed.

"They can't."

Maku raised her eyebrows to just below her bangs, touched her finger to her nose, and gave him a *'duh'* look.

"Well, maybe you, but you don't count. You can float around silently and stuff." Kaz waved her off.

"Besides, I was cleaning —" His eyes widened. "My katana!" He feverishly scanned the floor for his katana, finding it under a tangle of net, and carefully pulled it free.

Maku winced and looked away.

Kaz's scowl softened after inspecting the blade. "It looks okay. I'll have to start over, but it will be dark soon. It'll have to wait until morning."

"I'm sorry, again."

Kaz gave her a single nod and returned to inspecting the katana. He sighed. "Never mind. My fingerprints are all over it. I'll have to remove them right away or they'll damage the blade."

Maku waved her hand to get his attention. "I saw her," she signed.

"Wait. What?" Kaz stumbled on the net, walking over to her, his widened eyes pushing his eyebrows to the upper limit of his forehead. He didn't need to ask who — he already knew. "You saw the blue-eyed girl?"

She leaned toward him and nodded excitedly, her hands shaking at her sides.

"We never talked about you going to see her," Kaz said. "She's my responsibility." *The mirror, she needed the mirror to get to the other world!* "You took the mirror without asking me?"

"I couldn't help myself. I just had to see her. And I thought... you could use the help."

"Did you put the mirror back in the box?"

"Of course."

Kaz narrowed his eyes at Maku, having suspicions on why she chose to visit Cassidy, beyond being helpful and curious. He suspected it had something to do with a pillow. "And?"

"She's pretty."

Kaz pulled back in disgust and scoffed. "Like I care. What else?"

Maku smiled mischievously at her feet peeking out from underneath the end of her kimono. Her feet moved in that twisty way when the owner of the feet felt guilty about something.

"Maku?" Kaz said in an accusatory tone.

Maku tried to fight it, but her smile grew.

"Maku, tell me you didn't move her pillow."

She gave in with a grand smile and nodded rapidly.

Kaz deflated. "I told you to stop doing that."

"Hello? It's what I do," Maku signed exhaustedly.

In fact, it was what she did. Maku gained her mischievous spirit reputation by moving pillows from underneath sleeping children's heads to under their feet. A harmless act of a prankster. Sure, she had other abilities: to shake beds, flip the child instead of the pillow. All that aside, Maku was gentle despite her naturally frightening appearance.

Kaz rolled his eyes. "Anything else?"

Maku smiled at her feet and wiggled her toes. "She has a soft and cushy floor." She squeezed her eyes shut as she shook her hands excitedly, then signed, "I love it so much."

Kaz looked up in frustration, waiting for her excitement to fade. "Anything else that's *important*?"

Maku tapped a finger on her lips and she looked away. Her face brightened. "She has lots of shoes, or…" she scratched her head, "they looked like shoes."

"Ugh." Kaz dropped to the floor and carefully placed the katana across his lap.

Maku slowly floated down next to him and put her arm around his shoulders. Even when she was more ethereal than solid, she could still feel and be felt, just not as much. She leaned forward and signed, "Sorry. She was sleeping. There wasn't much to do other than watch her sleep."

"And move her pillow," Kaz said sourly.

Maku scoffed, pushing him away. Kaz put a hand down to brace himself from falling to his side.

"I saw the box," Maku signed. "In her room."

Kaz wasn't as excited as he'd imagined he'd be. The event Iwa had been preparing him for had come, and so far, there was *still* a lot of waiting around. Years ago, Iwa told him about her interaction with the satori, and that Cassidy was next to inherit the powers. Iwa wasn't entirely sure what to expect but knew her powers would fade as Cassidy aged and the power shifted. Iwa tried to hide it, but she had looked concerned at the thought. Kaz was worried too. What would happen to the barrier if Iwa lost her power? Would it just go away, letting in all the bad it has been keeping out?

Iwa said Kaz would be helpful because he and Cassidy were near the same age. Eventually, the day would come when they'd meet, and Cassidy would need a friend. Iwa even taught Kaz English, the language she'd learned while in her world, Cassidy's world.

Kaz pushed a stray strand of hair behind his ear. "Of course the box is in her room." He shrugged. "Where else would it be?" He said nothing for a minute, searching for answers in the silence. "We need to do something. We need to know how she is handling the powers and that she's okay. We need someone to watch her, undetected, and report back."

Maku excitedly waved her hands.

"Not you."

Maku pouted and signed something about Cassidy's soft floor.

"We don't have time to worry about soft floors." Kaz slowly nodded as he continued. "We need someone quiet, someone small. Someone who can watch over her and tell us everything she says."

Their eyes met as a knowing smile crept across their faces. "Yama," they agreed.

"Yama is perfect," Kaz said, striking his fist to his palm. "He's small enough to hide in tight places, and he can tell us everything she or anyone says."

Maku scrunched her face. "What if he can't hold it all in and explodes?" She mimed an explosion coming from her mouth. "They'll hear him and then —"

Kaz shook his head. "No. That was just the one time we had him spy on the Shiba twins, and they talk way too much. Yama can do this. I know it."

"Okay. I trust you."

A gust of wind caught their attention. Blooms blown from the cherry blossom trees flitted through the air.

Maku signed in Kaz's peripheral. "We should talk to her."

"Talk to her?" He frowned. "We can't talk to her. Not yet."

Maku shook her head. "Not Cassidy. Iwa."

Kaz's head fell into his awaiting hands. "I know." He groaned. "I guess I've been avoiding it. I hate the trip to her house; it's so far. Besides, it's not like we need help from her with anything."

"But what if something is wrong with Iwa? What if losing her powers is making her weak or sick?"

Kaz had never considered anything being wrong with Iwa, other than her lessening powers. He couldn't help but be a little concerned. "You're right. I have been expecting her sea eagle to deliver a message, but I haven't seen the bird in more than a week."

Before Kaz got a chance to use his best pleading eyes to ask Maku to update and check on Iwa, she offered to make the trip. He didn't need to give Maku all the reasons he didn't want to make the trip; she knew. Yes, the long journey was far easier for her, but also, he still held some resentment toward Iwa, the only parent he had known, for leaving him.

After his parents died, Kaz lived with Iwa in the village for seven of the first eight years of his life. Soon after his eighth birthday, Iwa said she needed to get away from the endless thoughts of the villagers and focus on maintaining the barrier. Kaz stayed behind with those same villagers. He wanted Iwa to stay too but assured her he could take care of himself. From the day she left, Kaz worked toward proving that and began training to be a samurai. Not long after, he caught Maku moving his pillow in the middle of the night, and they'd been friends ever since. Maku denied it, but Kaz always suspected that Iwa sent her to befriend and watch over him. At least it made him less angry toward Iwa, believing she cared enough to do so.

"Thank you for going," Kaz said.

"You're welcome. Besides, I can get there quicker than you."

Kaz smiled. "You sure can."

"Slow human." Maku smirked.

Kaz slouched and frowned, faking insult.

Smiling, Maku mussed his hair and pushed him again.

Kaz deftly righted himself and pushed her back, only to fall through her like a hand through water. He righted himself again and wiped away the ghostly residue he imagined was covering his body like warm tofu soup.

They shared a smile, and he laughed. His expression softened before turning serious. "We're actually doing something. Not just talking about doing something or practicing doing something, we're doing something."

Maku placed a hand on her bicep, flexed her arm twice, then signed, "We're a big deal."

Kaz's mouth fell to a straight line. "One step above moving pillows."

Maku scoffed and pushed him firmly, sending his katana sliding across the floor and him rolling and screaming. He settled to a stop and met her eyeline.

"No more jokes," Maku signed. "Finish cleaning your katana and find Yama, I'm off to the mountains to see Iwa. Last one back makes us tofu for dinner."

Chapter 22

After school, Anessa introduced Cassidy and Maisy to her mom. Cassidy gave Anessa's mom her dad's phone number; they talked and agreed Anessa could come over for a few hours. Dad was shopping with Grandma, but would be home shortly after the girls made it home. Another hurdle of "Operation Dress Anessa" was surpassed.

Anessa walked into Cassidy's house wide-eyed and openmouthed as if she had walked into a two-story toy store. "Wow, you must be rich."

An enormous, elaborate light fixture hung from the home's two-story-high entrance. Resembling an octopus, bent polished steel arms with LED lights at the ends reached out in varied directions from a spherical center. Polished dark hardwood floors led to other rooms, and carpeted stairs led to the second floor.

Cassidy shrugged her response. "I guess my parents are. My allowance is only ten dollars a week, so…"

Anessa scoffed. "That's ten dollars more than my weekly allowance."

Cassidy smiled awkwardly. "Yeah, so, wanna go to my room?"

"Sure, this should be cool," Anessa said excitedly.

They dropped their backpacks in a pile on the floor.

"Okay but shoes off first. Sorry, Japanese house." Cassidy removed her shoes and slid them under the bench next to the stairs. Above the bench were hooks for hanging hats, coats, and random hangable things her dad would eventually tell her to put away. In all honesty, most of the things lying around the house that needed to be put away were Cassidy's. There were even two guest rooms that Cassidy used for storage. She had explained to her parents that the amount of stuff in her life exceeded the limitation of a single bedroom… or two.

Maisy knew the drill and had already removed her sandals to reveal dandelion-yellow painted toenails. Cassidy watched as Anessa removed her shoes by alternately stepping on the back of each heel — the standard method for those too lazy or too in a hurry to untie the laces. She hadn't noticed the duct tape fastened to the front of Anessa's right shoe. It was colored blue to match and apparently was holding the shoe together. *At least her socks are clean.*

Maisy coughed.

Cassidy looked at the waiting eyes of Maisy, who was giving a *get-going* look. *Oh my gosh!* Had she not thought, but instead said aloud, the comment about Anessa's socks? A horrible queasy, sick feeling crawled inside her as she replayed the words in her head. A second later, Cassidy determined that she, in fact, only thought it. *Thank goodness.*

"So, your room?" Anessa said, looking confused.

Great, another one of my space-out moments. "Sorry. Yeah. Let's go upstairs. Just don't be too disappointed. It's just a bedroom."

"Just a warning," Maisy said, "I call it a messroom."

"A messroom? Why?" Anessa asked.

"It's not that messy," Cassidy said, frowning.

Maisy laughed.

Cassidy led the way, followed by Anessa and Maisy. A square canvas print on her bedroom door read, "And though she be but little, she is fierce." Mom hung the print last year after a room makeover in which they painted the bedroom walls lavender. Cassidy had reminded Mom that the growth chart at her most recent doctor visit had her at above-average height. Mom clarified that the quote was a reminder to not let anyone tell her what she can or can't do. For a moment, the quote reminded Cassidy of Iwa.

Cassidy pushed open her bedroom door and extended her arm, ushering Anessa and Maisy in.

"Wow, cool," uttered Anessa.

"Uh, Cassidy. What happened in here?" Maisy asked.

"What do you —" Cassidy started, then stopped after entering her bedroom, having the question answered at the same time.

"You cleaned your room?" Maisy marveled.

Cassidy scanned her room in amazement. "What the Frappuccino?"

Her dozens of books were neatly arranged on bookshelves flanking her bed, instead of in random, uneven stacks. Dirty clothes were missing from the floor, the queen-sized bed was made with the pillow properly at the head, and the various tabletops — the dresser on the right side of the room and desk to the left — were free of food containers, candy wrappers, and empty drink pouches. Properly deposited trash filled her short, white plastic garbage can. If vacuumed, her room would have been spotless.

"Yeah. What the frappe?" Maisy turned in circles, taking in all the clean. "This is literally the cleanest I've seen your room in years. Even my mom would approve."

"Yeah, but I didn't do it."

Anessa plopped onto the bed and sat with her feet dangling inches above the floor. "What should we do?"

Cassidy, still perplexed by the state of her room, spoke distractedly. "We can… make funny videos."

Maisy grabbed Cassidy's tablet from the dresser and waved it at her. "This was surprisingly easy to find."

Cassidy gave a crooked smile. "Funny, Maze."

They sat on opposite sides of Anessa, and Maisy loaded their favorite video app.

"I think there are some funny new filters," Maisy said.

"Filters?" Anessa asked.

Cassidy and Maisy glanced at each other in disbelief.

"Filters, ya know? Like dog faces and rainbow vomit," Cassidy said.

"Uh, okay," Anessa said in a confused but agreeable tone.

"Here, watch." Maisy held the tablet in front of her. "Come in closer."

Cassidy leaned close to Anessa, without touching for fear of inciting visions, and Anessa leaned into Maisy. Their smiling faces appeared on the screen, but where their human noses should have been were animated dog noses, and where their human ears should have been were floppy brown dog ears. Cassidy flashed a peace sign before Maisy pressed the screen to take the photo.

A gleeful expression exploded across Anessa's face, and they all broke into laughter, falling back onto the bed. Anessa popped back up, begging Maisy to show her more.

For over a half hour they wore alien faces, cat faces, glitter faces, wide faces, distorted faces, and even swapped faces. When Cassidy and Maisy swapped faces, they agreed they looked much better with their own. Something was disturbing about Cassidy's face with Maisy's hair. "Only I can pull this off so beautifully," Maisy said, patting her hair escaping from the back of a white headband.

Cassidy laughed, faltered, then stopped when eyeing her closet. The closet's interior was barely visible beyond the inch or two gap between the door and the door frame, but something was different. She stood and took careful steps toward it, leaving Maisy and Anessa laughing on the bed.

Cassidy reached for the door handle but hesitated. The hair on her arms prickled, sensing something or someone in her closet. Pulling her hand back, she shook away the nervousness and wiped her sweaty palm on her jeans. *What am I so scared of? No one is in my closet. It's just my stupid imagination.* She blew out a breath, quickly grabbed the handle, and opened the door. "What the?"

Her astonishment wasn't the result of what was or wasn't in the closet; her astonishment was about its organization. Her closet was as functional as it had ever been. Her shoes were in order, placed side by side with the shoelaces tucked into the openings. The piles of dirty or possibly dirty clothes were in a hamper in the corner. Her clean clothes had been hung and arranged by type and length. Random stuff that had accumulated in obscured corners was neatly placed in a large purple plastic bin. Cassidy imagined if she took the time to search, she'd find things long forgotten.

"This. Is. Crazy," she said to herself, before sensing Maisy and Anessa standing at her sides.

Maisy appeared even more amazed. "I guess you didn't do this either."

Cassidy shook her head. "Yeah… I mean, no. I don't know who —"

"Are the clothes arranged by color?" Maisy wondered aloud.

"What is that dress?" Anessa asked.

Cassidy followed Anessa's gaze to a silk, flower-patterned kimono hanging sideways and set it apart from the other clothes. "It's not a dress, it's a kimono."

"What's it for?"

"I wear it a couple of times a year. Just a few weeks ago, I wore it at the Obon Festival."

"Obon?" Anessa asked.

"Obon," Maisy answered for Cassidy, "is a Japanese Buddhist festival to honor ancestors. It's a lot of fun. There's dancing and food and," Maisy snapped her fingers, "what are those drums called?"

"Taiko drums," Cassidy answered, still distracted.

"Yeah, a taiko drumming performance. It's so cool. I go every year with Cassidy."

"Do you wear a kimono?" Anessa asked Maisy.

"No. Cassidy said I could, but I'd feel kinda strange not being Japanese."

"Are you Buddhist?" Anessa asked Cassidy.

Cassidy mulled over the question. Some of her extended family was Buddhist; they went to temple every week. Grandma used to go, but not anymore. Maybe that's why Mom and Dad didn't go to temple. "I guess I'm not, but it's not that I don't want to be, I just don't go to temple much. Does that make any sense?"

"I guess," Anessa said, glancing between them.

"Don't look at me," Maisy said. "My family is Catholic."

Cassidy turned the hanger in the proper direction and pushed the kimono even with the other clothes.

"Wow. You have a lot of shoes," Anessa said.

Cassidy grinned. *Funny you should mention that.* She touched her fingertips to her lips. *Ugh. How do I say this? So… Anessa, we noticed your shoes are falling apart. How about you have a pair of mine?* She scratched the back of her neck and scrunched her face. *It is what I want to say. It is the truth.*

Anessa looked to Cassidy, to Maisy, and back to Cassidy. She tilted her head to the right. "What's going on? Are we going to do anything else, or stand here and look at the —"

"Anessa, your shoes, they're… well, they're horrible," Cassidy blurted, then winced.

Anessa's face turned a ripe red. Her jaw dropped and would have fallen off if it wasn't attached to her head. "I — I think I should go." She walked toward the bedroom door, head bowed and shoulders slumped.

"Do something," Maisy mouthed.

The voice in Cassidy's head cried out. *"Help her!"*

"No, Anessa, wait," Cassidy said urgently, wringing her hands.

Anessa turned toward them, her face set in anguish and her hands close to her chest, gripping a fistful of her shirt. Tears welled in her eyes above flushed cheeks. "I thought," she started, looking to the floor, then up at them again, "I thought you invited me over because you wanted to be my friend. Not" — her voice cracked — "to make fun of me."

Cassidy had managed to ignore the haze surrounding Anessa, but now it was growing and making a show of itself. Wisps resembling tentacles whipped around her angrily. If the haze wasn't enough for Cassidy to contend with, sadness radiated from Anessa like heat from a bonfire. The haze's horrible sound was only eclipsed by the voice inside Cassidy's head telling her, urging her, screaming at her to take action. She had to fix it, she had to make it right. She had to do something.

The voice came again, urgent. *"Help her!"*

"Just stop, I'm trying!" Cassidy said a bit louder than she intended, trying to speak over the insistent voice in her head.

Maisy and Anessa looked stunned.

"No. Sorry, I wasn't saying that to you. I was talking to —" Cassidy paused, taking a breath. "That's not why we invited you… not to make fun of you." She dropped her head as she dug her toes into the carpet, trying to find the words to say, the right ones this time. "Anessa, I don't *want* to be your friend." A burst of bravery brought her to look into Anessa's eyes. "I am your friend."

Anessa chewed on her bottom lip as she wiped away a tear rolling down her cheek.

"You see how many shoes I have," Cassidy continued, glancing toward the closet. "I never wear most of them. Heck, a lot of them don't fit me anymore. So, I thought, you know —" She stepped toward Anessa. "I'd like to give some of them to you."

Anessa turned away, crossing her arms. "Yeah, well, I don't need a handout."

Cassidy couldn't blame Anessa for feeling hurt or angry. Unprepared to handle the situation, Cassidy looked to Maisy, silently begging for help.

Maisy nodded. "Cassie and I share clothes *all* the time. I bet some of the clothes in her closet are mine." She laughed uncomfortably. "Maybe even some of the shoes." She placed a hand on Anessa's shoulder. "It's what we do. We share." Her eyes met Anessa's. "Friends share."

"Anessa, I get it. More than you know, I get it," Cassidy said. She had seen Anessa's sadness and was currently feeling the brunt of it. "Some of the kids at school are jerks, two of them specifically, so," she smiled with uncertainty, "if you sit on the bed, Maisy and I want to help you try on shoes."

Anessa looked away, wiping away lingering tears. "Sharing?"

Cassidy and Maisy smiled at each other. "Totally," they said in unison.

Anessa's arms dropped to her sides, and with a hint of a smile, she hopped onto the bed. "Then bring me some cute size twos."

"You got it." Cassidy unleashed a grateful smile as an oppressive weight seemingly fell from her shoulders — the final hurdle of Operation Dress Anessa was cleared. She hurried into the closet and searched for size twos — the size she outgrew last summer. "Wait. Are the shoes in order by size?" She grabbed a pair of purple canvas shoes with pink and yellow flowers embroidered on the sides. She handed the pair to Maisy, who flashed a smile and whispered, "Nice save."

Cassidy stopped mid-grab for a second pair and shook her head. *Gosh. I have a lot of shoes. Too many, really.* Most of them still fit, but she always wanted the next cute pair to match a new shirt, pants, or backpack. For her, a new pair of shoes was never out of a need to replace an old worn-out pair, a new pair of shoes was about fitting in at school and being normal.

She grabbed a pair of pink canvas high-tops with thick purple shoestrings that she had gotten for Christmas last year, or maybe for her birthday. *How horrible that I can't remember who gave them to me. Or when.* She had worn them a few times, but only now did she admire them. "These are so cute," she muttered, inspecting the tongue. "Size two."

Cassidy brought out the pink high-tops as Maisy finished tying the shoelaces of the first pair.

"Nice kicks," Cassidy said, admiring her shoes on Anessa's feet.

Anessa flashed a shy smile. "They are really cute."

Maisy stood. "Okay, walk around a little. Make sure they fit."

Anessa slid from the bed and walked in a circle. She flared out her ankles and stood on the sides of the shoes with her hands outstretched. "So?"

"Keepers," Cassidy said, nodding.

Maisy nodded in agreement.

"My turn," Cassidy said, holding up the next pair.

Anessa smiled wide and hopped onto the bed. Her fingers rapidly worked at loosening the laces, and she placed the shoes on the floor.

Cassidy knelt at the bedside, placing one shoe on the floor. Peeking up at the now slightly calmer haze surrounding Anessa, it happened again — the visions. They came the moment she touched Anessa's heel to bring her foot into place.

Cassidy's room was gone in a blink, replaced by a memory of Anessa in her home or apartment — wherever it was she lived. Anessa was sitting on a mattress on the floor in what resembled a bedroom. Dim light from a lamppost shone through thin white curtains. Clothes were strewn across the floor. Moving boxes, open and unopened, were stacked against one of the walls.

A voice came from another room, someone speaking in short, terse sentences. Anessa crept to her bedroom door and peeked through the opening. Her mom stood in the kitchen with a cellphone pressed against her ear.

"Just stay away. You've done enough to us already," Anessa's mom said. "You picked what you wanted, and it wasn't me or your daughter." She firmly pressed the screen and slammed the phone onto the counter. A long silent moment was broken by a tired sigh escaping her lips as she leaned against the counter and wiped a hand down her face.

Defeating, immobilizing pain and sadness coursed through Anessa as she stared at her mother for an uncomfortable amount of time.

Wait a minute. Anessa's sad, but more for her mom than herself. This isn't just about shoes or clothes, this I about. . . a whole frappin' lot. What am I supposed to do about —

Her mom turned around to see Anessa watching her. They looked into each other's tear-filled eyes before Anessa pulled back into her room and gently closed the door.

"Anessa," her mom called as the vision faded.

"Sis," a voice said.

"Hello?" said another.

"Cassidy. Cass!"

The trance holding Cassidy released its grip. "W-what?" She looked rapidly back and forth between Maisy and Anessa as the brightness of the vision faded.

"You okay, sis? You're sweating."

Cassidy dropped the shoe and released her firm grip on Anessa's heel. Feeling a dozen breaths behind, she deeply inhaled and blinked hard, over and over, bringing the realness of her world back into focus. In her peripheral, Anessa looked questioningly at Maisy.

"Cassie, maybe you're still feeling a little sick." Maisy smiled as her hands fumbled with Cassidy's, trying to help her up. "Maybe you should get a cold washcloth while I help Anessa with the shoes."

A cold washcloth couldn't fix the dizziness and her throbbing temples. Still, Cassidy appreciated Maisy's excuse for being weird around Anessa… again. "That's — That's a good idea." Cassidy stood on weak legs and forced a smile, meeting Anessa's eyes before leaving the room.

She collapsed against the bathroom wall, still catching her breath. This second time in Anessa's memory was worse than the first. The first time felt like being hit in the head — with help from the school bathroom floor — but this time, the sadness ran her over like a school bus. *Oh my gosh. This is gonna be harder than I thought.*

The girl in the bathroom mirror was the version of herself Cassidy hated — a reflection of a scared, overwhelmed, and defeated little girl. This time, crowds of people were not the problem, and she wasn't lost. At least, not that kind of lost. Her father would often tell her before a difficult task, "You become what you think: If you think you can do it, you will. If you think you can't, then you won't. You can do this." *Can I do this? Can I really do this?* According to Dad, she had already failed just by questioning herself.

The voice inside her head returned as a gentle reminder that she still had something to do. "Okay. I know. Just give me a minute. Geez."

She cooled her face with a splash of water from the sink and dried off with a bath towel. After a final look in the mirror, she pushed her hair behind her ears and gave a self-supporting smile. Feeling somewhat better, Cassidy returned to the shoe try-on in time to see a smiling Anessa walking around in the pink canvas high-tops.

"Those look —" Cassidy paused at a movement under her bed. She squinted, then rubbed her closed eyes.

"Cass. You okay?" Maisy asked.

Cassidy opened her eyes, scrutinized the floor under her bed, and then looked at Maisy. "Yeah, sorry. I thought I saw something."

Maisy looked toward the bed and turned back to Cassidy with a shrug. "All I see are cute shoes."

Anessa modeled the shoes. "How do they look?"

"Too cute." Cassidy smiled despite the tempest of anxiety and doubt raging through her.

The shoes were cute, and Anessa appeared to be better. But they were just shoes, and a pair of shoes wouldn't fix all of Anessa's problems. *What am I going to do, now?*

Chapter 23

The girls managed to cram as much fun and outfit trying-on in as they could before Anessa's mom arrived to pick her up. Not only did Anessa find a couple of size two shoes to take home, but also a t-shirt and purposefully hole-filled jeans that were a skosh too small for Cassidy. She packed the mini haul into her backpack, zipped it up, and slung it onto her shoulder. Of the two pairs of shoes, she wore the pink high-tops. Cassidy offered to throw out the old shoes, but Anessa wanted to keep them for playing outside.

The girls stepped out of the front door into the late afternoon sun. Anessa's mom waved at them from the car. Anessa trotted down the concrete stairs, stopped, and trotted back to Cassidy and Maisy. "Thanks," she said, first looking at the ground, then to Cassidy. "The shoes are great, and… you know… thanks a lot."

"We're friends," Cassidy said.

"We got ya," Maisy added.

Anessa smiled and gave them each a quick hug. Cassidy recoiled at the embrace, expecting a blast of sadness. Nothing happened, even with the dark haze still clinging to Anessa. It was as if Cassidy had already been shown what the power needed her to see.

Anessa ran back down the stairs and into her mom's car. She slung her backpack onto the back seat and closed the door behind her. Cassidy intently watched the conversation between Anessa and her mom. The words leaving their mouths were barely audible, though they were quite clear the moment before they spoke them, inside Cassidy's head.

"Did you have fun," Cassidy said, repeating the conversation loud enough for Maisy to hear. "I had a *great* time."

They returned a wave goodbye from Anessa and her smiling mom.

"They have a beautiful house," Cassidy continued, repeating Anessa's mom and then Anessa, "It's huge inside."

"Put on your seatbelt and we'll head home," Anessa's mom said.

The car pulled away as the conversation continued to flow.

"Did you get the job?" Anessa asked.

"I won't know for a few days, sweetie. Oh. Whose shoes are those?"

"They're Cassidy's. She —"

Those were the last audible words before the car and the thoughts were out of reach.

I guess there is a distance limit on my power.

"That went well," Maisy said.

"Ya think?" Cassidy said questioningly.

Maisy pursed her lips. "The beginning and the end did. The middle… was tragic."

"Yeah, the middle," Cassidy groaned. "The middle *was* tragic."

"What happened? When you blanked out?"

Cassidy hugged herself. "I was, well, I saw through Anessa's eyes. She was at home. She was sad about her mom. She — Her mom was on the phone; I think with Anessa's dad."

"Was the vision or whatever bad?"

Cassidy nodded at the ground. "I don't think shoes are going to fix Anessa's sadness."

Maisy hugged her and pulled back, placing her hands on Cassidy's shoulders. "Hey. We'll figure this out. You saw how much fun she had today."

Cassidy grinned and nodded, though she had serious doubt on the figuring it out part.

Maisy grabbed her backpack and slung it over her shoulder. "We'll talk about this tomorrow. I have to get home for dinner before my mom calls your dad, asking where I am and lecturing me about overstaying my welcome."

They hugged again and said goodnight before Maisy ran home, and Cassidy plodded into hers. She paused in the doorway, reflecting on her time spent with Anessa and the new vision, the terrible vision. A sinking helplessness crept into the corners of her mind. For the briefest moment, she opened the door to even more negative thoughts, then slammed it shut and shook her head. "No. I'm not going to dwell on the bad. Like Maisy said, Anessa went home happy, or at least happier. Maybe the journal will help me figure out what to do. I can do this." Cassidy stood tall and walked to the kitchen, making a beeline for the fridge. "Hi, Dad."

"Hey, Cass," Dad replied. "Did your friend go home?"

"Yeah." She grabbed a Capri Sun — her like two-millionth of the day — from the fridge. "Her mom just picked her up."

"Is she okay? She seemed happy on the way out."

"Well, let's just say that she's a work in progress."

"Progress is a good thing." Dad stopped prepping dinner and leaned against the counter. "Is there anything else on your mind?"

Cassidy slouched and leaned back onto the fridge. "What's not on my mind lately?"

Dad opened his mouth and paused, holding up a finger. He scrunched his face. "Wait. This doesn't have anything to do with boys, does it?"

Cassidy revulsed. "Ugh. No. Gross."

Dad smiled and may have performed a little dance, clearly pleased with her response. "So, it's about your superpowers."

"I guess."

"You guess?"

Cassidy poked the plastic straw into the juice pack and took a sip. "Yeah, it is. I guess I just have to deal with it." She mindlessly stared at the floor, tracing shapes with her foot.

Dad walked over and hugged her before stooping down to look into her eyes. "I can't say I know how to help you with this, Blue. And I hate saying that. I'm your dad; I'm supposed to protect you."

"It's okay, Dad. It's weird, you know. And scary at times, but… a lot of the time, I feel like I'm doing the right thing. Like I'm doing what I'm supposed to be doing." She exhaled forcefully, flapping her lips. "I don't know if that makes any sense."

Dad tapped his temple. "Remember when we talked about finding purpose in life?"

He had told her about a ton of stuff. A lot of it had to do with spirituality and doing the right thing. The spirituality stuff didn't make a lot of sense to her and didn't seem all that important when her conversations with Maisy were much more fun, however, she did remember some of it. She scrunched her face. "I was a kid. Tell me again."

He laughed. "You *were* a kid?"

"I have powers now. I'm practically an adult," she said with a proud smile.

Dad smiled back. "Between you and I, the adults in the room, everyone is born with a path in life. Very few of us find our path early on; it can take years, decades even. Some of us find the path, fall off it, and never return. Some fall off the path and return to it later in life, like people with addictions. Think of it this way. Being on the path means that you are doing the right things: being kind to others, helping people, the Ten Commandments, The Noble Eightfold Path, all of that." He paused. "Make sense so far?"

She nodded. "So far."

Dad paced, his arms and hands becoming animated as they did when preparing to *really* get into explaining things. "The best thing about staying on the path is finding your purpose, which is not that complicated. We all find our purpose in helping others and making lives better. A comedian makes us laugh and feel happy. A surgeon repairs broken bodies. Teachers... teach. And so on."

"Aaaand what does that mean for me?"

"It means there is an order to the universe and that each of us is part of it. We all can follow the path and contribute to the universe. We are all granted a way to positively affect the lives of those around us, to serve others. This power you have could very well be your purpose."

Cassidy didn't know what to say about universes and purposes. Sure, she didn't know everything, but some stuff was just... a lot. And *this* was a lot. She smiled crookedly. "Mind if I think it over?"

Dad laughed. "Absolutely. This is some deep stuff. But you don't need to give me an answer. It's just something to think about."

Cassidy gave a thumbs up. "Got it."

"And just know, if you ever want to hang out, go for frozen yogurt, or talk about stuff that's more lit, I'm here for you. Mom too."

"Thanks, Dad."

He mussed her hair.

"Hey!" she said, hand combing her hair back into place.

He laughed. "Where are you headed?"

"To my room. I have a journal to read."

"Okay, dinner in about thirty."

"Got it. Oh, and Dad?"

"Hmm?"

"Did you clean my room?"

"Uh, no. I'm not allowed in your room. I know better."

She tapped her fist against her lips. *How strange.* If it wasn't Dad who cleaned her room, it could only be one other person. But before walking away, Dad needed to hear one more thing. "And, Dad, don't say 'lit' anymore."

On the way to her bedroom, Cassidy stopped to talk to Grandma, sitting comfortably on the couch in the living room. "Hi, Grandma."

"Hi, Cassie. Did your friends leave?"

Cassidy nodded. "Mhm."

"The blonde girl, that was Anessa?"

"Yeah. I should have introduced you. I never have anyone over other than Maisy, so I guess I don't have a lot of practice with introductions."

"I'm just a grandma, not a celebrity. She'll forgive you."

"You're an *amazing* grandma."

Grandma smiled at the compliment. "And how is Anessa doing?"

Cassidy collapsed onto the couch next to her. "She's okay, I guess. It's complicated."

"Want to talk about it?"

Cassidy shook her head. "Not really. I think I need a break from thinking about her." Oddly, a Christmas movie was playing on the TV. One of those sappy love stories where the guy and girl like each other, but they have to mess things up before realizing it. And, almost every time, a kid has to show them how dumb they are being. But it was August, way too early for Christmas shows, right? "Whatcha watching?"

Grandma waved her hand dismissively. "This? It's just an August Christmas marathon."

Nope, not too early.

"This one is almost over." Grandma said. "Want to watch the next one?"

Cassidy scrunched her face and shook her head. She loved Christmas movies, but mainly the ones in December involving Santa, kids outsmarting adults, and adults who thought they were elves. "I would, but I have a really old journal to read."

"Well, don't let sappy love stories keep you from that."

"Maybe tomorrow?"

"I'm leaving tomorrow, sweetheart."

"What?" Cassidy's heart sank. "But you just got here."

Grandma squeezed her shoulder. "You poor thing. I came here so quickly that I didn't have much time to make plans to stay, and my little dogs must miss me. But I won't be gone for too long. I'll be back in a couple of months for Thanksgiving."

Cassidy nodded languidly, any remaining happy energy being sapped from her. Grandma wrapped her in a hug.

While Grandma didn't have the powers, her eyes as brown as caramel, what little she knew about what was going on was more than anyone else. Grandma was also someone else to talk to. Cassidy had hoped for more time with her, and although she didn't want to talk about Anessa, she had lingering questions.

She mulled over her question, not quite sure how to phrase it. "Do you think I have a choice? In having the power? I mean, what if one day I decide I don't want it anymore, you know, seeing people's sadness and hearing what they are going to say. Which to be honest, hearing what someone is about to say is almost useless and can be seriously embarrassing."

Grandma laced her fingers and brought her hands to her chin. "I can't say for certain, but I think Iwa would have stopped using the power if she had a choice."

"That's what I mean. I'm so confused. It's like one part of my brain is fighting with the other. Helping feels like the right thing to do, but at the same time, it feels like I don't have a choice. It doesn't feel fair. You know?"

"You're right. It's not fair that you don't have a choice, but when there isn't a choice in the matter, you have to face the problem. It won't go away simply by ignoring it. It will remain a burden until you decide to take control."

"I'm like the worst person to get the power. Why couldn't I have had an older brother or sister to get it?"

Grandma shook her head, pointing at Cassidy. "I have to disagree. You are thoughtful, kind, and always concerned with everyone else's feelings. It's like you were born for this." She shrugged. "Maybe you were."

Cassidy smirked. "*Maybe* I don't have to ignore problems if I can avoid them. Other than Maisy, I literally avoid people." She looked at Grandma with idea-widened eyes. "I got it. I can hide from the world. Like Iwa's dad made her do. I'll convince Dad and Mom to let me homeschool, and I'll stay inside all day."

"Now that's one plan. Unfortunately, there's no hiding from sadness."

"I just need to hide from sad people."

Grandma shook her head. "Sadness is part of life for everyone. The key is to make them sad moments and not carry the sadness with you forever."

Cassidy groaned. "Being sad sucks." She examined Grandma's bespectacled eyes. "Did you want the power when you were a kid?"

Grandma smiled nostalgically. "You bet I did. I would lay in bed at night, sometimes in tears, wishing that I could have been the one with powers. I imagined how special I would be and how remarkable everyone would think I was for being able to hear thoughts."

"Yeah, but what about the sadness part?"

"I focused on the exciting part of the powers and convinced myself I could handle everything that came with it." Grandma grinned. "I was a tough little girl."

"I bet you were." Cassidy laughed, then grew quiet.

"If you could," Grandma asked, "would you give up the powers?"

The choice brought about a battle within Cassidy's mind. The part of her before all of this started, regular old Cassidy, screamed *yes! Please take it away!* But the voice that had been urging her into action rejected the idea of giving her powers away. "I'm not sure. It's kinda hard to decide, at least for now."

Grandma narrowed her eyes and tapped the tip of Cassidy's nose. "If there's an option, it's your decision. Maybe the answer is in the journal. Get to reading it so you can tell me more before I leave."

Cassidy's frown returned at the reminder of Grandma leaving. "Okay. I'll be in my room. See you at dinner." She stood and said as she walked away, "Oh, and thanks for cleaning my room."

She didn't hear a reaffirming response and didn't wait for one. It had to have been Grandma.

Chapter 24

Yama, a brown, short-haired creature, larger than a ferret and smaller than a fox but resembling both, returned to Kazuyasu to share the details of his mission to spy on Cassidy. He finished playing back the conversations among Cassidy, Maisy, and Anessa, that he had heard while hiding under Cassidy's bed. Yama could speak any language — human, animal, or other. Though saying Yama could speak any language was not quite accurate as Yama's ability was to repeat what he had heard. Specifically, Yama could remember and play back voices and sounds as if his mind had a built-in recorder. When Yama spoke Cassidy's words, they were in Cassidy's voice. When he spoke Maisy's words, they were in Maisy's voice.

Kaz stared at Yama as if he had been speaking a different language. Technically, he had, with Japanese being Kaz's first language and English, his second. His third was sign language so that he could understand Maku. Though Yama's words were clearly English, some of the words and references were foreign to him.

Maku couldn't take her eyes from Yama, hanging on his every word, her face wearing a full smile.

Kaz groaned. "Most of that was silly girl talk. I don't think anything was important in all of that nonsense."

Maku scowled at him.

Kaz stood and paced the wooden floor of his home's veranda. He stopped after four paces and turned to Yama. "Repeat that part before Cassidy goes to the closet for the — what did she call them? Jeans?"

Yama's furry brown face scrunched. His ears, too long for his size, intertwined above his head. When his mouth moved, his ears fell to his sides; Anessa's voice came from somewhere inside him. "Wow, you have a lot of shoes."

Maku's eyes widened as she smiled. She clapped and pitter-pattered her ghostly feet on the floor.

Kaz shrugged. "Why is that exciting, Maku? You don't even wear shoes."

Maku pouted and waved off his comment.

"And, Yama, about her shoes and clothes," Kaz said. "Please tell me you didn't put them in order."

Yama, known for being obsessive-compulsive, shrugged his furry shoulders and averted his eyes from Kaz's accusatory stare. Those who knew Yama often used him for clean-up jobs. If someone had a room in disorder, they'd invite Yama over for some unrelated reason and let his compulsion takeover. He would clean and straighten until nothing was left to clean or straighten.

Kaz eyed Maku, who glared at him, undoubtedly waiting for an apology for the shoe comment. Yama's expression was no friendlier. "You two are making me crazy. Maku, you with the pillow moving, and Yama, you with organizing her closet and room. She's going to find out about us before she's ready. She has enough to worry about. What do you think would happen if she saw a..." he searched for the words to identify Yama and Maku, only to realize he never asked exactly what they were. "One of you two? It would not be good." He stood rigidly and balled his hands into fists. "I will not allow either of you to go back."

Maku made fists of her own and stomped her feet. As if bewitched, her hair moved wildly around her pale face.

Cassidy's voice came from Yama's mouth as he scowled at Kaz. "I don't *want* to be your friend."

Kaz closed his eyes and crossed his arms over his head. "Enough!" Silence lingered between them before he softened and looked forgivingly to Yama. "Now, back to what I asked you to repeat. The part before Cassidy went to the closet for the... jeans."

Begrudgingly, Yama opened his mouth, and the girls' voices played. Maku looked delighted.

Kaz listened intently. "There, stop," he urged. He rubbed his narrow chin, just as the samurai did when in thought. "What does she mean, 'those kicks are snatched'?"

Maku and Yama performed simultaneous shrugs.

Kaz huffed. "You two are no help. Yama, I need you to return to Cassidy's and bring back more.

Other than the part about her not feeling well, we don't know enough about how she is handling her abilities. Iwa wants to know as much as possible so she can decide when Cassidy is ready."

Maku smiled and waved her hand above her head, volunteering.

Kaz shook his head. "Not yet, Maku. You're still too visible. *Maybe* you can go back and watch when there is less of the moon." The moon image on the front of Maku's kimono changed to match the stage of the actual moon, and her level of transparency changed along with it. The less visible was the moon; the less visible was Maku.

Yama smiled, or what resembled a smile on a weasel-like creature, and said in Anessa's voice, "I love your rug; it's so soft."

Maku pointed excitedly at Yama with an *ooooh* expression and signed, "Yes!" She smiled and signed a heart, wiggling her toes, pretending they were digging into Cassidy's rug.

"Totally," came Cassidy's and Maisy's voice from Yama.

Kaz slapped his forehead. "What am I going to do with you two?" He narrowed his eyes at Yama, who was poking a red stick into a silver pouch. "Yama. What is that?"

Yama stopped mid-sip and looked sheepishly at Kaz. He answered in Cassidy's voice. "Capri Sun."

Chapter 25

"Hey Maze," Cassidy said to her best friend through the tablet screen.

"Hey sis." Maisy was lying in bed on her stomach with her feet kicking in the air behind her. "What's up?"

Cassidy stood from her desk, took a couple of steps, and fell onto her back with her tablet in hand. She sighed. "Not much. Getting ready for bed."

"Did you read more of the journal?"

"Yeah, I read a little before dinner. I'm going to read more before bed."

"Whadya learn?"

"Not much." Cassidy rolled onto her stomach and elbows, keeping hold of the tablet. "I think I need to skip around. She — Iwa wrote about a lot of stuff that doesn't help me much. Like helping her boss with trade negotiations, whatever that means, and regular stuff, like how her day was and the weather."

"Eh... fun."

"And listen to this. She had a secret crush on her boss's son."

Maisy perked. She sat up, holding her tablet in her lap. "You didn't tell me it's a romance novel."

"Ew, no. Like, no. He could be the same boy she eventually marries, which would make him my lots of greats grandpa, but I don't have time for that. I need to figure out what's going on with my powers, not about what to do when secretly liking a boy."

"Well, don't let me keep you from reading about sweet hugs and kisses," Maisy said, making a kissy face.

"Funny."

Maisy laughed.

"Oh, and Iwa hasn't mentioned reading minds. Only what I can do, so far. Hearing what people are about to say and seeing what makes them sad when she touches them. But, yeah, I should get back to it."

"Okay... oh, hey. You still going to my dance comp tomorrow?"

Cassidy shot her a *'duh'* face. "Yeah, of course."

Maisy smiled. "Awesome."

"When have I ever missed one?"

"Absolutely *never.*"

"Exactly."

"Okay. Come over around ten. You can ride with us."

"Hey." Cassidy tugged at her hair. *I hope she is okay with this.* "I sorta invited Anessa."

"Oh." Maisy didn't hide her surprise. A surprise on the level of '*you have a cavity*', not '*we're going to Disneyland.*'

"I thought she might have fun, you know?"

"Yeah, I guess." Maisy's tablet fell a little farther from her face.

"And maybe I can figure out, like, how to help her."

"Sure. Okay. She can ride in the back with us."

Cassidy knew her friend as well as she knew her favorite food — cheesy nachos — and the names and birthdays of all her favorite YouTubers. Without a doubt, Maisy wasn't entirely thrilled to have Anessa tagging along. "Are you sure? I mean, her mom said she'd call in the morning and let us know. I can tell her our plans changed or...."

Maisy smiled, barely. "I'm sure. She'll get a chance to see me dance. One more person to witness my greatness."

Cassidy reflexively smiled back, hoping but unsure if Maisy was okay with the plan. "Okay. I'll — We'll come by at ten. If she can go, of course."

"Okay. Bye, sis."

"Bye, Maze."

As Maisy ended the call, Cassidy saw her smile fade to a frown. Maisy's frown didn't regularly make an appearance. Why exactly was it rearing its frowniness now?

Cassidy held the now lifeless tablet. "Maybe I shouldn't have asked Anessa to go with me." Having more than one friend was turning out to be unimaginably difficult, especially with Anessa needing more of her attention. But she couldn't give up on Anessa, not now. Could she, even if she wanted to? With the voice telling her to help, the urgent feeling of needing to help, and what Iwa said in her journal… there seemed to be no way out of this. Cassidy nodded resolutely. *Anessa's my priority. Besides, she's my friend too.* "Maisy will be okay. She's Maisy."

She slid from her bed and flicked on the lamp. After turning off the overhead light, she exchanged the tablet with the translated journal lying on her dresser. Something soft gave way underneath her foot. Cassidy lifted her foot, picked whatever it was from the carpet, and brought it into the light. "How did you get there?" A smooshed pink flower about the size of a big thumb lay in the palm of her hand. It didn't belong in her yard, much less her bedroom floor. She placed the flower onto her dresser with an idea to ask Mom or Dad about it tomorrow. With a skip and a hop, she flopped onto her bed. "Okay, Iwa. Tell me something good."

She opened the journal, flipped to the page she left off on, and immediately grew bored. She decided to flip through the pages and scan the sentences and paragraphs for anything about the black haze. Cassidy promised herself she'd read the entire journal eventually, but she needed substantial info on her powers *now*.

Two-thirds through the journal, she came to a page that read, "On the following pages, I will explain the secrets of our powers — the good and the bad."

Cassidy sat up, mindlessly grabbing for a scrunchie — often several were hiding in the space between her bed and the wall — and fastened her hair into a ponytail. "Yes, here we go." She read the end of the sentence a second time. "The good and the bad." She scoffed. "Good? I'd like to know one good thing about —" The heading of the next page caused her to pause. It read "The Light and the Darkness." The pages held precisely what Cassidy had been searching for — information on the black haze. Only, that wasn't what Iwa called it. Instead, she described it as people of light and, those with a haze, people of darkness.

Iwa wrote that other than infants and young children, who were the brightest of all, the people of light were as uncommon as the people of darkness. Most people were neither light nor darkness; they just... were. "Avoid the people of darkness," Iwa warned, "or you will be unable to resist the desire to help them. Their sorrow, their pain, is a plague upon my heart and mind. I often prayed to the gods that the people of darkness would pass through my village and not stay for an extended time. If they remained, there could be no rest, no sleep until I helped them or they left. This ability to hear the thoughts of others, feel their pain, and even see their life's sorrows is a curse, not the desired power I asked the satori to give me. If I could find the satori, I'd ask it, no, I'd beg it to receive it back. But spilt water will not return to the tray."

Cassidy blew flyaway strands of hair from her mouth. "A curse. That makes sense. I'm cursed. Well, that's just great."

She continued reading. "Seek out and befriend those who are of the light, especially those of the brightest, as they can help diminish the darkness in your life. But know that the thoughts of the light are shielded from you."

Cassidy perked up at this bit of knowledge. *Maisy will be so happy.*

"And be warned, those who are of the most tumultuous dark, though rare, are a danger. They intend great harm on others, and in turn, do great harm to themselves. They are a job for someone else as we cannot help them."

How would she know who the people were with the most tumultuous dark? Cassidy would hate to see someone with a bigger haze than Anessa. What if Anessa was who Iwa was warning her about?

"You will surely know them when you see them. They will appear to be more darkness than human."

Oh. I guess that answers it. Cassidy's bedroom door opened, letting in the light from the hallway. Mom leaned into the room with one hand on the door frame and the other on the knob. "Hey, sweetie."

"Hey, Mom."

Mom wore baggy black cotton shorts and an oversized t-shirt with the address of the Sherlock guy on it. It was Mom's 'relaxing before bed' outfit. "Whatcha doing?"

Cassidy grinned sideways and held up the journal. "Trying to figure out stuff."

"I see. Anything new?" Mom settled her feet. Now she wouldn't say goodnight without getting some nugget of information.

Cassidy sat up and crisscrossed her legs. "So…"

"So?"

"You know how you can tell if someone is happy or sad just by looking at them?"

Mom nodded. "Yes. By their expressions — smiles or frowns."

"Yeah, so, I can do more. I mean… I can see more."

Mom crossed her arms and leaned against the door frame. "You can *see* more?"

Cassidy sat the journal at her side and held her hands out in front of her. "Like, most of us are normal. We're not happy or sad. We're just okay, ya know?"

"Right."

"But when someone is sad, really sad, they'll have a darkness around them."

"A darkness? What does it look like?"

"It's like a haze." Cassidy's hands became animated as she struggled to explain something only she could see. She scrunched her face and grunted, unable to show what she meant. "Oh," she exclaimed. "It's like coloring books."

Mom's forehead wrinkled. "Coloring books?"

"Yes, but just the outlines. The black lines you have to color inside of." Cassidy's right hand made jerky movements as she pretended to color in the air. "When you're done coloring, the dark lines are still there."

"And people who are sad have these lines?"

Cassidy pursed her lips, half nodded, and half shook her head. "Kinda, but not solid lines. It's more like a cloud of smoke. And the sadder the person is, the bigger the haze, and the more it moves." She paused on a thought. "Like it's bothered or angry."

Mom slowly nodded and looked away.

Cassidy was becoming familiar with Mom's mannerisms when discussing the powers, and she seemed bothered. Silence filled the space between them.

"How are you doing with all of this?" Mom finally asked, sounding concerned.

Cassidy picked up the journal and placed it on her lap. She nodded once, less than confident. "I'm good. I'm figuring out a little at a time."

"You know, Dad and I are here whenever you need us."

Cassidy smiled warmly. "Yep. Thanks."

Mom walked over to Cassidy's dresser. She picked up the pink flower and held it in the light. "What's this?"

"A flower. It was on my floor. I stepped on it, so it's a little smooshed."

Mom examined the flower. "It looks like a cherry blossom, or what's left of it."

"Know where it came from?"

"A few of our neighbors have cherry blossom trees, but they bloom in the spring, so that can't be right." Mom shook her head and returned it to the dresser. "I guess I'm not sure. Strange." She returned her focus to Cassidy. "Are you going to Maisy's competition tomorrow?"

Cassidy nodded and smiled excitedly. "Yep."

Mom pulled her phone from the pocket of her baggy pants. "Well, it's getting late. You should get to sleep soon."

"Okay. A few minutes more."

Mom kissed the top of Cassidy's head. "Goodnight. I love you."

"Night. Love you too."

"And Cass… I'm sorry about freaking out after Grandma told the story about Iwa. I worry about you and don't want you to struggle with anything."

"I understand. Thank you."

As Mom left the room, one thing was certain — she had neither a haze nor a glow. A horrible thought pulled Cassidy's stomach into a knot. What if before the stress from this ancestral stuff, Mom had a glow, and now it was gone? Cassidy couldn't know, and it wasn't like she could ask her. She wanted for Mom to have a glow, for Dad to have a glow, heck, for everyone to have a glow.

Though not entirely sure how to help Anessa, she knew how to help Mom and Dad through this. She had to be better than she had been since 'that day.' She had to learn how to interact with people and not be afraid to be around them because of what she imagined could happen. She had to be strong; she had to be brave.

After finishing reading the part about the darkness, Cassidy grabbed her tablet and sent a message to Maisy. *Hey. I couldn't wait to tell you. I won't be able to hear your thoughts. I'll explain more tomorrow when we can talk alone. Good night.*

She set the tablet aside and picked up her own journal.

Journal Entry August 24

Hello... again. I can see and hear people's sadness. YAY! Not really. It's kind of a pain. To be fair, I can also see the glow of happy people, like Maisy. And the great news is that I won't be able to hear Maisy's thoughts because of her glow.

The bad news is I think Maisy got upset tonight when I told her Anessa might go with us to her dance competition.

I'll have to talk to her about it. I don't want my sis to be sad.

Grandma leaves tomorrow.☹

Anyway. I don't know everything to write in a journal, so... night.

Cassidy

Chapter 26

Niji awoke to a noise. She hopped up on all fours with her ears pointing up and alert, turning atop her bed mat in a circle. It was midnight dark in her bedroom on the grounds of the Palace of the Divine. A flash of lightning, closer than she liked, brightened her room and was gone in an instant. The rumble of thunder came a couple of seconds later.

She didn't dream of the noise that had woken her. If Niji knew one thing with hearing as keen as hers, it was noises. This noise was intentional, a rhythmic knock to get her attention. She closed her eyes and sniffed the air, using all of her senses to solve the mystery. Her eyes opened and adjusted to the lack of light. Slowly she moved around the room, keeping her head and tail low, and her ears plastered against her body. Her fur was as black as deep space.

Sureto wouldn't have knocked if he had come to tell her of his grand time in the valley. He wouldn't return for days or months, if he returned at all. Besides, the trace odor of sweat lingering in the air was not from a bird. *Wait. Do birds sweat?* A flash of lightning shone through the paper squares of the latticed door of her room, followed almost immediately by a wall-shaking boom of thunder. *That was too close. Please gods, do not strike the emperor's trees.*

Niji walked the wooden floor at the edge of her dark room, feeling the safety of having something substantial, the wall, on one side of her. She peered at the sliding door leading to the hallway outside. Every eight hours, a new set of ten guards walked down that hallway to and from their watch over the palace grounds. But a guard passing by in the hallway would not have knocked on her door. Though brutish, the guards were respectfully quiet between shifts. Sure, there were heavy footfalls and the occasional murmur of words, but these were sounds Niji had come to know and ignore. No, the knock that had awakened her was intentional, and had come from the sliding door leading to the palace's grounds outside, not the hallway.

Niji crept to the door to the grounds as the pitter-patter of rain struck the slate roof. Her ears pulled from her sides and stuck straight upward. Though she loved the splashing of rain and how it muffled all other sounds, allowing her to sleep undisturbed, it was now a hindrance in hearing what she needed to. It also didn't help that her bed seemed to call to her, inviting her to a rainy night of sleep, but something was sneaking around in the night that had to be dealt with first.

Reaching the door, Niji nudged it open with her tiny black nose and was met with a crisp, stiff breeze. She squinted, peeking through the gap. Rainwater splattered on the wooden porch walkway. The sky was dark and tumultuous, blanketed by ominous rain-filled clouds streaking by. A flash of distant lightning backlit the clouds, briefly giving them a bright white outline. She pushed open the door just enough to fit through, stepped onto the porch, and was met by rain pushed by the breeze and intermittent gusts.

Next to her room, a garden of miniature trees, stones of various sizes, and a pond was free of shady intruders. The trees swayed with the wind, and koi in the pond swirled madly in delight from the rain striking the water's surface. With her ears straight upward, twitching and turning, Niji crept down the walkway, hugging the wall, staying under the overhang of the roof to avoid the worst of the rain. She passed doors to other darkened rooms where guards were sleeping or doing whatever the guards did in the late hours of the night.

A faint noise behind Niji made her freeze at the edge of the garden. Her heart almost stopped before beating double-time, as if to catch up. Quickly she turned, ready to fight or run away screaming, maybe a little bit of both, but nothing was lurking behind her — no teeth and no beak. The tension in her body eased as she released a held breath. *What am I doing out here? What if*

I did find something dangerous? I should have stayed in my room.

Her bravery faded along with her desire to locate the source of the noise; she would be safer in her room. She scampered back toward her room, only to abruptly stop a few feet away. She squealed, curling into a shaking ball of fur at the brilliant flash and booming sound from a strike of silvery-blue lightening inside the grounds of the palace. Slowly uncurling and nervously scanning the sky for the next lightning strike, her frightened eyes caught sight of a tall, dark figure leaning against her doorway. She bared her sharp teeth. *Now I remember the owner of that sweaty smell.* Unafraid, but with her usual healthy amount of caution, Niji moved closer to the outline at her doorway until it came into better view. She stared up at her visitor — a tengu.

The tengu resembled but was taller than an average man, the crown of his head nearly reaching the top of the doorway. He wore a black kimono without an undershirt, and a red hakama. He had a lava-red face that appeared more maroon in the dark, and his black hair was pulled into a knot at the top of his head. He looked down at Niji with yellow eyes set underneath thick black eyebrows. An inches-long nose protruded from his face as if he had told a few too many lies. His lips curled into a creepy smile revealing pointy white, gleaming teeth. "Hello, Trouble," he said in a deep voice at the speed of a slow-burning fire.

Like most of Niji's acquaintances, the tengu failed to address her by her actual name.

"Hello, Clown," Niji countered, the term one of endearment that she'd made up during a previous interaction. She had claimed that the tengu, whose real name was Tsurugi, must have been wearing the mask of a clown to look so ridiculous.

"Oh, Niji, I only address you based on one of your outstanding qualities," Tsurugi said.

"And I address you based on your laughable face."

Tsurugi leered at her, but not out of anger. Niji knew mild insults were what he expected from her. Niji stepped past Tsurugi and into her room. She lowered her hind legs into a sit and shook the rain from her front paws. "Tell me, Tsurugi, why have you blessed me with your presence?"

Tsurugi pushed open the door, letting in the humid breeze from the storm. He rubbed his chin and leaned into the door frame as if he wasn't in the slightest hurry. "On my rounds in the forest the other day, I watched you run past. And seeing you is not easy, you being nearly the size of… nothing." Niji rolled her eyes as he continued. "I presumed you were on your way to the clearing for your beloved poison fire coral, and I decided to follow."

Niji's chest tightened as distressing thoughts scampered through her mind. *He watched me going to the clearing! That tree that fell… I forgot. That* was *Tsurugi. Did he see my fight with Sureto? Does he know about the hole in the barrier? He can't know. If he did, why would he be here and not there?* She calmed and collected herself and said, "I would expect no less from you, and of course, I knew you were there," she lied, scoffing. "The sound of the falling tree, it was you."

Tsurugi slowly blinked as a smile played at the corners of his mouth. Again, a flash of lightning, farther away this time, was followed by a low rumble of thunder.

"I was going for my regular visit to the clearing," Niji continued, then smiled playfully. "You should be careful following me around like that; others may think you're growing fond of me."

Tsurugi guffawed and crossed his arms. "Oh, what a scandal that would be. But alas, dear Niji, my only interest was in causing a bit of mischief." Mischief for the tengu usually meant bothering someone who was minding their own business.

Niji shook the rain from her ears, sending water droplets spraying across Tsurugi's hakama, and laid them flat against her back. She raised a furry eyebrow. "Is this why you're here? To tell me you saw me in the woods on the way to the clearing?" She rolled her eyes again. "Really?"

Tsurugi, ignoring Niji's attempt to draw his ire by splashing him, pulled away from the door frame to reveal a sheathed katana fastened at his side. He stretched his arms wide, and a pair of white-feathered wings spread out from his back. The wings shook, sending rain droplets to the ground, then returned to hiding behind his lean, muscular torso. "I'm no longer interested in the going-to the clearing; instead, my interest lies in the coming-back to the palace. He rubbed at his chin as he looked away. "You ran past me on your way back from the clearing not long after you arrived." He peered down at her with eyes full of accusation. "Why was that, Niji? What caused you to leave in such a hurry without a single finger of poison fire coral in your possession?"

Niji could lie with the best of them if given the time to formulate a story; however, Tsurugi's visit was unexpected, along with the question he posed. Her ears tangled into a knot behind her head as she scrambled for a fitting answer to his question. It came to her a moment later. "A tiger," she blurted. "When I got to the clearing, I spied a tiger." She averted her eyes from Tsurugi's look of disbelief. "At first... I heard it, and then I saw it, at the edge of the clearing... like it had been waiting for me."

Tsurugi raised a thick eyebrow of his own. "A... tiger?"

"Yes." Niji nodded once and mocked his slow cadence. "A... tiger."

Tsurugi stepped into her room, uninvited, leaving behind wet footprints as he ambled about. "The forests are my home. I know everything that lives within them." He stopped and looked down at Niji, tapping the side of his head with a long, sharp fingernail attached to his long red finger. "I know the tigers of that forest, and they were nowhere near the clearing." He eased his right hand to the hilt of his katana. "How about the truth this time?"

Niji swallowed hard. Deciding it was time to stop playing nice, she stepped back with her tail tucked, speaking through gritted teeth. "I could scream, and there would be a dozen guards here in seconds to strike you down."

Tsurugi scoffed. "The guards? The same guards I trained in the art of sword fighting? *Tsk, tsk.* You would be calling them to their doom. I would know their intended blow before they swung their sword. I trained all of them to be efficient swordsmen, but I only taught them a fraction of what I know."

Niji's eyes darted around the room. "But — but," she stammered. "The empress, the emperor, they would come to my defense, and you know you can't beat them."

Tsurugi sighed. "Oh, Niji. That may be true." He pulled the katana from its sheath as a lightning strike illuminated the room and reflected off the blade's pristine surface. "However, by the time they arrived, I would be your dying memory, gone in the dark of the night." He sat cross-legged in front of her, still gripping the katana as he laid it across his lap.

Niji eyed her reflection on the blade, then looked helplessly at her red-faced guest.

He smiled. "Now, Trouble, tell me everything. Tell me the truth."

Chapter 27

As Cassidy had done at every one of Maisy's competitions, she sat in the back row. She could come and go without dozens of eyes on her and could easily escape the auditorium after the competition. Anessa questioned the seating choice but didn't complain. After the announcement of the Best Dancer Award, Cassidy quickly snuck out of the auditorium with Anessa in tow. They slipped into a side hallway as hundreds of the dancers' relatives piled out of the auditorium.

Yes, Cassidy had told herself the night before that she had to learn had to interact with people, but she meant on an individual or small group basis. A hallway crammed with hundreds of loud, talking people was not the best place to test herself. Considering her power, she wanted to avoid the crowd more than ever. At first thought, the chance of encountering someone sad at a dance competition, a fun and exciting event, seemed ridiculous. However, competitions had winners, and if taken poorly, losers who would be far less than happy.

"OH MUH GEE, you were so good," Anessa gushed as Maisy walked up.

Maisy wore a blue spandex outfit covered with sequins of various sizes in flowing patterns and a matching short frilly skirt. A sash over her shoulder, crossing her chest at an angle, read 'Queen'. On her head sat a bejeweled tiara. And only for Cassidy to see, a warm undulating glow surrounded her.

"Yeah, sis, you did great," Cassidy said.

Maisy beamed underneath her rouged cheeks. "Thanks."

Mr. and Mrs. Davis walked over, Maisy's dad carrying a red bouquet of roses and a ridiculously large glittery gold and purple trophy. Her mom, who always looked elegant, wore beige slacks and a white blouse. Her hair was short against her head, and her skin was a radiant black. Her father, brown-skinned and tall, wore faded jeans and a blue button-up long-sleeve shirt. He set the trophy on the floor, handed the bouquet to Maisy, and kissed her cheek. "You were wonderful, Maisy."

"Thank you, Papa," Maisy said, now glowing inside and out.

"You still have to work on your turns," Cassidy said in a whisper only she could hear.

"You still have to work on your turns. Though, overall, you danced beautifully," Maisy's mom said, the dance instructor in her coming out.

Heat rose in Cassidy's cheeks. She looked wide-eyed in her peripheral, fearing someone had heard her say what Maisy's mother was going to say. She breathed a silent breath, relieved that no one had. *That was close.*

"Let's get a photo of the three of you together," Mr. Davis said, fidgeting with his camera, one of those professional-looking ones with a big lens. Cassidy stood at Maisy's left and held her at the waist. Anessa stood at Maisy's right and snuggled in next to her. Mr. Davis took a few steps back, holding the camera in his outstretched arms. "Okay, girls, smile. Say 'dance queen.'"

The girls giggled, then in unison said, "Dance queen," drawing out 'queen'.

The camera clicked a few times, and Maisy's dad smiled, apparently pleased with the shots. "Perfect."

"How about we go for a celebratory late lunch," Mrs. Davis said.

Maisy's arms fell to her sides, and her shoulders slumped. "Ugh, yes, please. I haven't had anything to eat in hours."

"Sure, sounds good," Cassidy agreed.

Anessa was staring at the ground. "I… I don't have any money. You can just take me home."

"Don't be silly," Mrs. Davis said. "It's our treat. We wouldn't think of asking you to pay."

"Of course not." Mr. Davis smiled warmly. "Unless you're secretly an eating champion and devour six plates of food."

Anessa smiled bashfully. "No, I'm not, but I can't —"

"It's settled then," Mrs. Davis said. She placed her hand on Mr. Davis' shoulder. "Reggie, would you take Maisy's trophy to the SUV and pull up to get us?"

"You got it." He hefted the trophy that was literally taller than Maisy and walked away.

Maisy stood motionless, in a daze.

"You okay?" Cassidy asked.

Maisy grinned at her. "Yeah, I'm good. Just tired." Her head flopped to the side. "And I'm hun-guh-ree."

Cassidy had no doubt Maisy was hungry and tired, but she sensed more. Whatever had bothered Maisy last night still was bothering her today. Anessa had something to do with it. She had to. Maisy had never acted this way, and the only difference was Anessa.

"Okay, girls, let's go," Mrs. Davis said.

Maisy, resembling a queen in her tiara, walked next to her mom. Cassidy, arms in a self-hug, walked beside Anessa, weaving through the crowd. She hadn't seen anyone with a haze, but regardless, she wasn't interested in taking any chances. She focused on the floor until they reached the exit, where she audibly exhaled.

In her peripheral, Anessa examined her.

"Are you good?" Anessa asked.

Cassidy plastered a grin over her anguish. "Yeah. I'm just not good with crowds. Horrible, to be honest."

Anessa looked poised to ask why when Maisy's dad pulled up.

Cassidy nodded toward the opened SUV doors. "It's a long story. I'll tell you another time, okay?"

Though, she wasn't sure she wanted to tell Anessa about 'that day' and her social anxiety. She had been trying so hard, and failing, at being normal around Anessa. What if this additional nugget of information made her look even more like a freak? But, what if it didn't? Didn't friends share more than clothes with each other? Didn't they also share secrets?

Despite her social anxiety having little to do with how she had been acting toward Anessa, maybe it would explain all the weirdness — the blanking out and nearly fainting. She'd tell Anessa, Cassidy decided, but only about her social anxiety and not about her powers. Never could she tell Anessa about her powers, friend or not.

Late lunch, which Cassidy called linner with it being close to dinner time, was at Maisy's favorite Mexican restaurant. After linner, they went to a frozen yogurt shop in a gigantic outdoor two-story shopping mall. A sprawling fountain display near the mall's center entertained shoppers with dozens of pulsating water streams illuminated by multi-colored lights. Three bronze statues stood in the fountain: a young boy riding a goose, an old man fishing in overalls, and a little girl with a floppy-eared dog. Trees for shade and colorful flowers surrounded the fountain, giving it the appearance of an enchanted garden.

Next to the fountain, Cassidy, Maisy, and Anessa sat on uncomfortable rod iron chairs. Mr. and Mrs. Davis sat across the way in a more comfortable outdoor furniture love seat.

Cassidy and Maisy were scooping their frozen yogurt from cups while Anessa attacked, from all angles, two scoops atop a cone. Anessa's eyes followed the streams of water as they danced by on their way around the perimeter of the fountain. She turned to Cassidy, placing her hand above her eyes to shield them from the sun. "This place is *so* neat. We didn't have anything like this where I lived. I could come here every weekend."

Cassidy smiled. "So could I. Well, except for winter."

"Yeah, way too cold then." Anessa gazed at the fountain. "I wonder if the water freezes over."

Maisy had been uncommonly quiet between bites of yogurt.

"How about you, Maisy?" Anessa asked.

Maisy was chomping on a spoonful of yogurt and held up a finger. In the SUV, she had removed the frilly skirt and put on a t-shirt and jeans over her dance outfit. Her face, however, was still in full-blown dance queen mode — makeup and artificial eyelashes. She nodded and leaned back in her chair. "Yeah, I love it here, too." She surveyed the surroundings. "It's one place where I can go and not feel like I have to compete with someone or pass a test. You know? I don't have to worry about disappointing —" She paused. "It's just me, my frozen yogurt, and my friend —" She looked to Cassidy then to Anessa. "Friends."

"For me," Anessa said, "it's like there's nothing or nowhere else in the world beyond here. No mean people. No problems." She paused. "It feels safe, like this is some magical place and nothing bad could ever happen here."

Cassidy sensed an opening to pry a bit. Maybe she could find out more about the vision of Anessa's mom on the phone and figure out how to help her. "Anessa," she started, already second-guessing her decision to ask.

"Yeah?"

"How," Cassidy paused, "how's your mom been? You know, being new to Farmington."

A small dab of melting yogurt clung to the point of Anessa's nose as she answered. "I don't know, okay, I guess." The sparkle in her eyes faded as if the question took her from the safety and magic of the here and now. Not to mention, her dark haze lived here, even in this wondrous place. Though, unless the light and shadows were playing tricks with Cassidy's vision, the haze had lessened and appeared much more subdued.

I'm so stupid, Cassidy scolded herself. "Hey, I'm sorry. I didn't mean to ruin your fun. It's just… never mind." She motioned to Anessa's nose. "By the way, you have yogurt on the tip of your nose."

Anessa ran the back of her hand across her nose and wiped the yogurt away on her jeans. She giggled. "Thanks."

They sat in silence as they ate and watched passersby on their way to the next store to shop. Cassidy was more than okay with people-watching;

it was people-interacting she could do without. She wanted to know exactly what she was up against when going into public places. How many people out there were sad enough to have a haze and potentially bring her into their sadness?

She surreptitiously watched people, inspecting them for glows and darkness, using her peripheral and furtive glances, fearing someone might meet her gaze. What would happen if someone caught her watching? Would she turn to stone, burst into flames, or just be embarrassed? The first two possibilities were well beyond her typical worst-case scenarios, making the likelihood of embarrassment seem much more probable and manageable. So, she openly watched everyone — little kids, those her age, and adults. A few people caught her watching, but she didn't turn to stone or burst into flames. Though most times she turned away embarrassed, often so did the person who discovered her watching.

In the end, she made some curious observations. Like Iwa explained in the journal, most kids — the babies and toddlers — had a glow. But not the kids her age; most neither had a glow nor a haze. The adults were the worst — no glows, and several had varying levels of haze. Thankfully, none had the darkest haze that Iwa warned about.

Cassidy softly smiled and relaxed. A place with hundreds of people and only around ten with a haze? Maybe she could go out and live a regular life. Ten was a number she could avoid.

She gasped and sat up with urgency. "Omagosh! What time is it?"

Anessa and Maisy sat up, matching her urgency.

"It was five when we got here. I saw it on the clock in the car," Maisy said. "Why?"

"My grandma leaves for the airport at six. I have to get home to say goodbye."

"Okay, sis. I'll run and tell my mom and dad." Maisy stuffed a big spoonful of yogurt into her mouth and took off in a run.

"You better work on that yogurt," Cassidy told Anessa. "Maisy's mom won't let you take it in her Mercedes."

Anessa nodded and went to work on the final scoop of vanilla, getting it on more than just her nose.

Mr. Davis pulled into Cassidy's driveway just as her dad slid Grandma's suitcase in the back of their SUV. Cassidy unlocked her seatbelt and bolted from the SUV the moment it stopped. "Dad! Dad!" she yelled, running up to him. "Where's Grandma?"

"Hey, Cass. You made it. We were getting a little worried." Though Dad used the word 'worried', his calm expression revealed that her level of concern over the prospect of missing Grandma leave for the airport far exceeded his. "She should be—"

"I'm over here," Grandma announced, making her way down the front steps of the house. Her purse hung from her shoulder, and her grey and black hair was freshly permed. She was definitely ready to leave.

Dad waved at Mr. and Mrs. Davis. "Hey, neighbor. Dance competition go well?"

Mrs. Davis pointed to Maisy walking up the driveway with Anessa. "There's our queen, right there."

Cassidy decided to let the adults carry on without her, with little time remaining before Grandma had to leave. She ran up to Grandma and gave her a big hug. Not long ago, her hugs were at Grandma's waist. Since her last growth spurt, she was nearly as tall as Grandma.

"Hi, Cassie. You've come to say goodbye?"

Cassidy pulled back from the hug, pouting. "I thought I was going to miss you."

Grandma's finger tapped Cassidy's nose. "You nearly did."

Maisy and Anessa stopped a step behind Cassidy.

"Hi, Maisy, dear," Grandma said. "You look beautiful today."

"Hi, Grandma," Maisy said.

"And you must be —"

Cassidy followed Grandma's stare. "Grandma, this is Anessa. Anessa, this is my grandma."

Anessa and Grandma exchanged smiles and hellos.

"Mom," Dad called to Grandma. "We should get going. The line to get through security can be long on Saturdays."

Cassidy frowned. "I'm going to miss you."

"I'll miss you too. Pick up that phone and call me if you ever need me or want to talk about you know what," Grandma said conspiratorially, glancing at Anessa and Maisy before her eyes found their way back to Cassidy's.

Cassidy grinned and nodded knowingly.

"You take good care of Cassidy," Grandma said to Maisy.

"I promise," Maisy said.

"Anessa," Grandma said. "You have two good friends here in Cassidy and Maisy."

"I know I do," Anessa said, smiling bashfully.

Grandma sighed. "Well, I'd better get going." She kissed Cassidy's forehead. "I love you."

"I love you too," Cassidy said.

Dad helped Grandma climb into the SUV and closed the door behind her. Cassidy stepped back and stood between Anessa and Maisy as Dad started the engine and followed Maisy's parents out of the driveway.

Cassidy's heart sunk as they waved and the SUV pulled away. It wasn't so many years ago that Grandma had practically helped raise her while Mom and Dad worked. When Dad started working from home, Grandma had moved back to Oregon. She would now be gone until Thanksgiving.

"Maisy! Are you riding with us?" Mrs. Davis called from the car.

"Hey, Cass," Maisy said. "I'm going home."

Cassidy wiped away a tear. "Oh, okay." She studied Maisy's expression for anything wrong. "You sure you can't come in for a little bit... or want to?"

"You know, I got all this makeup on, and I could seriously use a shower."

They hugged, and Maisy whispered, "We need to talk about what you told me last night."

"Okay," Cassidy whispered back. She pulled away, plugging her nose. "Yep, you need a shower."

Maisy grinned. "Told ya. Maybe see you tomorrow? See you Monday, Anessa."

"Okay. Thanks for the fun day," Anessa said.

Maisy smiled and walked away, still with a bit of a strut of a queen.

Anessa's face brightened. "She really is a good dancer."

"The best I know," Cassidy said.

Anessa's mom pulled up and parked in the street.

"That's my mom." Anessa frowned. "Guess I gotta go, too."

Cassidy felt like a character at the end of the final episode of a TV show, when everyone goes their separate ways, leaving the last person on camera to deal with their thoughts and emotions on their own. Many nights she sat on her couch watching final episodes, with tears running down her face as she said goodbye to characters she had watched for years. At the moment, real life wasn't much different, though she mostly held back the tears, mostly. "Okay. Thanks for coming today. Maybe we can hang out again next weekend."

Anessa's smile reached her eyes. "That'd be awesome."

Cassidy waved to Anessa's mom in the car.

"Um… bye," Anessa said with a goofy smile, giving an awkward wave with her hand at her waist.

"Okay, bye."

Anessa hugged Cassidy without warning. When she pulled away, the difference was evident and profound. The haze, Anessa's dark, sooty haze that had been covering her like a coat of pollution, was gone. She didn't glow like Maisy, but most people didn't.

Seeing Anessa like most everyone else was what Cassidy wanted. And she'd bet, no, she knew, Anessa wanted that too — to be happy and accepted for who she was. They said final goodbyes, and Anessa ran to her mom's car and they pulled away. Then, yes, it felt exactly like the end of the final episode of a TV show.

Cassidy managed to stand taller and feel stronger, regardless. A happy warmth at seeing Anessa's haze gone surpassed the sadness from Grandma and Maisy leaving. The urge to help Anessa was absent as well. As was the voice. That demanding voice was silent, and Cassidy didn't miss it one bit. "Maybe I can do this," she muttered.

Later that night, Cassidy lay in bed and dove back into the translated journal, right back into the pages that discussed the powers. The first line, after the pages that explained the haze and glow — the people of light and dark — started, "Fret not over hearing what someone is prepared to speak, fear hearing the unspoken thoughts of everyone."

She dropped the journal to her chest and gazed at the ceiling. "What? Are you serious?" It was the first mention, other than the story Grandma told, that hearing all thoughts was an ability she would have. Iwa said that the satori could hear people's thoughts and read their minds. She threatened to not help the satori if it didn't give her those exact abilities. The satori warned her, but she ignored it. Now, in her journal, she says to be afraid.

Reading further, Iwa explained that she had discovered the ability to hear thoughts, all of them, and how it caused the worst day of her life. *I guess Iwa had her own 'that day'*, Cassidy thought. Iwa described a day in town during her first year living with the merchant and his family. The town was bustling with commotion because the Dutch would soon arrive on grand ships to trade goods. When the Dutch ships arrived that night, a fear grew within her, knowing the town would become even more crowded with people. The next day, merchants made their way to the village, and by the light of the day, loud and bustling people crammed the walkways.

Iwa stayed in the back of the shop, hiding from view. She peeked into the front of the shop from around a folding screen as six visiting merchants haggled prices. It was then that her boss summoned her. Hesitantly, Iwa edged from the back room and was ordered to go to the storeroom next door for a bolt of red fabric. The thought of entering the throng of people outside terrified her. She pleaded with the merchant to send his son to retrieve the bolt, but he was already busy making trades. Only after getting a disapproving glare from him, which she had never seen directed toward her, did she agree to retrieve the fabric.

Iwa hugged the shop's inside and outside walls all the way to the storeroom, like a timid animal avoiding predators. When she had retrieved the bolt and was on her way back, a line had formed outside of the shop blocking her way back in. People were forcing their way through the line on both sides, and someone pushed her from the back.

Sweat poured from her skin as she struggled to find space, somewhere she could stand and avoid anyone and everyone's touch. There were loud voices, not only from mouths but from the minds around her. It was sound layered with sound. Iwa's head pulsed with pain, and she panicked. She dropped the bolt of fabric, pressed her hands over her ears, and screamed until the world around her went black.

A twinge of panic fluttered in Cassidy's stomach like a kaleidoscope of butterflies. "Oh my gosh. I *will* be able to hear thoughts, all of them. This is not good."

Iwa wrote that the merchant allowed her to remain in the shop during the busiest days from that point forward. She recalled the satori telling her to clear her mind and find the silence. On Iwa's 'that day', the satori's advice became as clear as still water – the advice was meditation.

Cassidy's dad once taught her a basic meditation that she tried a few times but never made a regular practice. She would need to take meditation seriously if a chance existed of experiencing what Iwa did.

A knock sounded on her door, and Dad stuck his head through the opening. "Hey, you."

"Hey Dad."

"May I enter?"

Cassidy made a flourishing sweep with her hand. "Come hither."

"Tada!" Dad entered with the bronze mirror, now clean and pristine, in his hand.

"Wow!" Cassidy took the mirror and examined both sides again and again. "It looks amazing." The green was gone entirely. It was nearly as reflective as a glass mirror; she could actually see herself on the smooth side. She hugged the mirror to her chest and repaid Dad with a smile and a thank you.

"You are most welcome. Need help with anything else?"

"No, I'm — Actually, could you teach me how to meditate?"

"I have taught you how to meditate."

"I know, but… like for real this time."

Dad laughed a small laugh. "It was for real the other time I taught you."

"No, I just mean that I want to really learn this time, take it seriously."

"Any reason why?"

Cassidy held up the journal. "Iwa said it was a good idea to learn. To help with the powers." She didn't elaborate. Sharing that she would eventually have the power to hear all thoughts was not at the top of her to-do list. Who would want to be around her knowing nothing in their head was private?

"Cool. We'll start tomorrow." He leaned in and kissed the top of her head. "Goodnight."

"Goodnight. Thanks again for the mirror."

Journal Entry August 25

Anessa's haze is gone!!!

It was so cool to see her happy. I can't wait to see her at school Monday.

I tried to tell Maisy, but she didn't answer my calls. I guess she's tired from the work it took to be a queen.

Dad cleaned the mirror and said he would teach me to meditate. I guess I will be able to hear ALL thoughts. I'm not looking forward to it, but I need to be ready.

Anyway. Maybe I really can do this!
Until next time.

Cassidy

Chapter 28

I can't do this. "I don't get it," Cassidy said as Anessa entered the classroom later than usual on Wednesday morning and headed straight for Mrs. Higgins.

"Get what?" Maisy asked.

Cassidy nodded toward Anessa, shook her head, and huffed. "She was fine Monday and Tuesday. Good even. Now, something's wrong."

Maisy turned in her chair toward Anessa and tilted her head. "How can you tell? Is the haze back?"

"Yeah. It is." Cassidy had explained the haze to Maisy when they talked on Sunday and told her about her glow, which Maisy immediately modeled, pretending everyone could see it. Maisy was thrilled to hear that Cassidy wouldn't be able to listen to her thoughts… as long as she stayed perfectly happy and kept her glow.

A faint black outline surrounded Anessa. Her thoughts reached Cassidy's mind without any mental focus before she said them.

Maisy leaned close. "What is she saying?"

"She — She's going to Saint George this weekend. She has to leave on Saturday and should be back in time for school on Monday, but she's letting Mrs. Higgins know in case they don't get back in time."

"Saint George? Why is she going there?"

"Her dad lives there." Cassidy released a held breath and slid down in her chair, lightly rapping her forehead with her knuckles. "She's going there this weekend with her mom to pick up the last of their stuff."

"She must have a major problem with her dad."

Cassidy locked eyes with Maisy as she mulled over what she knew about Anessa's relationship with her dad. She sat up. "I don't know. I've only seen her sad about her mom *because* of her dad." She bit her lower lip and stared at her desk. "I guess in a kinda way, she does."

"I don't know how you —"

Cassidy shook her head at Maisy as Anessa approached. "Hey, Anessa." *Hi, stupid haze.*

"Hi, Cass. Hi, Maze," Anessa said, officially in the single syllable nickname friendship level. She let her backpack plunk to the ground.

"You okay?" Maisy deftly asked, drawing out the words, pretending she didn't already know.

Anessa sighed. "Yes… no. I have to go to Saint George this weekend to get the rest of our stuff."

"I bet it will feel good to bring all of your stuff here," Cassidy said, trying to impart a silver lining in place of the black one. She looked to Maisy for support.

"Yeah… yeah. I bet there are some things you've been missing. Clothes and stuff," Maisy added.

"Not clothes so much, but my bed and dresser are still there." She bobbed her head side to side, then nodded. "So, that will be nice — to have an actual bed again, instead of a blow-up mattress. And somewhere to put my clothes instead of on the floor."

The voice was there, reminding Cassidy of her obligation to help Anessa, but she ignored it. Instead, she triumphantly tapped her pencil on her desk and grinned. "See. It's not all bad."

Anessa managed to smile, though the faint haze still undulated around her.

The lunch bell rang three hours later to the cheers of the class. Kids rushed from their seats to grab their lunch bags from their cubbies or ran to the lunchroom to get a good spot in line. As usual, Brody was first up and out of the door, charging for the lunchroom as if the cafeteria staff served flawless one-liners, cut downs, and insults to the kid first in line to use on their classmates.

Cassidy calmly grabbed her lunch bag, but she too had somewhere she needed to rush off to before eating. "I have to go to the office for a few minutes. Meet ya in the lunchroom?"

Maisy scrunched her forehead. "What for?"

After seeing the return of Anessa's haze, Cassidy decided she needed help from someone with the knowledge of helping others; she needed to speak with Ms. Jennie. But she couldn't explain this to Maisy with Anessa around. Both Maisy and Anessa eyed her, waiting for an answer.

Cassidy didn't have a lie, so she went with a half-truth. "I... Ms. Jennie wanted to see me."

"Want us to go with you?" Anessa asked.

"No. You two go. I will be quick, I promise."

Maisy didn't act thrilled at the idea of eating lunch alone with Anessa, even if only for a few minutes. She and Maisy had eaten lunch together every school day for the last five years. Lunch was their time to catch up, gossip, and plan for later.

Cassidy had been meaning to talk to Maisy after school about Anessa, but Maisy had been quiet lately. She didn't even ask to hang out Monday or Tuesday afternoon. If it weren't for the walk to and from school and lunch, Cassidy and Maisy wouldn't have talked much at all.

Maisy's creased forehead softened. "Okay. But hurry. It's our time to talk and stuff."

Cassidy placed her hand on Maisy's shoulder. "Thanks, sis."

Maisy grinned and nodded.

Cassidy smiled at Anessa and left.

A few minutes later Cassidy reached the school office, unassumingly walked past the office secretary who was busy helping a visitor and stopped outside Ms. Jennie's office. She peeked in at Ms. Jennie writing in her planner. Cassidy moved her hand to knock but stopped. Then, closing her eyes and taking a deep breath, she mustered up her confidence. *Come on, Cassidy; you can do it.*

Ms. Jennie spoke before Cassidy's knuckles reached the door.

"Cassidy? May I help you?"

Cassidy dropped her head and formed a smile before looking up. "Hi, Ms. Jennie. I know I don't have an appointment scheduled or anything, I just —"

"I have a few minutes. Come in."

Cassidy tittered and smiled in relief. She walked into the office, her lunch bag in hand. "Thank you." She held up her empty hand to make a vow. "I promise, only a few minutes."

"Good. I see we both have something to eat."

Cassidy held up her lunch bag and nodded. "Yeah. Maisy and Anessa are waiting for me in the lunchroom. I told them I would be quick."

"Have a seat."

"Thanks." Cassidy sat on the edge of the couch with her feet firmly on the floor. This was no time to get comfy.

"What's on your mind, Miss Cassidy Kenner?" Ms. Jennie asked.

What was on her mind? Cassidy hadn't taken the time to think over what she'd ask. What did she want to ask? *Oh yeah,* that. *But how without talking about my powers?*

"So, Ms. Jennie, you help people. Right?" Cassidy asked with a crooked grin.

Ms. Jennie raised her eyebrows and chuckled. "Um, yes. In a way, I do."

"Yeah, so, what do you do when there is someone you don't know how to help, or… can't help?"

Ms. Jennie placed her hands on her desk, left over right. "Well, Cassidy, that is a great question."

Cassidy remained silent, waiting for the answer.

"To be honest, I can't help everyone."

Cassidy's lips parted, and both eyebrows rose. How could that be? Ms. Jennie helped everyone she met in one way or another.

Ms. Jennie grinned. "Don't look so surprised. I appreciate your belief in me and what I do, but I can't help everyone. That's not possible."

Cassidy deflated.

"Cassidy, no one can help everyone. There are complex situations that create trouble for and in people. Some people need more help than I can give. More than you can give. And, often, they have to be willing to help themselves."

These were not the words of comfort Cassidy had hoped for. What made her think she could help Anessa, or anyone for that matter, if Ms. Jennie couldn't help everyone?

Ms. Jennie craned her neck forward. "Does that answer your question? Does it help at all?"

"I guess," Cassidy said, as discouragingly as those two words sound when combined.

They sat quietly for a moment.

"Lunch?" Ms. Jennie hinted.

Cassidy nodded, rose from the couch, and trudged toward the door.

"Cassidy," Ms. Jennie said.

Cassidy turned back to face her.

"Even though we can't help someone with all of their problems, that doesn't mean we can't be there for them. To hold their hand. To hug them. To encourage them. To let them know they have a friend in this world who cares about them. And I know for a fact that someone we both know appreciates you. Now, does that help?"

Ms. Jennie's words swirled around Cassidy's thoughts until they found a home in comfort. Cassidy smiled warmly and nodded. "That helps."

And it did; it helped a bunch. She left for the lunchroom with a determined step, where two kids were waiting on a good friend.

Chapter 29

With Ms. Jennie's words as her guide, her weapon, and her armor, Cassidy spent the next three days being a friend to Anessa, a best friend. It wasn't all that difficult because she *was* her friend. Cassidy didn't think about her powers or the journal. The voice reminding her to help Anessa became more of a companion than an annoyance.

Cassidy listened when Anessa talked about what upset her and offered support by reminding her she'd be there to say goodbye when she left for Saint George, and be at their desks in class when she got back.

They talked and laughed during lunch, and Anessa came over after school on Friday. Dad dropped them off at the mall where they ate frozen yogurt and, with encouragement from Anessa, they danced next to the fountain without caring who watched. As streams of water shot into the air, synchronized to music, they sang about bravery with Sara Bareilles and about showing your colors with Katy Perry. When Dad picked them up to take them home, their hands and faces were sticky from yogurt, and sweat drenched their hair and clothes.

Cassidy had asked Maisy to come over, but she said she had to practice for an upcoming dance competition. Maisy was still acting un-Maisy-ish, so Cassidy decided to make every effort to talk to her while Anessa was away. Maisy still glowed, but her glow was softer, like one of Dad's flashlights when the battery was almost dead.

Cassidy wasn't sure how hearing all thoughts worked, but she wouldn't want Maisy to lose her glow and happiness just so she could find out what was wrong. That would be a horrible trade. Cassidy didn't want to admit it, but she wasn't sure what was wrong with Maisy. Maisy had started acting weird, different, since they started hanging out with Anessa. And, lately, only Cassidy had been hanging out with Anessa. Just like today.

"That's got to be it," Cassidy whispered.

Anessa, lying on Cassidy's bed and searching for the next video to make them laugh and forget about her trip tomorrow, looked up from the tablet. "What's got to be it?"

"Oh. It's just —" She shook her head dismissively. "Something I have to do tomorrow."

Anessa scoffed. "I hope it's more fun than what I'm doing. Five hours in a moving truck, both ways."

Cassidy grinned. "No, nothing like that, thank goodness."

"Thank *greatness*, you mean."

And just like that, Cassidy thought of Maisy.

"I wish Maisy was here," Anessa said. "She's so much fun."

Cassidy nodded. "Yeah, she's the best." She had all but ignored Maisy the last two days, other than asking if she wanted to come over. Being so focused on Anessa meant that Maisy got pushed from the forefront of her mind to the background. *I should have paid attention and included her more. I'm so dumb.*

"What's wrong?" Anessa sat up, placing the tablet on her lap.

Cassidy frowned. *Great, now Anessa can see when I'm upset. Wait. Do I have a haze?* There didn't seem to be one, but maybe she couldn't see her own sadness, her own haze. "Nothing. I'm good," she said, convincing enough, she hoped.

"Well, good, because our favorite YouTuber just posted a new video." Anessa patted the spot on the mattress next to her.

Cassidy smiled and flopped onto the bed.

They flipped onto their stomachs, and Anessa pushed play. They sang along to and laughed at videos up until Cassidy's dad announced the arrival of Anessa's mom. It was time for her to go.

"Where's the moving truck?" Anessa asked her mom, who was waiting on the front porch.

"Hi, Mrs. Chestnut," Cassidy said.

"Hi, Cassidy." Mrs. Chestnut pulled Anessa into a hug.

Maybe they aren't going. "Yeah, where's the truck?"

Anessa pushed free of her mom's loving grip and straightened her hair.

"I don't pick it up until the mornin'. No need to pay for an extra day," Mrs. Chestnut said.

Cassidy sighed internally; Anessa *would* leave tomorrow. Though, it wasn't all bad; she needed the time to fix the mess she made of her friendship with Maisy. "When are you coming back?"

"If everything goes as planned, we'll be back Sunday night," Anessa's mom said.

"Cool. Then I'll see you at school Monday," Cassidy said, smiling at Anessa.

Anessa fake gagged. "Ugh, school. I'm hoping we're really late, then. Sorry, Cass."

"Not a chance, young lady," Mrs. Chestnut said. "School on Monday, for sure."

Anessa pouted. "Fine."

"Okay, I'll go cool down the inside of the car while you say goodbye. It gets hot fast in this heat."

"Guess I'll see you Monday," Anessa said somberly. "I have something for you." She rummaged around in her pink pants pocket, pulled out a bracelet, and handed it to Cassidy.

A flamingo pendant dangled from a pink and purple braided rope bracelet. Cassidy slipped the bracelet onto her forefinger. She eyed Anessa. "What is this for?"

"I read that flamingos are a lot like people. They search for other flamingos to be their friends for life. I thought that was so cool." She smiled bashfully. "I think of you that way. You're my friend for life, and I'm glad you found me."

Cassidy's heart radiated warmth within her chest. "Thank you. I love it. I'll wear it all the time." She gave Anessa the briefest of hugs, hoping to avoid seeing what was on Anessa's mind. But, even with the briefest hug, a flash of a vision came and went. The voice urged her to pull at it, to see it clearly, but Cassidy squashed the urge, wanting the memories of the fun day they had together front and center in her mind. The bad stuff could wait until Anessa returned. She slipped the bracelet onto her wrist and smiled at its perfect fit. "See ya Monday."

"Say hi to Maisy. Oh, we were having so much fun I forgot. We never talked about why you hate crowds."

"Oh. Right. I forgot too." Though, Cassidy was okay with forgetting. "How about when you get back?" Maybe, just maybe, Anessa would forget about it over the weekend.

"Deal." Agreement made, Anessa ran to the car.

They exchanged waves as the car pulled away, and a moment later, the Chestnuts were gone.

Cassidy stood there, thinking about nothing in particular, then she thought hard. "Maisy!" She sprinted into the house and to her bedroom. She grabbed her tablet from the dresser and gave the writing box a glance, feeling guilty about not having read the journal the last few days. But she was choosing to live her life and deal with her powers, instead of just reading about them. Cassidy loaded the video-chat app, pushed an image of Maisy's smiling face, and plopped onto her bed.

Ring, ring, ring.

"Come on, Maisy. Where are you?"

Ring, ring, ring.

The ringing stopped. Her finger pressed the image of Maisy's face again. Cassidy had a friendship to repair and waiting until tomorrow to get started was out of the question.

Ring, ring, ring.

Ring, ring, ring.

Cassidy closed the app and turned off the tablet; the blank screen stared back at her. Falling back onto her bed, she gazed at the ceiling. "Why won't you answer?"

Her bedroom door opened.

"Maisy?" she said urgently, sitting up. "Oh, hi, Dad." Her face sagged into a frown.

"I'm happy to see you, too," Dad said sarcastically.

"Sorry, I thought you were Maisy."

He stepped into the doorway. "Is there something wrong between you and Maisy?"

Cassidy sighed. "I think so."

"Why so?"

She pulled at her hair, then her arms dropped to her sides like limp noodles. "I — You know, Anessa has needed me lately."

"Okay."

"I sort of forgot to pay attention to Maisy."

"I see."

"I was being a good friend to Anessa and a bad friend to Maisy." Cassidy wiped a falling tear from her cheek.

Dad knelt in front of her and patted her knee. "Cass, you and Maisy have been friends for years. Best friends. You have spent nearly every day of your lives together since you were four."

"I know." She sniffled. "But she won't answer when I call." She held the tablet up to him.

He gently took it. "If she won't answer, then leave her a message and tell her how you feel. Tell her you're sorry. Give her a couple of days to think it over."

Cassidy pouted, then nodded. "What if she doesn't listen to the message?"

"She'll listen to it." He wiped her tears and snot with his sleeve. "Gross."

She giggled through the sadness. "Get that away from me and go change your shirt."

Dad laughed.

"Cassidy," he said, appearing thoughtful. "There may be more going on with Maisy than you know. The way we *regular* people know what's bothering someone is by asking them. And even more important, listening to them. It's what friends do. So, ask her, and don't judge, just listen."

"I will." She pulled him into a hug, snotty shirt and all. "Thanks, Dad." He always knew what to say, and sometimes, like now, it made sense.

"Dinner in thirty minutes. Leave that message." He kissed her forehead and left her alone with her thoughts and tablet.

Chapter 30

Sunday was half over, and Cassidy hadn't heard from Maisy or Anessa. Her favorite activities of watching videos and reading got boring crazy fast. The realization sunk in that she did not live an exciting life or even a somewhat exciting life outside of her friends. The word excitement and her life were as far apart as the moon was to Earth.

Yesterday, Dad taught her a meditation. It was one he said would be easy for her because it only required focusing on her breath. She asked him to teach her another type because she already knew how to breathe to calm her anxiety, but he promised the meditation was a more advanced technique, like leveling up in a video game. She had to remind him that she didn't play video games.

"Ugh! I am *so* bored." Cassidy slid from the bed and peeked out of the blinds to the sunny outside. Sundays in the neighborhood were typically quiet, with most of the neighborhood at church or temple.

Uncharacteristically, she hoped for something to happen or for someone to walk by, giving her something to do, even if just an opportunity to watch them.

Her face brightened at an idea. "Frozen yogurt at the fountain." *Just me, yogurt, and Sue and the Eight-Headed Dragon.* She threw on a clean shirt with two capital Ws emblazoned on the front, brushed out her hair, pinned back her bangs with two precisely placed mint barrettes, and called for her dad.

"Are you sure you'll be okay alone?" Dad asked in the way of questioning her sanity.

He was right to. This was like nothing she had ever done. The look on Dad's face was comical when she asked him to drop her off alone at the yogurt shop. It was like part of his brain exploded from confusion, and he had to use an alternative part to make sense of it.

"I'll be fine," she assured him. "It's not like you'll be that far away."

She had said he could go home, but Dad protested leaving her alone at the mall. He planned to park close and wait in the car. It wasn't like she was flying to another country; it was just the yogurt shop but being alone in public was kind of a big deal. It was a challenge, and she wanted to do this, so she agreed to his terms.

"Okay. Be back here in 30 minutes. There's a clock in the shop. I'll park right over there." Dad pointed to a row of parking spaces.

Cassidy gave a thumbs up. "Got it." She grabbed her book, slid out of the car, and closed the door behind her. She gave Dad a little you-can-go wave and walked to the frozen yogurt shop, pausing at the door. Peering inside, it wasn't crowded — six, maybe seven people. She could feel Dad's eyes on the back of her head, but she wouldn't turn around; she wouldn't let him see her questioning herself now that she was at the door. "Here goes nothing," she muttered, and opened the door with a sweaty palm.

The cold yogurt-flavored air covered Cassidy providing relief from the heat of the outside. To her left, a mother paid for a small cup of frozen yogurt for her son, who looked no more than five. He jumped around his mother while tugging her shirt as if he was already on a sugar high.

Pink and purple circular tables with chairs were to her right where a teenage couple and a father with his two daughters were sitting. To Cassidy's relief, everyone appeared to be perfectly happy. Honestly, could anyone be sad while eating frozen yogurt?

She walked to the back, crammed her book into her armpit, and grabbed a medium-sized cup — the small cup was a perfect size for little kids, which she was not, and the large cup was just too much. She got the large cup once, thinking bigger must always be better, but she ate little more than half and left with a sore tummy.

Cassidy filled her cup halfway from a dispenser labeled chocolate, half from a dispenser labeled cookie dough, and topped it off with cookie crumbles. With the line to pay empty, she walked right up and shyly handed the girl behind the counter a ten-dollar bill. The girl tried to make small talk, saying something about the weather and cooling off, but Cassidy only managed to say "yeah" and "thank you". She got her change and found a seat in the corner, away from everyone.

Cassidy stuffed a spoonful of chocolate and cookie dough into her mouth and casually scanned the shop — no glows, and thank goodness, no hazes. The tension in her shoulders eased, and she managed a contented smile. She was doing it — just hanging out in public like a normal person. No voices, no sadness, no crowds. It was just how it should be.

She flipped open Sue and the Eight-Headed Dragon where she last left off, about a third of the way through. Sue had just stumbled back to camp after sneaking off alone to battle a swamp troll. Sue thought she could take down the troll on her own and not risk the lives of her friends, but what she thought would be a single troll turned out to be three ugly and unforgiving green trolls. Sue took a beating but managed to get away with only bruises and dings to her armor and ego. Sue's friends reminded her that she could never have enough friends to help, no matter the extent of her powers. Cassidy scoffed. "Come on, Sue. Trust your friends."

Cassidy read two more chapters before her spoon scraped the bottom of the cup, leaving a thin pool of brownish goop with little soggy chunks of cookie. She brought the cup up to her mouth to finish it off, freezing when it touched her lips. "She is so pretty," a voice said to her right, piercing the near silence.

The two girls were focused intently on their phones. Their dad, having no chance at their attention, was also using his. But it couldn't have been the dad; the voice sounded too young.

The teenage couple was still slowly eating their frozen yogurt, apparently enjoying each other's company and in no hurry to leave. They made cutesy faces and whispered stuff like "No, *you're* the cutest," and "I like *you* more".

Gross. Can we not have love-talk while I'm eating? Cassidy hadn't had too much yogurt but wanted to throw up all the same.

Maybe it was the guy who said it. It was difficult to make out their voices, barely over a whisper. Which was perfectly fine with Cassidy; she preferred not to hear the fluff they were saying to each other more than once. She would turn off the power if she knew how.

The girl stood from her chair and said, "I'm going to wash my hands. Don't leave me Cutie Mac Cute Stuff."

Cassidy gagged. *Please, no more of that ridiculous talk.* She studied the boy as he watched his girlfriend walk away. When the girl disappeared behind the bathroom door, he ran his hands through his brown hair and thought, *I hope my hair looks good.*

The yogurt cup dropped from Cassidy's hand, bounced across the purple table, and splashed her with yogurt remnants before falling to the floor. *What the frappe?* Cassidy heard every word… as if he said them. But he didn't say the words, not even in a whisper. His lips did not move. The boy hoping his hair looked good was one hundred percent a thought.

"No. Way," she muttered.

The boy hid a laugh at her behind his hand. Cassidy hardly noticed him or the liquid sugar dribbling down her shirt and onto her pants. She sat there, mulling over this new ability. Iwa's journal made it clear that she would eventually have the power to hear all thoughts, but she didn't care to and absolutely not this soon. *I have to tell Maisy. Thankfully she is safe around me. Oh my gosh! What about Mom and Dad? What do I tell them? When do I tell —*

"I'll get that for you," said a voice.

Cassidy woke from her daze.

The girl from the register had picked up the cup and was wiping the yogurt slop from the floor. She wore a visor over her blonde hair that was pulled back into a tight ponytail. She stood and glanced at Cassidy with hazel eyes. However, the girl's beautiful eyes couldn't hide her curled lips and pinched eyebrows as she wiped the table with a clean cloth.

"I'm so sorry," Cassidy said. "I was just —"

The girl said not to worry about it, but with a hint of frustration. Then her thoughts gave away exactly how she felt. *Dumb kids, coming in here all the time, making a mess.*

Cassidy scowled, and before she could think twice, blurted, "I am not a dumb kid."

The girl stopped mid-wipe, her eyes bulging. She stammered, "You heard — Did I say that —"

"That – that's not very nice," Cassidy continued, stammering, shocked at suddenly hearing thoughts and disappointed in what she heard.

The girl's face turned red, resembling one heck of a sunburn. She apologized, and nearly in tears, ran to the back of the shop.

Cassidy's heart hurt and her cheeks burned red. She instantly regretted upsetting the girl, who seemed to be having a super bad day, but she didn't wait around to apologize. She had to leave; she had to be alone.

The teenage couple saw what had happened and were gawking at Cassidy with annoying smiles on their faces. Cassidy licked a smudge of yogurt from her pointer finger, picked up Sally and the Eight-Headed Dragon, and rushed to the exit, pausing at the door. "Tell the girl," she said to the room, "not to be upset. It's okay." She turned toward the teenage couple and smiled awkwardly at the boy. "Your hair… it looks fine." She left and didn't look back.

It had only been twenty minutes. Cassidy couldn't go back to the SUV and have Dad see her all flustered. Instead, she ran to the fountain and plopped down in her regular uncomfortable chair. Her heart thumped like that of a caffeinated rabbit. Someone had to be following her. The girl that worked at the yogurt shop or the guy with the hair. They would chase her down and ask how she did it. How did she hear what they thought? No way could she explain it; she couldn't tell them. A minute passed, then two... no one came for her. Cassidy's heart calmed. She slid down in the seat, released a long sigh, then laughed. *That was crazy.*

Dad asked Cassidy about her solo adventure. She lied a little, saying it was good. The yogurt was good, the book was good, being on her own was good. The hearing thoughts and upsetting people... not so good. He gave a questioning look but didn't pry. It wasn't the time to tell him about hearing actual thoughts, not yet. She needed time to figure out how to control it. Then she would tell him and Mom so they wouldn't be freaked out being around her, worrying about her snooping around in their head. Which she would absolutely not do and had no interest in doing. With her best fake smile, she assured him, "I'm fine, promise."

Journal Entry August 31

I'm worried. I left Maze a message two days ago and she hasn't replied.

I said I was sorry for ignoring her and that I would be a better friend and that I wanted to hear all about what was making her upset...

This is hard. How can I be a best friend to two people?

Anessa's back tomorrow. I guess I have to figure it out.

On top of ALL of that, I heard thoughts today, actual thoughts. Ugh. Can this stink any more than it already does?

Anyway ... goodnight journal. Thanks for listening or whatever.

Cassidy

Chapter 31

Cassidy walked to school alone on Monday. Maisy's mom called Cassidy's dad to explain that Maisy had a student council meeting before school. The election was only a couple of weeks away. The kids running for office positions had to go over the rules for campaigning. If the rules were the same as previous years' elections, the school hallways and doors would be covered by posters with clever and not so clever catchphrases like "Vote Tommy Hewitt for Class President, He Can Do It", or "Don't Be Lazy, Vote for Maisy". Maisy would never allow such an unimaginative slogan to touch a school wall or door, though. "Fight the School Daze and Vote for Maze". That one would be a maybe. Maisy would win the election. Everyone knew her, and everyone liked her except for maybe the bullies.

Cassidy rehearsed what she'd say to Maisy the entire walk, right up until she reached the classroom and sat at her desk. Only a couple of kids were in the room, but not Maisy or Anessa. Cassidy waved at Alex, who gave her a big smile. Alex acted the part of Cassidy's valentine the last couple of years. They even had frozen yogurt together, kind of. Alex happened to be at the yogurt shop with his parents at the same time she was with hers. They sat at the table next to hers. He said 'hello', or 'hey Cassidy', something like that. She smiled and waved to be polite. Honestly, she didn't have an interest in being anyone's valentine beyond getting a card and a piece of candy.

The five-minute warning bell rang. The rest of the class would soon come clambering through the door. In moments she'd start working on fixing this Maisy and Anessa thing.

Brody and Adam stumbled in, laughing at something or someone. Alice and Josie walked in next. Josie was trying for class president too. *What rhymes with Josie Pemberton?*

Maisy entered behind Josie as bright and confident as ever. "Hi Cass," she said, with a little less affection than usual. But she said words, and that was a start.

"Hi, Maze," Cassidy said, encouraged. "How was the meeting, future class president?"

Maisy pursed her lips as she situated her books and pencils on her desk. "It was good. I can't wait to get started on my campaign."

Cassidy smiled and touched her hand. "You'll win. I know it."

Maisy returned a smile, though not her signature blast of white.

Maybe she didn't listen to my message. "Hey, Maze —"

The bell rang.

Uncharacteristically, Mrs. Higgins was missing, and some of the class was already expressing their desire for a substitute teacher. School days were always easier with a substitute who wasn't familiar with the curriculum. They'd read chapters from their books or be given math worksheets. Boring, monotonous stuff, but a break from 'do this' and 'do that'.

"Wait. Where's Anessa?" Cassidy asked, scanning the room.

Maisy shrugged.

Maybe they were delayed. Cassidy smiled. *Anessa's getting Monday off like she wanted.*

A full ten minutes after the bell rang, Mrs. Higgins finally entered the room, greeted by moans of disappointment. She gave a glare that hushed the class.

Ms. Jennie walked in after her, which was strange because the counselor usually only came to class when a kid forgot they had time scheduled with her, for presentations on being better at life and school, or to discuss community projects. It was way too early in the day for a presentation. Her eyes were irritated red, and there was something more, something worse. Surrounding Ms. Jennie like a personal dust storm was a faint dark haze. On top of that, Mrs. Higgins had a haze of her own.

The hair on Cassidy's arm stood straight, her skin tingling. *Something is wrong. Something is very wrong.* Cassidy sat forward in her seat and clutched at the front of her shirt.

Mrs. Higgins raised a haze-shrouded hand, resembling that of a dark wizard, and asked for everyone's quiet attention.

"What's going on, Cass?" Maisy asked.

Cassidy shrugged and shook her head. She focused on Mrs. Higgins, anticipating her every word, knowing for certain she'd be the first to hear them.

"Class," Mrs. Higgins said hesitantly. "Ms. Jennie has joined me today to share tragic news with you."

Ms. Jennie, her face strained, nodded.

Anessa's seat was still empty. No backpack, no books, and no Anessa.

"Many of you know," Mrs. Higgins paused, attempting to compose herself. She looked at Cassidy and Maisy. "Many of you know and are friends with Anessa Chestnut."

From that moment, Cassidy heard her teacher's words twice — once as a thought and once from her mouth — and her heart slowly and painfully broke into tiny pieces.

"There was an accident on their way home from Saint George. Their truck —" Mrs. Higgins' voice broke as a tear trickled down her cheek, the haze undulating around her. "And they — Unfortunately, she and her mother didn't make it."

"Didn't make it," Cassidy repeated to herself, making it the third time she heard those words. Words that she didn't know how to handle. Words that didn't make sense. Words that were certainly a mistake or a cruel joke because they couldn't be real. How could they be real? She had seen Anessa three days ago. She laughed with her, sang with her, played with her, and hugged her goodbye. *I hugged her goodbye.* An unbearable heaviness grew inside of her, weighing her down to her seat.

Everyone's eyes fell on Cassidy, including Maisy, who had placed a caring hand on hers. Maisy looked devastated at witnessing the pain and heartbreak of her best friend.

Cassidy's lower lip quivered. *Why is everyone looking at me?*

"Sis. Are you okay?" Maisy asked.

"Why… is everyone… looking at me?" Cassidy asked Maisy through tears and rapid breaths. "Why are you all looking at me?" she yelled.

Some kids turned away; others continued to look at her through watery eyes of their own.

"Now, everyone," Mrs. Higgins said, gaining back the attention of most of the class. "Ms. Jennie will be available in her office all day, and we're bringing in additional counselors for you to talk to should you feel the need."

Cassidy shook her head at Maisy and fought to speak. "M-Maisy. Th-this isn't ha-happening. I-I just saw her F-Friday."

Maisy stood, and with effort, pulled her up by the hand and into a tight hug. Maisy was saying something, as was Ms. Jennie, who placed a hand on Cassidy's shoulder. But none of it felt real. People were saying words, and words were stupid; everything was stupid, and she had heard enough.

Cassidy pushed away from Maisy and bolted from the room, wailing as she ran. Running away just as Anessa did on her first day. She reached the end of the hallway before Ms. Jennie caught her, picked her up into a hug, and carried her to the office.

Chapter 32

Cassidy was once again on Ms. Jennie's couch, curled up in a ball, hugging her legs, with her head resting on a pillow at the armrest.

Miss. Jennie, having left her alone a few minutes earlier, walked in. "I called your mom. She's on her way."

Cassidy lifted her head, leaving behind a tear-soaked pillow. "My mom? Sh-she's at work. She's way too busy."

"I couldn't reach your dad. She said he must be in the dentist's chair. But she wanted me to tell you that it's okay, and she'll be here soon."

Cassidy flipped the pillow over to the dry side and laid her head down again. She chewed on a lock of her hair as thoughts of Anessa, and now Mom leaving work early, raced through her mind. It was difficult for Mom to leave work in the middle of the day. She'd have to reschedule so many appointments. Just knowing that Mom was coming to get her was comforting. When life was at its worst — from being sick to being lost in a crowd — Mom was there for her, always.

Cassidy searched the room until her gaze fell on Ms. Jennie, whose eyes were still a little red, as Cassidy imagined her own were but worse. The haze still hovered around Ms. Jennie, but only just, like the last tendrils of fog fading in the morning sunlight, nothing at all compared to… Anessa.

"Want to talk about it?" Ms. Jennie asked.

Cassidy slid her forefinger underneath her pink and purple bracelet and rubbed it with her thumb. The beaked face of the flamingo pendant stared up at her. She did; she really did want to talk about it. She wanted to understand how this could happen. Her mouth didn't want to cooperate at first, but she managed to create words. "I can't stop thinking about her. My chest — My heart hurts. She was at my house on Friday. She was happier, and I almost had her —" Cassidy stopped herself. This was not the time to try to explain her powers. In fact, there would never be a good time to discuss her powers with anyone other than her family, and Maisy, of course.

Ms. Jennie's forehead scrunched. "You almost had her what?"

Cassidy ran her hand across her nose, wiping away tears and snot. "Nothing. I don't know what I was going to say." *Yes, I do. Dang, I can't say anything without Ms. Jennie catching it.* She pondered over a question. "Ms. Jennie. How is it fair? I mean, Anessa was just a kid. She was *my* friend. And now… now she's gone. Just like that. Gone."

Ms. Jennie walked over and sat next to her on the couch. "I know this is difficult, and you feel horrible —"

"It's just," Cassidy pushed up from the pillow and sat, brushing away hair stuck to her tear-soaked cheeks. "She didn't have enough time. It's like a waste, a waste of time. None of it mattered."

Ms. Jennie pulled her into a side hug. "I know it feels that way, Cassidy, but no day in life is a waste of time. Every day we are alive is a blessing." She exhaled. "I know you are dealing with a lot of emotion right now, and what I am about to say might not seem important, but I want you to think about it."

Cassidy's mind was as scattered as box of puzzle pieces, but she nodded.

"Once when I was going through a difficult time, someone important to me explained that our lives are like stories. We are living our stories right now. Every day, every minute, every second. Each day of our lives is a page in our storybooks, and the chapters are the years. Along the way, people will come into and out of our lives. Some people are there for the whole story, some for a chapter or two, and some only for a page or a paragraph." She sighed. "Anessa's story was short, much too short. But I promise you, the pages of her book, the ones you are on, were some of her favorites."

They sat quietly until Cassidy broke the silence. "I think I get it, what you're saying, but it still isn't fair, and I'm still sad."

"Of course it isn't fair, and you should be sad, and you will be sad. The good thing about sadness, though, is it helps us grow an understanding and appreciation for happiness. Like most things in life, there can't be good without bad." Ms. Jennie squeezed her again and leaned away to meet her eyes. "And Cassidy, remember, your story isn't over. You have lots of pages to fill. And people who love you want to help you fill those pages." Ms. Jennie stood, straightened her clothes, and smoothed a few stray strands of Cassidy's hair. "You have a friend waiting to see you. I'll wait outside for your mom."

Cassidy's mouth fell short of a smile. She nodded, and Ms. Jennie left. Maisy, her friend, her sister, the person on more pages of her book than most, came in right after. Cassidy hopped from the couch, ran over to Maisy, and hugged her fiercely. Never again did she want to let go.

Chapter 33

Cassidy stayed home from school for the rest of the week. She insisted she would be okay with just Dad home so that Mom could go back to work. Cassidy had enough on her mind and didn't want to worry about Mom getting more behind.

On Tuesday, Maisy skipped school and spent the day with her. They sat around and watched TV as Dad kept them well supplied with snacks and drinks. They didn't talk much about Anessa — they didn't need to. They both knew how each other felt, both sad and confused at someone dying so young, especially with that someone being a friend.

On Wednesday, Maisy stopped by after school. She had met with Ms. Jennie to talk about Anessa and how she was handling it. Thankfully, Maisy still had her glow, even if it was more of a shimmer than a shine.

Ms. Jennie called Dad with the details for Anessa's funeral. Cassidy wasn't sure if she wanted to go at first, but Mom and Dad said they'd both take Friday off to travel to the funeral in Saint George. Maisy already had a trip planned to an out-of-state dance competition. She said she would cancel, but Cassidy wouldn't let her. Maisy promised she would be waiting for Cassidy the moment she got back.

Cassidy hadn't been to a funeral, at least not one she remembered. Her grandma, Dad's mom, died six years ago, but being a kid at the time, her memories of her grandma and the funeral were hazy. A photo of her grandma sat on the fireplace mantle and would catch Cassidy's attention every so often. She'd wonder what Dad's mom was like, and wish she'd had more time with her. Losing one grandma made her love and appreciate the one she still had even more.

After careful thought and input from Mom and Dad, Cassidy decided that attending the funeral was the right thing to do. Dad said funerals were a way to say goodbye to someone important to us. Cassidy cried at the thought of saying goodbye, but as Ms. Jennie and her parents told her, the sadness would never really go away, not entirely. It would just get easier. The memories of Anessa would keep her alive in her heart and mind.

The drive to Saint George took what seemed like forever. Cassidy sat in the back seat gazing at the passing landscape of fields with grazing cows, hills, and mountains, thinking over and over, *I'm going to the funeral of my friend.* As much as she didn't want to see it, she caught herself searching for signs of the accident, regarding every shred of tire and glitter of glass they passed on the road as a potential spot of the accident. She decided soon after that seeing the accident site wouldn't make her feel any better, and in fact, might make her feel worse. It would be a haunting image she wouldn't want to remember.

She passed the time by reading Sue and the Eight-Headed Dragon. Sue was a warrior who had to overcome overwhelming odds when very few people believed in her. Well, they wanted to believe in her; however to put it plainly, she and the evil dragon were not friends — not even one of the eight heads liked her — so defeating the dragon was an impossible task. Cassidy didn't reach the end of the story before they arrived in Saint George, but she was confident in the ending. Sue had a sword, a belief in herself, and friends who had her back — the dragon didn't stand a chance.

They reached the cemetery, drove a couple of minutes down a narrow road, and parked behind one of a dozen vehicles. Cassidy stepped from the SUV and under one of the shade trees offering relief from the late morning sun. She gazed at the hundreds of headstones sticking from the short grass like misspaced grey dominoes, but with names, dates, and final messages instead of spots.

Dad rested his hand on her shoulder. "All good?"

Cassidy gave Dad a pained look but nodded. She held Mom's hand as they walked up an incline, carefully stepping between gravestones for fear of disturbing… anyone. *Thank goodness I can't hear the dead. At least, I don't think I can. I better not be able to.*

She paused, gripping Mom's hand, and bringing her to an abrupt stop.

"What's wrong?" Mom asked.

Fifteen or so people were underneath and around a blue canopy only yards away, next to two dark wood caskets.

Mom followed Cassidy's gaze. "Lines in a coloring book?"

Cassidy nodded.

"All of them?" Mom asked.

Cassidy nodded again.

Everyone was dressed in black suits or black dresses, and they all wore a black haze as if they pulled it from a hanger in the same closet as their clothes and slipped it on. Cassidy couldn't determine where one haze began and where another ended. A layer of sweat formed between her hand and Mom's.

"Do you still want to do this?"

Cassidy looked up at Mom. "Would it make sense if I said I do, but I don't?"

"Perfect sense," Dad interjected. "Often, the right thing to do is difficult but necessary, and —"

"This is necessary," Cassidy completed. After a deep breath, she pulled Mom along, only to stop after a few steps. "But it won't hurt to stay back a bit. That's a lot of grief in one area."

Mom and Dad agreed.

As they came closer to the haze storm — a hurricane of dark, angry whisps — the horrible sounds grew louder. People talking in whispers, thoughts in whispers, and underneath it all, the awful sound of the haze — hundreds of fingernails scratching a chalkboard in a dozen storms. Cassidy slowed when the worst of it hit; worse than the noise and the haze storm was the urgent pull to help. The assault from the needy people stole the step from her feet and sucked the air from her lungs. *Iwa. I don't want what happened to Iwa to happen to me.*

Dad studied her for a quick second. "Are you okay?"

Cassidy licked her dry lips, released Mom's hand, and took two steps back. "Here," she managed to squeeze out.

Mom looked at Dad with concern. "Fine. We'll stay here."

"No," Cassidy blurted. Some of the funeral attendees looked at her from behind the haze. She turned away and softened her voice. "No. I want to be alone."

"Are you sure?" Mom asked.

Worse than the haze and its sound, and even worse than the urge to help everyone, was that Cassidy heard her parents' thoughts for the first time. The yogurt shop was proof enough that hearing private thoughts was as wrong as she suspected. Kids should not listen to their parents' thoughts, nor anyone else's for that matter.

"I'm positive." Cassidy looked directly into Mom's eyes, praying no thoughts passed to her. "It will feel weirder if you stay with me. I'm close enough to hear the priest but far enough away from," she waved her hand toward the crowd, "all of that."

Mom's eyes seemed to show understanding, but she couldn't understand, not entirely. Cassidy hadn't told her about hearing all thoughts. She felt guilty for keeping it a secret, and she would tell them, she would, but now was not the time.

Dad kissed the top of Cassidy's head. "Wave if you need us." He grabbed Mom's hand and headed toward the canopy, caskets, and nightmare haze.

Fewer people attended the funeral than Cassidy would have guessed. Apparently, Anessa and her mom didn't have a big family. Anessa's dad was with someone. His sister or girlfriend. Whatever. It wasn't important. His haze was the worst of them all, the worst that Cassidy had ever seen, but it still wasn't the tumultuous darkness Iwa described in her journal. Iwa said those with tumultuous darkness were dangerous, but Anessa's dad wasn't dangerous, just really sad. He cried loads of tears. Dad had once described someone acting like Anessa's dad as "inconsolable".

After the eulogy by the priest, bringing tears to every eye and doing nothing to help calm the massive haze, Mom and Dad came back to stand with Cassidy. Everyone else lined up near the caskets. Cassidy felt out of place. She didn't know anyone else. Her parents talked to a few people, undoubtedly introducing themselves and explaining the odd behavior of the girl avoiding everyone.

"What's going on? Why is everyone lined up?" Cassidy asked.

"To lay a flower on the caskets," Dad said, his eyes red and watery, "and to say a final goodbye. You should get in line."

Cassidy tugged at her hair, looking toward the line of people resembling a storm cloud. She wanted to say goodbye; she needed to say goodbye. But how could she? Iwa collapsed in a crowd that wasn't sad, just loud. Cassidy's crowd was a nightmare. "I — I don't think I can."

"We'll take you." Mom gave a gentle, reassuring grin.

This couldn't work, no way it could work. A sea of sadness waited for Cassidy by the caskets. Anessa's sadness alone had sent her to the nurse's office and nearly made her faint two other times. *Anessa.* Cassidy studied the flamingo bracelet. *This is my only chance to say goodbye. She deserves it. I deserve it.* She gave her parents a firm, confident nod. "Okay, but hold my hands."

Each step closer to the line of people came with an increased volume of sound from thoughts and haze. Most everyone was thinking what was expected: *she was too young; why did this happen? I miss you.* Cassidy held her breath. Every muscle in her body was tensed to the point of discomfort. Mom and Dad didn't complain, but she knew she was crushing their hands with her grip. Dad didn't say it, but Cassidy knew what he would say, "Breathe, Cassidy. Just breathe." So she did. She breathed in slowly, out slowly, and repeated, counting each breath. She looked forward but didn't focus on anything in particular. The tension eased using the meditation Dad had taught her. The sounds faded into the background. The world was a breath away.

"Are you in there?" a voice asked.

Cassidy blinked, focusing again on the world around her; several people were still ahead of her in line. She looked up at Dad, still readjusting to her surroundings. The lady first in line had her hand atop one of the caskets and her lips moved, but Cassidy couldn't hear the words or the lady's thoughts. *I guess meditation does work.*

Cassidy quickly glanced at everyone else milling around and chatting, hoping the meditation worked on all of them. Her eyes latched on to Anessa's dad. The voice awakened within her, along with a burning desire to help him feel better. *"Help him,"* the voice called, her voice. But what could she do? She didn't have the power to mend broken hearts; she couldn't bring Anessa back. Cassidy pulled her hands away from her parents and took an uncontrollable step toward him, then stopped and gritted her teeth. *No. I don't want to do this. Not here and not anywhere. Get out of my head.*

"Help him," the voice called again.

Cassidy squeezed her eyes shut, pressing her fists into her temples.

Mom touched her shoulder. "Cass, are you okay?"

"No. No. No. No," Cassidy muttered. *I can't help him. What am supposed to say?*

"Help him," the voice repeated flatly.

What am I supposed to — Cassidy looked to her wrist, her thumb and forefinger finding the bracelet Anessa gave her. Her vision tunneled to Anessa's dad in the crowd, still tearful, still sad, and the path she was called to take. "I'll be back," she said absentmindedly to her parents. They didn't reply, or maybe they did, and she didn't hear them as her feet carried her closer and closer to Anessa's dad. She stopped a few feet away. Haze surrounded him like a terrible, dark cloud. Unlike the angry tendrils of Anessa's haze, his were lazily swaying around him, like his sadness was different, depressed somehow.

He glanced down at her and looked back to the person he was talking to. He glanced at Cassidy twice more before pausing his conversation with a finger and a, "one sec".

"Hello… Anessa's dad." Cassidy realized after opening her mouth that she couldn't remember his first name and wasn't sure if his last name was also Chestnut. Anessa had shown her a picture of him on Facebook. Despite the haze, the resemblance to Anessa was there — something in the brown eyes. His name, however, was a blank.

He managed a slight smile. "Hi. You are?" Not only did Anessa resemble him, but she also clearly got his southern accent.

"Cassidy… I'm Cassidy."

"You can call me John." He looked toward her parents and asked like he knew, "You're here with your mom and dad?"

Cassidy nodded. She didn't know if her parents were near or not; her singular focus was Anessa's dad. Despite him trying to keep his composure, sadness radiated from him. The sound of his haze was a sorrowful storm. She dared not touch him, fearing what she would see... knowing what she would see. A touch wouldn't be necessary for what little she could do. "I was friends with Anessa."

He cleared his throat. "Anessa talked about you. You're the shoe girl."

Visions of Anessa in her bedroom the day of the shoe try-on floated through Cassidy's thoughts like ghosts, a time that was gone and only a fading memory. "Anessa was in my class in Farmington. We were," a lump formed in her throat, "we were friends."

His slight smile faded and tears formed in his eyes; his haze undulated. It was as if mentioning Anessa living in Farmington was a painful reminder of something. He wiped away the tears. "Yes, you were. And thank you. I know she needed a friend." Fake or real, he managed to find the smile again.

The bracelet. "I have something for you." She pulled the braided bracelet from her wrist and held it toward him. The dangling flamingo looked her way. "Anessa gave this to me. I want you to have it."

He studied the bracelet, taking it from her like a precious treasure. "You know what they say about flamingos."

"I do."

He chuckled. "Then you know why I want you to keep it."

She took the bracelet from his outstretched hand. "Friends forever. Right?" The bracelet fit snugly back on her wrist. She smiled at her own memory.

As she feared, Anessa's dad's sadness couldn't be cured with a simple, single interaction. Like Ms. Jennie said, not all problems could be helped. Cassidy couldn't make him better or feel happy when he had good reason to be sad, but looking into his eyes, past the haze, a kind of understanding passed between them. Their lives were touched by having Anessa in them. What little Cassidy could do to help, had helped.

"I'm going to say goodbye." Cassidy glanced over her shoulder toward the caskets.

"It was nice meetin' you, Cassidy."

"You too. And thank you for the bracelet."

He shook his head and started to say something but paused. "You're welcome. Now, don't forget to take some roses."

Cassidy nodded as she backed away.

The white tablecloth was lined with single roses of many colors. Cassidy took a pink rose from the table for Mrs. Chestnut, and a white rose for Anessa. She smelled them and tapped them on her cheek. The last person in front of her laid a rose on each casket. The power of the meditation must have faded as she heard them think, *I'll miss you,* right before they muttered it.

Cassidy slowly stepped forward and stood between the caskets. Unsure of exactly what to do, she laid a rose on each and scurried toward her parents.

She stopped midstep.

That couldn't be it. Just lay a rose and walk away. Their friendship amounted to more than just laying a rose. She took another rose from the table, a yellow one to lay for Maisy, to say a final thing to Anessa, a proper goodbye.

Cassidy stood before Anessa's casket again, holding the yellow rose above it.

"Hi, Anessa." She smiled a smile carrying the burden of heartbreak. "This rose is from Maisy. She loves yellow; I know she would have picked it for you if she could be here. If you can hear me, somehow, I miss you. You were my second-best friend." Her lip quivered before a smile returned. "Maisy would be way mad if I said you were my first." She looked around, concerned with being in someone's way, catching glances from grieving people. Mom had her arm intertwined with Dad's. They smiled her way.

Turning back to the casket, Cassidy continued, "I hope you're happy where you are… Heaven. That's where Maisy's mom says you are. I hope they have videos you can watch. And I hope everyone is really nice." She touched the flamingo pendant. "Thanks again for the bracelet. I will love it forever." It was too much to hope for, crazy even, but she listened intently for Anessa — for a word or a sign of her presence. She'd give anything to hear her voice again or see images of her life, even the bad ones. However, Cassidy's hopes were met with the sounds of the people around her.

"I'm sorry, but I have to go." Tears streamed down her cheeks; never had she felt as heartbroken at saying goodbye. "Bye, Anessa." She dropped the rose and slid her fingers across the casket as she walked away. Her walk switched to a tearful sprint into her mother's awaiting, consoling arms.

Cassidy had never thought about dying, much less how her parents would feel if anything happened to her. She was their only child. What would they do without her? Without having a child? And what about Maisy? Would Maisy feel this much hurt, or worse? Cassidy fought to rid the horrible thoughts from her mind

The drive home didn't seem as long because she slept most of the way. When they reached the driveway, she stayed in her seat as Mom and Dad took what little they had brought for the trip inside.

The last few weeks had been all about Anessa. Where was Anessa? How was Anessa feeling? Why was Anessa sad? And now…. Cassidy slumped in her seat, muscles weak. *I guess that's it.* They had gone to the funeral and made it home all in the same day, and there would be nothing else Anessa related to ever happen again. The part of her heart that Anessa had filled was an empty cavern.

A few minutes passed before Dad broke her from her daze and carried her inside like he did when she was a little kid. Usually, she wouldn't allow it, but between Ms. Jennie carrying her at school and now Dad carrying her inside, she came to again appreciate allowing herself to be carried by someone when life was a bit too much to take.

Chapter 34

The midday sun shined rays of light upon the valley. Maku sat with Kaz on the steps leading up to his veranda. As if a performer, Yama stood at the bottom of the steps repeating the words spoken by Cassidy, Maisy, and Cassidy's parents during the week after Anessa's death. After the last word squeaked from his mouth, his ears dropped limply to his sides, and he released a mournful-sounding sigh. Hearing their sorrow-filled words and then having to repeat them seemed nearly more than he could endure. He bolted for Maku and curled into a ball in her arms, wrapping his ears around himself like a blanket.

Kaz sat motionless, trying to find the sense in it all. He had never known anyone to die as young as Anessa. In fact, other than his parents, he didn't know of anyone who had died. People in his world lived long lives. Thoughts of Anessa had led him to thoughts of his parents and painful feelings. His brow furrowed as he slowly touched his face.

Tentatively he wiped away a single, trickling tear. He stared at his wet finger questioningly. "My parents are dead," he muttered. He knew that. Of course he knew. He often paid his respects to them at the shrine in his home. But tears? He felt strange.

He woke from his stupor and looked up at Maku with Yama in her arms. Tears fell from Maku's eyes, soaking Yama's fur, he pawed at his own tears wetting the fur below his eyes.

Kaz stood and showed them his tear-soaked finger. They examined it through their own tear-filled eyes, offering neither reassurance nor answers. He cleared his throat and released a shaky breath. "What's — What's going on? Why do I have tears?" He shook his hand, flinging away the tear. He peered into the distance, digging his fingers into his scalp. "Why do I feel this way? What is this feeling?"

Maku wore an uncommon frown; tears slid down her face and pooled in the corners of her mouth before rolling down and falling from her chin. Yama climbed up and curled around her neck like a shawl, freeing her hands. "I forgot this feeling," she signed. A vertical line creased the space between her eyes. "It's been so long."

"A very long time," Yama added in an unknown voice.

"We're… sad," Maku signed.

"Sad," Kaz repeated the word that was foreign to him. He had experienced happiness, frustration, anger, and, secretly, envy. Sadness, however, had been absent from his life, not even a consideration. Memories trickled into his mind, memories of his parents. They weren't much and weren't clear, but they were there. More tears formed and slid to his quivering lip.

Maku waved her hand to get Kaz's attention. "I don't understand what's going on. I'm so sad for you and for Cassidy, and I don't know what to do."

Something strange was happening, and whatever control Kaz had over the situation was falling apart.

"What do we do? Maku asked.

"I… I…." What did they expect from him? He didn't have an answer for this. He wanted to run to his room, curl up on his bed, and hide from this sadness until it went away.

Yama appeared desperate, awaiting an answer.

"We have to do something," Maku signed.

Scanning the surroundings offered no solace or immediate answer to Kaz. *What do we do? What do I do? Was this part of what Iwa meant when she said things could get worse? Iwa! Of course!* "I'll tell Iwa."

Maku and Yama nodded vigorously.

"She'll know what to do. She'll know what's going on." He turned and took two urgent steps before a noise stopped him. In the distance rose a shrill voice. Not a cry, but a word yelled again and again. The voice became clearer and more audible as the seconds passed. A moment later, a young boy ran up to the steps leading to the veranda, screaming the word, a name.

"Kazuyasu-san," the boy said urgently, doubled over, gasping for breath. It was Michihiro, a kid two years younger than Kaz. They were playmates until Iwa left. Kaz then decided he no longer had time for 'kid stuff' and vowed to follow the path of becoming a samurai.

"Michihiro-kun. What's wrong? Why are you yelling my name?"

Michihiro, with his hands on his knees, fought for words as his lungs fought for air. "Ka — Kazuyasu-san."

Kaz's brow furrowed. "Yes, that's my name. I got that part. What is wrong?"

The boy stood upright, bowed, and took two deep breaths. "The samurai… there's… there's something wrong. Someone… is hurt. At the southern guard post."

Kaz's expression hardened as his hand slid to the hilt of his katana. "Someone's hurt, and the samurai asked you to find me? They need my help?"

Michihiro stood openmouthed as if Kaz claimed to have ridden on the back of a dragon. "What? No."

Kaz frowned; his shoulders drooped.

"They didn't say anything about you," Michihiro continued.

Kaz scowled and waved his hand in front of Michihiro's face. "Okay, okay, enough. Then why are you here?"

Michihiro, now in complete control of his breath, stood tall with his chest out and chin high. "Because you are my samurai. They may need your help." His posture broke as he leaned in toward Kaz. "Wait. Why are your eyes red? Allergies?"

Kaz's eyes narrowed as he regained his stature. Maku's and Yama's sad expressions had changed to ones of worried anticipation. "This is more urgent. I'll go to Iwa after. Follow me." He sprinted away.

Michihiro followed. Yama jumped to the floor and ran next to Maku. They ran for nearly fifteen minutes under the midday blue sky to reach their destination, which was a twenty-minute run from the barrier surrounding their mountain and valley.

A crowd of samurai and villagers came into view as the motley group neared one of the many typically quiet guard posts. Kaz, Michi, Maku, and Yama reached the end of the grass field, ran onto a gravel path, and stopped at the crowd. Some of the villagers and samurai in the crowd briefly acknowledged their presence.

"What's happened here?" Kaz asked, catching his breath.

Two villagers looked down at Kaz dismissively and returned to their conversation.

Kaz scowled and huffed. "Wait here," he said to Michi, Yama, and Maku. "Let me find a way through." He walked to the right and left of the impenetrable wall of bodies surrounding the focus of attention. "Excuse me. Let me through," he ordered, receiving no response.

He ran up to and bowed to two samurai, who had their swords sheathed. "What happened here?" he asked.

The samurai glowered. One of them waved Kaz off. "This is no place for a child."

Kaz gritted his teeth, his hands forming fists, and stood on the tips of his toes. "Let me through!" he yelled, loud enough for everyone in the crowd to hear, and possibly anyone still in the village more than a mile away. Bothered faces turned to show their displeasure. "Go home" and "keep quiet" were some of the words hurled at Kaz.

Another voice came from the crowd, one softer and kinder that cut through the conglomeration of bodies. "Is that Kazuyasu? Let him through. Let him through," Iwa yelled.

The crowd slowly parted, forming a path. At the end were Iwa, Wada Nakataka — samurai and lord of the village — and a samurai slumped to the ground with his back against a short cobblestone wall.

As Kaz drew closer, he recognized the downed samurai as Hayashi Kagenaka. His eyes were open terrifyingly wide, the pupils white and swirling like a milky universe lived within them. His kimono and hakama were clean and untorn, and his katana sheathed. *He didn't draw his sword. There was no battle.*

"Wada-sama," Kaz addressed respectfully and bowed deeply. Wada, a giant of a man, wasn't wearing his armor; surely he wasn't planning for battle. Instead, he wore a grey linen kimono with a black sash and matching grey hakama. A single katana was tucked into the black sash around his waist and hung horizontally to the ground. His black hair with streaks of silver was pulled back into a topknot. Wada acknowledged Kaz with only a glance.

"Iwa-sama," Kaz said, bowing to her. Iwa's next expected visit was weeks away, but here she was. Someone else must have alerted her, or somehow she knew. "Wha — What's happened here?"

Wada looked to Iwa.

Iwa wore an orange linen kimono, a yellow sash, and white trousers underneath. She had tan, wrinkled skin and long white hair tied into a bun on top of her head. She was kneeling next to Hayashi with her hand on his shoulder and a worried expression. She spoke softly, her voice raspy. "We're not entirely sure." She removed her hand from Hayashi's shoulder, returned it, and repeated. "I can't see clearly."

"You're still losing your powers?" Kaz asked, concerned. Iwa had explained to Kaz that from the moment of Cassidy's birth, her powers had begun to lessen, and when the power fully activated within Cassidy, Iwa's own powers would rapidly decline. If she couldn't see what happened to Hayashi, then her powers had lessened significantly since her last visit.

Iwa sighed. "Yes. I'm afraid I am. And it's gotten worse in the last couple of weeks." She looked mournfully at Hayashi. The samurai lay unresponsive, the pupils of his eyes still swirling, still ghostly.

"Is the barrier… is it still there, still protecting us?"

Iwa frowned. "I meditated on it this morning, just like every morning. However, with my powers mostly gone," she shrugged, "I can't be sure."

The crowd murmured worries of the barrier protecting them being gone, something they knew would eventually happen. Iwa had told them she would do everything in her power to keep the barrier in place and everyone protected. So far she had succeeded, but help from Cassidy was part of the contingency plan.

Iwa narrowed her eyes at Kaz. "Your eyes… have you been crying?"

Kaz considered the word, crying, and opened his mouth to answer, but Wada interrupted, speaking in a deep, commanding voice. "I've sent two groups of samurai to check the status of the wall. They are to report back to me before sunset."

Kaz clutched his hands as he turned in a circle, the eyes of some of the crowd meeting his. What could he do? What knowledge could he summon on what or who could have done this to Hayashi? How could he help? Someone in the crowd mentioned seeing a giant raven in the sky. Most everyone laughed away the comment. He considered this bit of knowledge, but giant ravens didn't live in the valley or these mountains. Besides, a raven couldn't do this, not even a giant one. A horde of ideas bumped around his brain, but none of them were good. His eyes settled on Iwa's. "What do we do?"

Iwa pivoted on her knee, placed her hand on Kaz's shoulder, and squeezed. "It's time. Go get her. Bring her here."

Kaz's eyes widened. "Her? N-now?"

She looked to Wada, who nodded, then turned back to Kaz. "Yes. Now. Go. Hurry."

Kaz looked to Wada for permission. "May I go, Lord?"

Devoid of emotion, Wada waved a hand at him. "Go."

Kaz shuttered a gasp and bowed. His weak legs struggled to keep him upright. *I can't believe Wada-sama has given me an order. My first order as a —*

"Go. Now," Wada again ordered.

Kaz straightened and turned urgently to run, only to stumble and fall on his backside. He clambered to his feet and darted from the crowd. "Come on! Let's go!" he yelled to his friends as he ran past. Over his shoulder, he added, "Maku, hurry ahead and get the mirror. Bring it to the grove."

Chapter 35

Cassidy, ready for bed, yelled goodnight to her parents who were downstairs popping buttery popcorn for an at-home movie night. She reached for the light switch but paused, eyeing the calligraphy box sitting on her dresser. A wave of guilt washed over her. She hadn't been able to bring herself to look at the journal, much less read it. After Anessa died, she wanted nothing to do with her power. Why read and study the journal if she was out of the helping-sad-people-business? At least, she hoped it was that easy — just stop helping. However, the journal never mentioned a way to hide from the thoughts and sadness. Iwa's power grew without any control on her part. Like Dad said, maybe this was her path, whether she wanted it to be or not.

She clicked off the light and hopped into bed, pulling the covers over her head. The tablet screen, the only light in the room, illuminated the sheets above her. The week after losing Anessa was over, as was the weekend of her funeral. Back to school tomorrow. Back to life as if nothing had happened. Life would carry on without Anessa. *I wonder what she wanted to be when she grew up? I wish I would have asked her.*

Cassidy hadn't stopped to think about it since the funeral, but the voice, that annoying inner voice that had been there since the first day she saw Anessa, was gone. It made sense that it was gone, with no one sad around, other than herself. What sad person would she unexpectedly run into next, bringing back the voice and the undeniable desire to help? The thought tied her stomach into an uncomfortable, tight knot.

Ring.

Maisy's avatar illuminated the bottom left of the tablet. Cassidy smiled and eagerly pressed the image. Maisy's beaming face filled the screen.

"Hi, Maze."

"Hi, sis."

"Whatcha up to?"

Cassidy's head drooped. "Just trying to avoid thinking about going back to school."

Maisy scrunched her face. "I bet. *But,* it will be great to have you back. I've missed my girl."

Cassidy giggled. "I've missed you too."

"Sidewalk tomorrow morning?"

"Yep. Sidewalk."

"Kay. See you there."

Cassidy wasn't ready to say goodnight. Not yet. She wanted to find the words that would fix everything, all the wrong she had done but wasn't quite sure what exactly to say. "Hey… Maze?"

"Yeah?"

"I wanted to — It's just... I'm sorry, again, for putting you second."

Maisy's expression softened. "It's okay. You were trying to be a good friend to Anessa. I get it."

Cassidy smiled warmly. "You get it because *you're* a good friend."

Maisy unleashed a smile. "The greatest." Her smile faded. "Besides, I have other stuff on my mind, ya know?"

"Like what?" Cassidy asked, concerned.

"*Loads,*" Maisy said. "We can talk about it tomorrow if you want." She paused and continued tentatively. "If it's not too much."

Maisy's glow had diminished from where it was at the start of school, when all was right in the world. However, it was still there, still visible, and still keeping Cassidy from knowing what was on her mind. Cassidy would have to find out the old-fashioned way by talking to Maisy, and she loved that thought.

"Sure, tomorrow."

"Thanks." Maisy brightened. "Hey. Did you see the email I sent?"

"No. What email?"

Maisy smiled, like a gifter knowing the contents of a wrapped present. "Just check it out. See ya tomorrow."

"Okay. Night Maze."

"Night, Cass."

Maisy's pixelated face left the tablet screen, and Cassidy fervently clicked the inbox and opened the email from Maisy. The subject line read "Memories" followed by a smiley face emoji. She clicked the attachment. After a few seconds of the Wi-Fi working its magic, a photograph stretched across the screen of her tablet. It was the photo Maisy's dad took after the dance competition. Maisy was an image of accomplishment wearing her tiara and sash, and…. Goosebumps rose on Cassidy's arms. Anessa was in the photo, smiling, happy, and better than that, the haze, the awful haze, wasn't there. Apparently, the haze couldn't be captured in photos, not even for her to see. Cassidy reveled in the idea of having an image of Anessa to keep for the rest of her life. She would cherish it and the bracelet, always. Touching the image of Anessa with the tip of her pointer finger, she smiled wistfully and tapped the tablet off.

Her room fell dark except for a faint light from outside. Sadness crept in as she stared glumly at the lifeless tablet. The distractions of Maisy and the photo were gone, leaving the impending of tomorrow to fill the vacancy of her thoughts, like a monster climbing out from a dark place. Tomorrow would be like the first day of the rest of the school year.

After a minute of silence, she let her mind wander. Maybe she was trying to forget. Maybe she was avoiding sleep. Maybe she was avoiding —

Scrape.

Cassidy's eyes widened. *What was that?* She laid silent, motionless, waiting for whatever made the noise to make it again. Seconds passed. It didn't.

Slowly, she pulled the sheet from her head and pushed her hair from her face. Darkness shrouded the room, creating indiscernible shapes. *I need light to figure out what made the noise.* She swallowed. *I have to leave the bed.*

Her hands trembled and her heart raced as she slowly slid from the bed until her feet met the soft cushiness of the rug. Her eyes adjusted slightly, allowing the dark shapes to become recognizable objects and furniture instead of one of many impossible monsters from books and movies. She pulled the cover and blanket from her lap and stood motionless, as if whatever made the noise would make it again based on her lack of movement. It was silent aside from the hint of deep bass coming from the theater room two floors below.

She reached for the lamp, clicked it on, and hastily swiveled, scanning the room for something, anything. Nothing was there, no monster, no stranger, no eight-headed dragon, no jerk in the box. She exhaled a long-held breath.

Cassidy crept around her room, searching for anything that could have made the sound. She peeked into her closet, unsure of anything in it that would be scraping, but she wanted to be thorough. Mom had once told her, "If you ever leave something out of the equation, it could be the thing that costs you." Her mom was probably speaking financially, but it also applied to life. Like when searching for the source of scary noises.

Nearly giving up finding the noisemaker, the writing box caught her eye. She moved closer. It was still on the dresser, but not how she had left it. Something had clearly moved it, which was a frightening thought, or, thinking more crazily, it had moved itself. Slowly she reached for the box as if sneaking up to catch a bird. Her fingertips brushed along the smooth lacquered wood, and to her relief, nothing happened. It didn't come to life and introduce itself, apologizing for spying on her the whole time. She pushed the box back into place.

Scrape.

Cassidy's eyes widened as her breath left her. *That was the sound. It was the box.* Her eyes bulged. *Something moved it.* She wanted to run screaming to her parents, to hide between them in their bed as she did as a child after a nightmare, during a lightning storm, or after hearing a strange noise. But she didn't run to her parent's bed. They weren't in it anyway, and she didn't —

A burst of bright light shredded the near darkness of her room, sending a jagged spray of yellow across her, the wall above the dresser, and the ceiling. Cassidy screamed and swiveled, raising her hands to shield her eyes; light seeped through the spaces between her fingers.

Unless she was dreaming or crazy, sunlight was pouring into her room. But how was there sunlight? She was in bed minutes ago, ready for sleep. The moon was out, the stars. Her fingers spread, increasing her view. "What the Frappuccino?"

She allowed her hands to fall from her squinting eyes, rapidly adjusting to the bright daylight. The smell of earth poured into her room. A jagged line wide enough to walk through appeared to have been cut between her world and somewhere else, some other world. In the other world, long grass swayed underneath a tree with... pink blooms. *Cherry blossoms.* Her jaw dropped as a boy walked through the opening and into her room.

The boy stared at her, mirroring her surprise. Then his eyes narrowed. "Ca — Cassidy-chan?"

He said my name. How does he know my name? She hugged herself. "Yeah... yes."

He nodded once and extended his hand toward her. "C-come with me," he stuttered. "We need your help."

Cassidy stepped back, fighting the urge to scream for her parents. He *was* just a boy, twelve years old, thirteen maybe, and wearing what looked like a kimono. Unmistakably, a warm glow surrounded him. It wasn't blinding, but more like Maisy's. He had an accent as if English was not his first language. *Why does he seem familiar? He doesn't look danger — Wait. Is that a sword? Oh my gosh, this is crazy. That is a sword.* "Come with you? Where?"

He pulled back his hand and shrugged. "To my village, of course. Something... has happened."

Of course, to your village. How stupid of me. Cassidy looked at him in disbelief. "I can't just go with you. I don't even know you."

He grunted; his expression hardened. "I am Shimamura Kazuyasu. I am a samurai."

Her mind stumbled over his name. "Shima Kazuwhatsu?"

He waved a hand dismissively. "People call me Kaz; use it for now."

"Kaz. Got it." She regarded him carefully. "And, *you're a samurai?*"

He rolled his eyes.

"But you're just a —"

"Yes, yes. I am only a kid." He stepped closer. "Please, listen. Iwa sent me to get you. We must —"

Cassidy flinched. "Iwa? Did you say Iwa?"

He nodded once, firmly.

"You… know Iwa?" She blinked hard. "Wait. She's alive?"

"Yes." He huffed. "You ask many questions. But there is no time. We must go, now."

"Cassidy!" Mom yelled from downstairs.

Kaz stepped back and nervously glanced at what could only be described as a portal to another world.

Cassidy put a finger to her lips under wide eyes. "Yeah, Mom?"

"You okay in there?"

"Yes. Sorry. I just… scared myself." *Scared myself? Worst excuse ever.*

"Oookay. Let's get that light off."

Do you mean the light from another place, the light from another world? "Yes, ma'am."

"Goodnight."

"Night."

Kaz appeared ready to jump back into the world he stepped from.

"I can't go with you. My parents will see that I'm gone and think I've been kidnapped or something," Cassidy said.

"It will not take too long. They… your parents will think you are sleeping."

Cassidy laughed to herself and shook her head. With everything that had happened so far – hearing thoughts, seeing sadness – this moment topped it all. A boy literally walked into her bedroom from a hole to somewhere else. *Iwa. He knows Iwa.* She shook her head the moment she decided she just might go with him.

"But how do I go and how will I get back."

Kaz shook his head. "I will understand, I mean, explain later." His head bobbed side to side. "Well, Iwa will. It is complicated."

"Complicated. Of course." She looked down at her pink pajamas — *I can't go anywhere dressed like this* — and held up a finger. "One minute." She stepped into the closet and closed the door. A minute later, she emerged wearing a t-shirt that read 'Nachos Is My Favorite Food Group', jeans, and checkered Vans.

"Okay, I'm —" She paused. Kaz was smiling as he dug his toes into the rug.

He caught her staring and quickly looked away as he clumsily slipped back into his sandal, tying the rope around his ankle. "It *is* soft," he muttered. "You, uh, ready?"

Was she really going into what appeared to be another world with a boy she just met? Maybe the other world was Japan. That would explain his clothes. He looked Japanese, which made sense because he said he was a samurai, but samurai weren't a thing anymore. Were they? He claimed that Iwa sent him, which was crazy because she would be like 400 years old. What if Cassidy's many greats grandmother really needed her help? *What would Dad do? No, that would be boring. What would Sue do? I didn't get to the part of the book where she battled the eight-headed dragon. Ugh, I read too slow. What would I do? What should I do?*

Cassidy had been on an emotional roller-coaster. She started a new school year, inherited a not-so-fun ancient power, and struggled with helping a new friend while having a best friend. Her reward was finally helping Anessa, only to lose her. She had been through more turmoil and tragedy in one month than she had experienced in her entire life. 'That day' that had defined her and how she lived her life was nothing compared to the death of a friend. Yet, despite it all, her confidence had grown. She had become mentally stronger even though the world was still a scary place, scarier even. Ms. Jennie said she had blank pages to fill in her story. Cassidy knew what she had to do.

She stood firm, squared her shoulders, and nodded. "I'm ready."

"Right. You need one more thing. A stone or a gem." He pulled at a chain hanging from his neck until a golden amulet slid *from* underneath his top. An image of a dragon was carved into the center. "Something solid. Something…" His face strained as he tapped the side of his head. Like he had solved a brainteaser, he excitedly pointed at her. "Permanent."

Her eyes narrowed. "Why?"

"It is so you will have a," his brow furrowed, "connection to your world. Iwa can —"

"Iwa can explain. It's complicated. Right." She tapped her lips in thought. "Oh, I know. Just a sec." She rummaged around in the closet and stepped back out with a pet rock — complete with smiley face and googly eyes — in hand. She and Maisy had made some a couple of summers ago, and her rock had found its way to the corner of her closet, where forgotten things were stored. "I got it. A pet rock I made with Maisy."

"Yes," he nodded thoughtfully. "Maisy. I like her."

She blinked and tilted her head. "Wait, how do you know Maisy?"

He averted his eyes, mumbled something, then regained his composure. "Later. I will explain later. We have to go." He reached out his hand, silently asking her to take it.

"Wait. One more thing. Just in case." Cassidy rummaged around in the top drawer of her desk, grabbed a pencil and a blank piece of paper, and wrote: *Hi, Mom and Dad. If you found this and, surprise, I am not in my bed, I will be back soon. I promise. I have not been kidnapped. This has to do with Iwa and the mirror. Don't worry. Cassidy*

She placed the paper on the desk and the pencil on top. She bit her lower lip and looked around her room, saying a silent goodbye. *I'm really doing this.* "This is crazy," she muttered, shaking her head. *No,* she thought. *Be brave.* With a deep breath, she slipped the pet rock into her pocket and gripped Kaz's hand.

"Right. We go." He turned and quickly stepped into the light, Cassidy following with a jerk as the slack in their arms reached the limit.

She stepped into the light of the sun and onto a field of lush green grass. The slice of darkness behind her, her room and way back, sealed shut and disappeared. Cassidy reached for where it was, only to touch warm empty air. She gasped. "It's gone."

"Do not worry," Kaz said. "It is there, but difficult to see."

Her sweaty palms and rapid heartbeat revealed her worry, but she didn't have time for worry. Iwa was alive and needed her; she was set on finding out why.

A grove of cherry blossom trees was in full bloom only yards away, like an explosion of pink. The trees stood in perfectly spaced rows, resembling a hundred soldiers lined up for some kind of naturistic war. Above was the clearest, bluest sky she had ever seen. Towering snow-capped mountains cut across the horizon.

Wait. Is this Heaven? Am I dead, and that's why Iwa is here? Cassidy squeezed her eyes shut, and opened them after a few shakes of her head. *I can't be dead. I was just in my room talking to Maisy, not skydiving or anything crazy.* She faced Kaz, who was watching her as she adjusted to the surroundings. "Where is this? Where are we?"

"You are in the valley of my village, my home," he said.

Cassidy started to ask another question but stopped to admire a butterfly fluttering between them in jerky movements. She lifted her hand as the butterfly came closer and perched on her index finger as softly as a snowflake falling on a blossom. The butterfly's delicate wings were a splattering of colors; blue, white, brown, and green. She smiled and imagined it smiled back. Maybe it did. Kaz was studying her and muttered something in Japanese.

"Whadya say?" she asked.

He shook his head. "Nothing. Forget it. Ready?"

The butterfly, seemingly sensing her pending exit, flew from her finger. She waved goodbye as it disappeared into the cherry blossom trees amongst the hundreds of bees furiously buzzing in and around the pink blooms. Settling her gaze forward with her chin held high, she nodded. "Ready."

"Okay, follow." Kaz took off running. "Try to keep up."

Cassidy did her best to keep up him. He effortlessly navigated the tall grass while she plodded through like her feet were sinking in sand with each step. He stopped every time he got too far ahead and waited for her to get close.

He crossed his arms the third time he had to stop. "Come on. Hurry."

"Sorry. I don't have a lot of experience running in tall grass," Cassidy said. She remained polite but was bordering on telling him to stop being rude.

The grass shortened after another three minutes of running, and their pace increased; Cassidy nearly kept up with Kaz. Instead of watching her footing, her eyes devoured the hilly landscape, the tall mountains in almost every direction, and the brilliant blue sky. An exhilarating feeling coursed through her, a surge of energy she couldn't explain. Her senses heightened to a sharp point. Everything inside and out of her was in focus. A feeling swelled within her she couldn't quite describe. It was like she could do or be whatever she wanted to be, whatever she needed to be. She pulled even with Kaz and smiled at him. He looked surprised, then smirked as he started to slow.

He nodded ahead. "We are nearly there."

"Where?" It was the only word needed for her question and the only one she could manage to say after all reasonable thought escaped her. Her mouth gaped as she stared at three figures standing only yards away — a boy close to her age, surrounded by a glow, a frightening and strangely familiar looking girl with flowy, long black hair, and a long-eared fox or bunny looking thing that was... smiling at her. *Do fox-bunnies smile? Do fox-bunnies exist?* Kaz looked at the curious trio like nothing at all was out of the ordinary. Like he knew them.

"Cassidy, these are my friends. Michi, Maku, and Yama. Everyone, this is Cassidy."

She gave a quick wave to the three strangers looking at her, feeling like the new kid in the neighborhood, which she was. "Nice to meet you."

Michi bashfully said hello; Maku touched her hand to her forehead like a salute, then excitedly shook her hands at her side; Yama said, "Hey Cass," in Maisy's voice.

Cassidy blinked and blinked again. "Did —" Her questioning look was met by Kaz's awkward grin. "Did that, whatever it is, just say hi to me in Maisy's voice?"

Yama looked at the ground and intertwined his ears behind his back. Maku covered her mouth with both hands, her eyes wide.

"I will explain, but later," Kaz said.

Cassidy looked at him incredulously. "How much will you have to explain later?"

He scratched the back of his neck. "A lot, I fear. I promise I will, but Iwa needs you."

With the new experiences and acquaintances, Cassidy had forgotten about Iwa. She would soon meet the person responsible for all of this. She had read about Iwa's life not long ago, believing her life ended hundreds of years ago. None of this seemed real to Cassidy but questioning her current situation and surroundings would not get her anywhere. She refocused on the reason she stepped into this world to begin with. "Which way?"

Kaz appeared to be silently admonishing his friends but stopped and pointed to her right. "That way. Straight ahead."

Cassidy inhaled deeply, sprinted away, and yelled "Keep up," over her shoulder.

A minute later, a crowd of people came into view. Cassidy slowed and stopped on a gravel path as dozens of strangers turned to look at her, hundreds of eyes simultaneously examining her. She blinked once, hard. "Wow." Nearly everyone in the crowd wore a warm glow, and being tightly crowded, they resembled one big ball of light. "This must be the happiest place on… wherever this is."

The padding of feet and paws reached Cassidy. Kaz and Michi stopped on her left, Maku and Yama stopped at her right. They each offered a gentle smile, even the fox thing — she was sure it was a smile this time. Kaz nodded sideways toward the crowd that parted for an elderly woman with blue eyes.

Cassidy gasped. "Iwa."

Kaz nodded in her peripheral.

Iwa strode with a hitch in her step toward Cassidy, not once taking her blue eyes from her. Stopping a couple of steps away, she smiled warmly and bowed. "Cassidy-chan. It is nice to meet you."

Cassidy shook her head disbelievingly while performing an awkward bow. "Iwa? How is it you? How — How are you here? How are you alive?"

"We have so much to discuss. You've grown so much since the last time I saw you."

Cassidy's brow furrowed. "Since the last... what?"

"We will talk about it later."

Cassidy raised her eyebrows and gave Kaz and Iwa pointed stares. "We really need to talk later, because I have questions. A lot of questions."

A voice called out. On the far end of the crowd, a tall man wearing a sword at his waist, like Kaz's, was helping steady a man sitting atop a short stone wall. Heat rose in Cassidy's chest, all other sounds around her muffling, leaving space for the voice in her head that urged her forward, pushing her to help. After a first hesitant step, she strode forward with purpose. Like looking through a wrapping paper tube, her pinpoint focus was on the man steadying himself and rubbing the back of his neck. He said something in Japanese, which was an immediate and unanticipated problem. How could she possibly help him if she couldn't understand him?

She did her best to ignore the crowd's eyes on her and their combined blinding glow. Her concern was for the man in distress. She stopped before the tall man with the sword and the man who drew her in like gravity. The tall man looked at her curiously, then nodded, and in a deep voice said, "Cassidy-chan."

Iwa came to stand at her side. The tall man said something to Iwa, and she to him.

Something was wrong with the man atop the stone wall, but it wasn't the familiar sadness, it was uncertainty… fear. *What the Frappuccino?* Had she somehow gone from only seeing sadness to seeing other emotions? A hand touched her shoulder, and Cassidy met Iwa's eyes.

"I need your help," Iwa said.

"How can I help? What can I do that you can't?"

"Much more, now. Sadly, my powers are mostly gone. You have them now."

"What? How?" Cassidy asked.

"I did not know at first, but when I felt my powers weaken after you were born, I consulted the satori. It explained that my powers would lessen as yours grew, until eventually, I would have none. Now, I am all but powerless. You have taken my place."

"I'm… I'm sorry I didn't know. I didn't even know you were still alive."

"There is no need for apology."

"I don't understand why."

Iwa smiled mournfully. "I promise I will tell you more later, but for now, we need your help."

"I still don't understand how I can help." Cassidy pointed to the man sitting on the wall, still wavering as if he were floating atop a raft in the middle of a pool. "He's not sad. He's… confused or scared. I'm not sure how I know that, but I do."

"Cassidy, believe me when I tell you this. You can do much more than you know. You are more *powerful* than you know."

Cassidy mulled over Iwa's claim. Somehow, she knew it was true. This greater power grew within her the moment she stepped into this world, and it seemed to grow with every step after. An energy she had never felt burned inside her. Without further direction from Iwa, Cassidy stepped closer to the sitting man.

"He has no memory of what happened, but we believe he was attacked," Iwa said. "We need to know by what."

"Sir, I'm going to touch your shoulder," Cassidy said. "I need to see what you saw."

Iwa translated for Cassidy. The man looked up at Cassidy with unfocused eyes, nodding before his head slumped again. Iwa nodded her okay to proceed.

Cassidy flexed her fingers as she took two deep breaths. Despite the newfound power growing within her, a tinge of uncertainty lingered. Did she really want to see what had attacked the man and experience his emotions? She had felt the emotional drain after experiencing Anessa's sad moments. How would she feel after seeing whatever was in this man's memory?

Taking a final breath, Cassidy tentatively reached forward until her hand met his shoulder. With a sharp inhale, the outside world vanished, and she was transported into the man's mind and memories. She narrated the vision as it unfolded before her.

"He is sitting on a stool in a small room or building. It looks like a hut. He sees something looking at him from a window. An animal with silver eyes. He yelled and fell backward off the stool. He's stumbling around… now he's up and running from the hut. He… he's confused. He's shielding his eyes from the sun. Something… the animal came from the other side of the hut. It's growling at him. He's saying something to it. It —" Cassidy yelped and jumped backward, her heart pounding.

"What did he say?" Iwa asked.

Cassidy looked around wildly, scanning her surroundings for the frightening creature. Her eyes landed on the crowd, a concerned Kaz, Maku, Michi, Yama, and then found Iwa's gaze.

"Cassidy. Be calm." Iwa grabbed her wrist. "Be calm."

Cassidy's rapid breathing eased along with her fear. She wiped away a layer of sweat from her forehead and sat on the stone wall next to the man.

"What was it? What did this to him?" Iwa asked.

Nothing the man said was familiar to Cassidy. In Japanese, she didn't know a noun from a verb. She replayed his words in her mind, focusing on what he said when the creature revealed itself with silvery, piercing eyes. *What was that word?* "Cat? I think he said Cat-something."

"He said Cat?" Iwa asked.

The creature didn't look like any cat Cassidy knew. It was not a tiger, lion, or even a house cat. It looked more like a wolf or fox. Cassidy closed her eyes and shook her head. "No. It wasn't cat, it was something else."

She replayed the end of the vision in her mind and focused only on the man's voice. The word was clear this time, though unfamiliar to her. "It wasn't Cat, it was Kit. He said, Kitsoonay."

Iwa and the tall man repeated the word in unison, evoking gasps and murmurs from the crowd. Everyone wore a fearful expression, except for the tall man who was now gripping his sword's handle, still at his waist. Cassidy wasn't entirely sure what a kitsoonay was or if she had pronounced it correctly, however clearly, it was something to fear. In less than thirty minutes after entering this amazing new world, its beauty and wonder had been tarnished. Cassidy now knew one thing with absolute certainty: this world was not safe.

Chapter 36

Niji was first to the poison fire coral garden and the barrier. The night before, she had told the siblings the general location, and the empress sent her ahead to scout the area. If anything was suspicious or out of place, she was to backtrack and warn them.

Before leaving on the journey, she attempted to temper the sibling's inflated expectations, fearing the opening would seal itself shut before they could reach it. Her importance to the siblings wouldn't save her from a disappointed empress. The empress wouldn't harm Niji physically, but to make a point, she didn't need to. Losing favor with the empress and being treated lower than the lowest class, practically worthless, was a great teacher in not screwing up.

Niji sighed in relief — the barrier hole was there as she left it. She munched a piece of poison fire coral as she watched the opening to the Gadian Mountains. It hadn't changed much; maybe it had grown in the slightest. She marked it for easier detection by laying a piece of red cloth across it. Half of the fabric was on her side, half was on the other. The half on the mountainside flitted from the push of a gentle, cool breeze.

Niji had never been on the other side of the barrier; the barrier had been in place for the entirety of her life. The siblings saved her when she was just a pup after losing her parents when things went bad with the invaders of the valley. When the banishment from the valley came, the siblings gave her shelter and protection.

The siblings had known Niji's mother; she had been their friend. They said she had been killed by the invaders. They did not say much about her father other than admitting their disapproval of him. They didn't say he was dead exactly, just gone. Niji didn't care that he was gone. He was the reason she was such a freak. She was not one thing or another. She was some type of mutt who apparently would now and forever have a single tail. Maybe her father was alive and on the other side of the barrier. If so, did he care that she was gone? Did he even know she existed? When she crossed the barrier, she would hunt him down. She would ask him those questions. Those and many more.

Niji's head swiveled at the snap of a branch. Behind her, the emperor and empress paraded into the moss-covered clearing. The emperor wore his standard linen kimono and sash in shades of brown and green. The empress wore a green silk kimono that hung just above her ankles and a brown sash around her waist. Uncharacteristically, they traveled without guard. Access to the mountains and valley for now remained a secret between the three of them. Five, including the clown and crow, but Niji ignored that fact.

They carefully navigated the fungus garden, stepping over and between the red finger-like protrusions. The emperor stopped at the large cedar tree in the center, placing a hand upon it. "Hello, my friend," he said.

The empress rolled her eyes out of his view but gave him the moment. With the tree greeting complete, they joined Niji standing before the shrubs obscuring the barrier hole.

"Niji," the empress said. "I pray this is the location and that the hole in the barrier remains?"

Niji nodded, pushing the poison fire coral to the inside of her cheek with her tongue. "Yes. It's just behind these shrubs. I've marked it with a red sash."

The empress looked to her brother and nodded toward the shrubs.

"Of course," the emperor said. He approached the shrubs and passed his right hand across their leaves as if petting an animal. He whispered something and stepped back.

The shrubs' branches and leaves shuddered, and one by one their roots popped from the ground, flinging dirt and debris into the air. The exposed roots pressed onto the ground, lifting the shrubs from the earth, and walked a few yards away. The roots dug into the new soil like hungry worms, replanting themselves. With the shrubs removed, the red sash-marked hole was in clear view. The siblings gasped.

The empress brought her hand to her mouth, gently touching her lips. "There it is, brother. Our passage to redemption and revenge."

The emperor's eyes grew wide as he reached toward the opening. "I can feel them. I can hear them. My cherry blossoms are calling to me." Tears pooled in his eyes. "We've been apart far too long."

"What…" Niji said tentatively, fearing interrupting their moment, "is our plan? Shall I enter —"

"We wait for Yurei to return," the empress said.

Niji blinked, then shook her head. "Yurei? What about Yurei?"

The empress looked down at Niji as if the question was ridiculous. "We informed Yurei of the location and sent him ahead to scout the other side."

Niji dug her claws into the dirt and pressed her lips shut for several tense moments to prevent herself from saying something she would regret. And, she had something to say, and it indeed would be regretful. With nothing kind to say, she replied with gritted teeth, "Yurei. Of course."

Niji stood just behind the siblings so she could secretly glower at them. Her ears rolled up like two balled fists. She had offered to enter the opening for a scouting trip to surveil the land and report back, but the empress had expressed concerns

Niji thought she had put to rest their concerns about her ability to avoid, and if necessary, escape capture. She had assured them that she had never been caught. Well, except for last night by Tsurugi… and the other day by Sureto… but the empress didn't need to know that.

Venturing into the valley was Niji's right; she had found the opening and was nearly eaten after doing so. Scouting the valley would have been her opportunity to show her worth. But instead, they had sent the spirit kitsune, Kaze no Yurei. Sure, Yurei was an obvious choice for the job. He was fast, stealthy, and had useful powers if he were caught or seen. But his hearing was no match for Niji's, not even close, and his fur could not change color to match the surroundings. Secretly, she hoped he would be caught. Nothing more. She didn't want harm to come to Yurei. But, if he were captured, maybe that would teach the siblings a lesson for not believing in her.

The empress wrung her hands as her foot rapidly tapped the ground. "Where could he be?" she huffed. "How long has it been?"

"Not all that long, sister," the emperor said, attempting to soothe her. His voice had that effect on most. "Find your patience."

"It should have been me," the empress said, scowling. "I should have gone. The only way I can ensure something is done properly is to do it myself."

"That's nonsense," the emperor countered in his slow, even tone. "Had you crossed the barrier and been caught, not only would we have been discovered, but we would have lost our most powerful warrior."

The empress turned on her brother and glared at him. If any look had the power to hurt, this would have been the one. "You imagine your most powerful warrior so weak that she would be captured by any of the samurai or common folk on that side of the barrier?"

The emperor gingerly stepped back and deeply bowed. "No, sister, I would never."

Flames arose in the empress' palms. Slowly she circled her brother, glowering at him. "If I may add clarity to my decision, the only reason I chose Yurei over myself is that at first sight of one of those invaders, I would have found it difficult not to attack then and there." She stopped circling where she began and rubbed away the flames in her palms. Her shoulders relaxed. "That being said, you, my faithful brother, are correct. It would have been foolish of me to go. Though, not a single samurai in that village could defeat me... five or ten, maybe."

The emperor straightened, wearing a relaxed smile. "Ten... maybe."

Niji's ears sprang into the air. She spat the fungus she had been chewing onto the ground in a wet, red glob and stepped closer to the opening.

"What is it, Niji? What do you hear?' the empress asked.

Niji raised her palm toward the empress, cringed, and immediately lowered it. She apologized for the hush-hand and bowed. She refocused on the noise, her ears upright, twitching and turning. "Paws striking the ground… moving rapidly."

"How many?"

"Just one set."

"Kitsune?" The empress leaned closer, her breath hot on Niji's ears. "Is it Yurei?"

Niji wanted to say, *I could hear better if you sealed your mouth shut,* but instead just thought it. She closed her eyes and listened as intently as she ever had, listening for sounds underneath sounds. "It's Yurei." She breathed a sigh of relief.

A breath later, Yurei bounded through the opening, bringing with him the piece of red cloth snagged on one of his claws. He ran in a circle around the three of them, bowed to the siblings, and collapsed at their feet, gasping.

The empress asked Niji urgently, "Is he alone? Is anyone following him?"

Niji closed her eyes and shook her head. "No… no one is following him."

The tension eased from the empress's face and shoulders, and she focused on Yurei. "What is it? What brings you back in such a condition?"

Yurei stood on all four paws and shook, sending leaves and dirt flying from his translucent fur. He looked up at the queen with his silvery eyes and spoke in a whispery tone. "I was running in the shadows of the trees when I came upon a guard post. Nothing more than a tiny hut with a thatch roof. I thought it empty and moved for a closer view, but a guard was inside, a samurai."

"Foolish mistake! You were supposed to take all precautions to not be seen." The empress paced as she rubbed her palms together.

Yurei tucked his three tails, bowed, and remained so. "I am sorry, Empress."

"Continue."

"The samurai was as startled as I and reached for his sword. I had no choice but to possess his mind."

"And?"

"I cleared his memory of me and ran."

"And?"

Yurei glanced up. "And… I am here."

"Did anyone else see you?" the emperor asked.

Yurei shook his head. "No. I'm certain of it."

The empress narrowed her eyes and stared at Yurei for what felt like a season. "You may leave. Tell no one what you have seen." She waved him off, showing him her back and five impressive tails.

Yurei bowed, rambled across the clearing, and disappeared into the brush.

Niji suppressed her pleasure at Yurei's failure and gingerly stepped between the siblings, stood on her hind legs, and leaned back onto her tail. She spoke slowly, carefully, as to not enrage the empress. "Yurei *was* an obvious choice for the job."

"Silence Niji," the empress scolded.

Niji timidly dropped to all fours and bowed her head. She peeked at the emperor from the corner of her eye to take cue from him. The emperor knew when to speak and when to hold his tongue. He stood silently, so she followed his lead.

The empress placed a finger to her lips and paced. Her five tails slowly swayed behind her as if they too were in deep thought. A quiet minute later, she paused. "Niji."

Niji raised her head. "Yes, my Empress."

"I may have made a poor choice in sending Yurei when your skills of stealth are unmatched. Along with your cowardliness and fear of absolutely everything, you are certainly the best for a job in which avoiding attention is paramount."

The corners of Niji's mouth downturned only the slightest at the combination of compliment and insult. It was the empress's way of making sure those beneath her knew their place. Niji decided upon being politely agreeable. "That is a perfect description of my talents and why I'm the best for the task."

"Go, prepare the guard and bring them here," the empress ordered her brother. She turned to Niji. "Niji. Enter the valley. Keep a watchful eye, but do not be seen. Return upon the light of the new day." Her eyes narrowed as the corners of her mouth curled in an evil smile. "Tomorrow, we take back our beloved valley from the invaders and destroy the cursed mirrors that brought them here."

To be continued...